Company

Company

STORIES

Shannon Sanders

GRAYWOLF PRESS

This publication is made possible, in part, by the voters of Minnesota through a Minnesota State Arts Board Operating Support grant, thanks to a legislative appropriation from the arts and cultural heritage fund. Significant support has also been provided by the McKnight Foundation, the Lannan Foundation, the Amazon Literary Partnership, and other generous contributions from foundations, corporations, and individuals. To these organizations and individuals we offer our heartfelt thanks.

MINNESOTA
STATE ARTS BOARD

CLEAN
WATER
LAND &
LEGACY
AMENDMENT

Published by Graywolf Press
212 Third Avenue North, Suite 485
Minneapolis, Minnesota 55401

www.graywolfpress.org

Published in the United States of America

ISBN 978-1-64445-251-6 (cloth)
ISBN 978-1-64445-252-3 (ebook)

2 4 6 8 9 7 5 3 1
First Graywolf Printing, 2023

Library of Congress Control Number: 2022952325

Jacket design and illustration: Kimberly Glyder

For Fox, Calloway, and Miles

Contents

Opal Daughtry
m. Centennial Collins
```
        |
    ┌───┴───────────┐
```
Dr. Cassandra Collins   Felice Collins
m. Charles Heaven
```
    |
┌───┴───────────┐
```
Cecelia Heaven   Cyrus Heaven
```
    |
```
baby
(by Cole Chatwell)
```
                    ┌──────────┴──────┐
```
Miles MacHale   Thelonious
m. Lauren Keane   MacHale

Lela Collins
m. Linwood MacHale

Suzette Collins
m. Micah Lamb

Mariolive MacHale
m. Dante Hope

Caprice MacHale

child

Bellamy Lamb
m. Shane Joseph

AUBREY
Audrey Lamb

BABY

Company

The Good, Good Men

Theo had come all the way from New York with no luggage. From the parking lot Miles watched him spring from the train and weave past the other travelers, sidestepping their children and suitcases with practiced finesse, the first of anyone to make it across the steaming platform. His hair was shaved close on the sides, one thick strip left to grow skyward from the crown of his head. In his dark, lean clothing, hands shoved deep in his pockets, he was a long streak of black against the brightly colored crowd. He alone had reached their father's full height.

He made no eye contact with Miles as he strode to the car and yanked at the door handle. Still didn't as he folded himself in half and dropped heavily into the passenger seat, releasing a long breath. "Fucking hot," he said, pulling the door shut.

Miles threw the car into drive and steered out of the parking lot, out of the knot of station traffic. "Summertime," he said by way of assent.

These words, the first the brothers had spoken aloud to each other in over a year, hung in the air between them until the car reached the mouth of the highway. Their mother, Lee, had finally moved back out to the DC suburbs, to the end house in a single-family neighborhood all crisscrossed with telephone wires that Miles had seen often from the road. He was grateful for its proximity, only a four-mile drive from the train station. Last time around, searching for her dumpy apartment deep in the District, he and Theo had lost precious time to gridlock and confounding one-way streets and been beaten there by their sisters, turning the whole operation to chaos. A mess of shifting allegiances, tears, hysteria. Later, in the relative quiet of Miles's living room, Theo had complained of his ears ringing.

"No bag, nothing?" asked Miles now, nodding toward Theo's empty hands. "We need to stop for a toothbrush?"

"No," said Theo. "I'm good. I'm out tonight, right after Safeway."

Miles thought of Lauren back home, washing the guest linens and googling vegan dinner recipes since morning. "Okay," he said. "Quick trip, though."

"Just to keep it simple," said Theo. "We dragged it out last time. A task like that always expands to fill whatever time you allocate for it. You know? We gave it two days, and it took two days. We were inefficient." He reached for the dashboard and gave the AC knob a hard crank, calling up a blast of chilled air. "This time, two hours. We'll give it two hours, and we'll get it done in two hours."

Miles suppressed a shiver. Stealing a glance at his brother's outstretched arm, he saw an arc of freshly inked letters at the biceps, disappearing beneath a fitted sleeve. Lauren, who maintained aggressive Facebook surveillance of all her in-laws, had kept Miles apprised of each of Theo's new tattoos for years, undeterred by Miles's disinterest. Only this last had caught his attention.

"Bad stakeholder analysis, is what it was," Theo was muttering. "Last time, I mean."

"What's the new tattoo?" asked Miles, pointing.

Theo blinked at the graceless transition, then obligingly pushed up his sleeve. "Got it in Los Angeles, on a work trip. A girl I was with talked me into it. I had been thinking about this one for years." He traced his finger around the lettered circle, four words rendered to look like they'd been scrawled by hand in a familiar chicken scratch. *"Miles, Thelonious, Mariolive, Caprice.* For us, obviously."

"But where did you get Daddy's handwriting to show the tattoo artist?"

Theo let the sleeve drop and folded his arms across his chest. "From a check he sent to the old house for us, with our names in the memo line. I found it in a stack of Lee's work papers with a bunch of other ones and took it when I went to New York. It was in my wallet when I went on the Los Angeles trip."

Miles felt a swell of heat despite the frigid air. "You took a check from her and never gave it back?"

"Did you not hear me? It was with a bunch of other ones, and it was about eight years old. All the checks were years and years old, some of them reissues of older ones. He would write that in the memo line. He would send them, and she would put them someplace idiotic like tucked in the finished crossword puzzles or a pile of old magazines. And then, I guess, lose them, so he had to write new ones. She was always doing that kind of shit with checks. I found this one, and the others, all mixed in with the girls' old coloring books. I took *one* and left the others there for her to find never. Is that okay with you?"

Theo's posture had gone rigid, his face turned squarely in Miles's direction. Miles took his eyes off the road long enough to stare back; but like a traveler gone too long from his hometown, forgetting its habits and idioms, he had lost his fluency in the quirks of his brother's face. At one time he had been able to tell, from the slightest twitch of an eyelid, that Theo had been teased past his threshold and was about to cry; to hear an impending temper tantrum in the sharpness of his inhale. All that was years ago, when any impulse would buzz between them like a current, felt by one brother even before the other acted on it; when a germ passed to either inevitably would invade the other. A faraway, definitively ended time. The composition of Theo's face was the same as always, brooding features assembled slickly under a strong brow. But now it was like their father's face in the pictures: impassive, all traces of thought as strange and unreadable as hieroglyphics.

Lee had a new man, again, this one a fellow patron at the karaoke bar where she'd been throwing away money every week for months. It was known that he mixed good homemade cocktails and spoke a little French, which was probably what had done her in, because he wasn't particularly good-looking and didn't seem like anyone's genius. He had a dog as big as a wolf, supposedly, and for some reason wore too much purple and a signet ring on his little finger.

Miles's spotty intel had come from Mariolive and Caprice, who, working innocently but in tandem, were only a bit more effective than either of them was separately. Lauren, for her expert stalking efforts, couldn't find even a single Facebook reference to supplement what little was known about her mother-in-law's new relationship. It was not known where the new man came from, what he did for a living, or what wives and children lay crumbled in his wake. Nor what in God's name he was doing making regular appearances at karaoke bars, if not trolling for naïfs like Lee.

But without question he had established himself as a regular at Lee's new house out in the suburbs, as evidenced by his car's presence there on each of four spot checks Miles had conducted upon receipt of the intelligence. It was there on a Sunday afternoon, a black sedan parked casually in the carport behind Lee's dented Ford Explorer. There again the following Thursday as Miles inched homeward past the wire-crossed neighborhood in rush-hour traffic. There on a Friday after dark, the lights on in the little house behind it, a hint of movement within. And then, confirming Miles's nauseated suspicions, there again the next morning at sunup, the house still and silent.

Mariolive had said, *At least this one has a car.* Which was more than could be said of certain previous ones, like the one who'd needed Lee to drive him up to Philadelphia once a week to try to see his estranged son. Or the one who'd put the dents in the Ford Explorer driving down I-95 in the dark after cocktails.

But still: a grown man, well past any definition of middle age, living unashamedly off a woman with air between her ears. Who lived by the word of her daily horoscope and always kept a tambourine handy to punctuate moments of spontaneous group laughter.

And also: a karaoke bar. An unforgivable fall into the soulless and vulgar. Lee had met their father at a District jazz lounge that no longer existed, a place Miles had long imagined as dark and deliciously moody, like the man himself, with threads of light piano melody curling through the air between sets. He was the MacHale third of the regular Tuesday-night trio Somebody, Somebody & MacHale (Miles thought he would never forgive Lee for this offense alone, her willful forgetting of the group's full name, which no amount of internet searching could recover), the long-fingered bassist who looked a little like Gil Scott-Heron and stood almost as tall as his instrument. MacHale never talked between sets, but he had a smile like a swallow of top-shelf whiskey. Lee had learned from him about melody and improvisation, about modality, how bebop could crush you, how the blues could lift you.

From that she had found her way, albeit over some thirty-five years, into the drunken sump of some suburban karaoke bar. A place where, by very expectation, the music was shit.

Mariolive estimated she'd been hearing consistent mentions of Mister Signet Ring for two months. Caprice, marginally more reliable in temporal matters, thought it had been four. In his email to Theo, Miles had taken liberties: *Bro. Hope you are well. Yet another motherfucker living up in Lee's house for the past six months. You have time to go to Safeway?*

Theo, perpetually glued to his devices for work purposes, had written back within a minute: *I'll make time. When?*

He was explaining again about the stakeholder grid. "It's about maximizing your tools to push your agenda forward," he said, drawing squares in the air with long fingers. "You look for the intersection of interest and influence—the people who want what you want and have some power toward achieving it—and you mobilize them. High interest, high influence: That's your first quadrant. That's who you need on your side. They can help you mobilize the folks in the other quadrants. As long as you keep your first quadrant happy, you'll always have some muscle behind your agenda."

"Got it," said Miles.

"My mistake last time," said Theo, "was thinking the girls were in the first quadrant. I thought they were with us and that I could use them that way."

"When really . . . ?"

"*Low* interest, high influence. Not actually on the same page as us, not actually ready to go to goddamn Safeway, but influential. You know? Noisy. They have Lee's ear, she listens to them, wrong as they are. They're third quadrant. You keep third quadrant as far away from the task as possible, because otherwise they'll destroy it."

"Ah."

"Which is why, this time, no girls."

As Theo said, their mistake last time had been inviting their sisters. Mariolive and Caprice were a storm of emotion, almost as changeable and ridiculous as their mother. The last time, with things coming to light fisticuffs between Theo and the squatter who had infiltrated Lee's shoebox apartment in the District, both girls had simultaneously burst into tears. *No, Theo, stop*, they wailed, each clutching one of Lee's shaking hands. *It's fine, it's fine, just let him stay.* When only days earlier, they'd agreed that the non-rent-paying leech of a boyfriend needed to be escorted out of the too-small apartment. When only minutes earlier, they'd been helping Miles gather the boyfriend's belongings—tattered books, crusted-over cookware—and toss them unscrupulously into the cardboard boxes brought for this purpose. Mariolive had thrown herself in front of the boxes, her thick black braid darting from side to side with each shake of her hair. *Let him stay with Mommy.* Which was why it had taken a total of two days, two trips back to the apartment, two separate escalations of physical contact, to get the lowlife to leave, believably for good.

The time before that: uneventful. The brothers working alone, their sisters away at college, had sent the motherfucker packing for Philadelphia within twenty minutes of focused intimidation. Then, as now, Theo had been wearing head-to-toe black, and incidentally Miles had, too (he had come straight from coaching football practice), and to the infiltrator they had appeared a powerful and unified posse. The infiltrator had actually cowered—a foot shorter than Theo, who had reached his full MacHale height at that point—and promised he would never again take advantage of Lee's generosity. Lee herself, crying and wringing her hands in the corner of the room, had been easy to ignore; both brothers had a lifetime's practice.

Once, MacHale had sent Miles a letter. The letter, etched in blue ballpoint in MacHale's erratic, challenging script, confirmed Lee's memory of their first meeting at the long-gone jazz lounge. She had been the girl who turned up to all his gigs in halter dresses she'd made by hand from colorful see-through scarves, swaying her considerable hips at front-and-center as though they'd hired her as a dancer. Perfect rhythm, and stacked as all hell; but too pretty, an almost unbearable distraction. And too silly to be bothered by the fact that everyone—including MacHale, losing notes on his bass—was watching her. He had never seen anything like her, a Black girl with glowing cinnamon skin and hair the color of a well-traveled penny. Sometimes she wore an Afro with a shiny turquoise pick in it, even though it was the eighties and people weren't doing that so much in the District anymore, and on those days he couldn't look at anything but her.

She claimed not to know anything about jazz but somehow could hum all the staple melodies after hearing them once. Often, she brought her own tambourine and accompanied the trio from the lounge floor. The Black men and even some of the white ones stared greedily at her, hollering their approval, and even then she didn't stop, her craving for attention apparently bottomless.

I'm sure you know the feeling, read the letter in MacHale's labored handwriting. And even on his first read, Miles *had* known the feeling, having experienced Lee's oblivious attention-seeking many times over, and having also experienced the misery of watching girls he wanted flirt with other men. He understood why his father had seen no other option but to set aside his bass one day and leave the lounge with her, thirty minutes before the gig was scheduled to end, and to marry her six months later and quit the gig altogether. He certainly didn't need her, the someday mother of his children, swaying and twirling her hips into a future of infinite Tuesday nights.

Belatedly, something dawned on Miles. "Wait," he said. "So you think *I'm* in *your* first quadrant."

Theo, thumbing through emails on his phone, grunted in reply. "If this is done in two hours," he said, "I can get the 7:05 back to New York. There's a gin-tasting event in Brooklyn that I want to get to by midnight."

"Gin at midnight is worth rushing back for?"

"Networking. There's these guys who'll be there that I need to maximize face time with to kick off some new stuff I'm doing in the coding space, and if I hit them up while they're a little bit loose, I might be able to—" He faltered audibly, looked at his brother. "Anyway, yeah," he concluded. "I definitely want to get back for that."

Miles's hand twitched toward the phone in his pocket but then tightened instead around the steering wheel. Lauren called this—the type of work people like Theo did in places like Brooklyn, which no amount of description could clarify to outsiders—*alternawork*.

"Unlike Lee," Theo continued, "I can't just leave money on the table. I think about those checks she never cashed, and I just—man." He whistled, a low, pensive sound.

Miles sensed, in the shifts of Theo's upper body, that some familiar, troubled presence had joined them in the car. The mishandling of money had always offended Theo deeply; as a boy, he'd been brought to tears many times by Lee's fretful comments about bills. And from amid the high-piled detritus of the many chintzy apartments Lee had occupied

over the years, Theo had somehow sniffed out, and pilfered, MacHale's
forgotten child-support checks. There was something so pathetic in it
that Miles was almost, *almost* moved to touch his brother's shoulder and
to apologize for it, for all of it, on Lee's behalf.

For years the brothers had been inseparable everywhere but at school,
where they were two grades apart. Living the other two-thirds of their
lives in symbiosis, Miles the mouthpiece for both of them. From playing
like the best of friends to fighting savagely at the drop of a hat, their feet
and elbows always in each other's faces, a constant bodily closeness like
nothing Miles would ever experience again. Like a first marriage.

Among other things, MacHale and his wife had argued about this,
whether brothers should be together so much, immersing themselves so
fully in their two-person games. Lee had discouraged it, having gotten
it into her mind that Miles's engineer's brain was stifling Theo's fanciful
imagination, or that they were conspiring daily to rearrange the carefully
curated array of crystals and candles on her dresser into an unintelligible
mess. She wanted them to be apart sometimes, at least long enough for
Miles to complete his homework assignments without Theo's scribbles
winding up all over them. She believed fiercely in the importance of
regular aloneness, shutting herself into the bedroom with the crystals for
occasional twenty-minute stretches while both boys pawed at the door,
indignant.

But in those days she had left them to their own devices for hours
while she worked—sometimes impossibly long shifts at the Macy's
makeup counter; other times sorting garments at the consignment shop
in Northeast, using her pretty face and her honeyed words to sell them to
their second owners. Each day, after she was out the door, her long skirts
trailing behind her like plumage, MacHale had gathered both boys, not
giving a fuck about their aloneness, and sat them before the bass in his
practice room to listen while he did his finger warm-ups, his spiderlike
scales and arpeggios.

He would play a song or two at a time, then go fix himself a Sazerac,
and then do another few songs, delighting the boys by weaving made-
up lyrics about Lee into the classics. Into "I Cover the Waterfront" he
worked lines about how Lee left all her men home alone too much; "So

What" became a song about her big butt and how she wore those skirts to show it off to the men at Macy's.

MacHale gave the boys little nips of his Sazeracs (nasty, and then gradually less nasty) and told them jokes he'd heard at the clubs where sometimes he still played jazz. He disliked television but every so often let them watch episodes of *The Cosby Show*; he sneaked them out to two Spike Lee movies in the space of a year. He said no to buying them a Nintendo, no and no and no again, each of thirty thousand times they asked; but in the afternoons before his gigs, he let them sit on his back to watch cartoons while he snoozed on the couch.

And yes, sometimes he sent them into the master bedroom to swap any two of Lee's crystals, laughing riotously and giving them double high-fives when they returned triumphant.

And then Lee, returning late at night from doing inventory at the consignment shop, was a wild card who often shattered the consistent peace of daytime. She might be happy and pull out her tambourine, shaking it and her hips when the whole family was laughing. But she might just as readily make a beeline for the stove and wordlessly slam a pan onto it, storm clouds nearly visible over her slick copper-colored bun as she began to stir-fry chicken and peppers. MacHale making the boys laugh by mimicking her cooking posture with exaggerated flourishes or pretending to bite the nape of her bare neck like a vampire.

Her high drama, her hysterical turns of phrase. *Tell it to the devil, you piece of shit*, Miles once heard her scream on the front porch under his bedroom window, the words slicing their way into his dream and waking him up. Her idea of a welcome-home as MacHale returned from one of the many gigs that didn't end till well past midnight. She ranted with wild passion, her words otherwise shrill and indistinct, while MacHale responded at a blessedly normal volume, his low, moody murmur so comforting that before Miles knew it he had drifted back to sleep. In the morning it was as though nothing had happened. Lee served the boys their eggs and toast with a wide artificial smile, pretty as ever with a purple ribbon braided into her hair.

At one of these gigs, MacHale broke his left tibia and fibula and landed himself in the hospital for a stay that dragged on like a prison sentence, forcing Lee to quit the Macy's job and surrender several of her shifts at the consignment shop. (*Are we going to be poor?* Theo asked, again in tears; and Lee laughed one of her untamed, destabilizing laughs. *You thought we were rich before this?*)

After that MacHale was on the couch, suffering the television he so disliked with his leg stretched stiff before him, eating half of what Lee offered him and rejecting the rest, irritable each time she reminded him he could not drink whiskey—not even in cocktail form—on meds as strong as the ones he'd been prescribed.

She was moving more slowly than usual, in the first bloom of visible pregnancy with the girls, and she complained often about her aching back and feet in a way that seemed to Miles to be wildly insensitive, considering. MacHale called the boys to him on a Saturday morning. *We need eggs and sausage and green onions*, he said, making eye contact first with Miles, then with Theo, looking back and forth between them; nothing he had ever told them had seemed so important. *But I don't like your mama swishing around in the streets like she does. You boys go with Lee to Safeway and you don't let nothing happen to her. Nobody looking funny at her, nothing. You understand?*

The boys, with their small chests puffed out, gangly Theo actually walking on tiptoe to appear taller, flanked her dutifully on the walk to Safeway.

The eggs were found easily, but in an aisle full of loitering men; so Theo stayed behind with Lee while Miles darted ahead and grabbed a carton, checking the contents for cracks as he'd been shown to do. *Aren't you helpful*, said Lee.

She forgot her purse in the aisle with the sausages but realized it only once they'd reached the green onions five aisles over; Miles, able to see in his memory's eye the maroon felt satchel slung over one of the shelves, deployed Theo back to that aisle, holding Lee in place with produce-related questions till his brother reappeared with the purse.

In the checkout line they stood behind Lee, shoulder to shoulder between her and the other customers, because she was wearing one of those skirts and it just seemed like the thing to do.

At home, their chests puffed out ever farther, they each received praise and a kiss on the forehead from MacHale, and pride nearly overpowered Miles's eight-year-old body.

A week later, wobbling a bit on his new crutches, MacHale took his sons to the toy store and led them straight up to the checkout counter, behind which was kept all the costliest merchandise. With each hand palming one of his sons' flocked heads, MacHale got the cashier's attention and nodded up to the top shelf. *A—what do you call it, Miles? A Super Nintendo Entertainment System, please. We'll take one of those for these good, good boys.*

Happiness hummed between Miles and Theo, their feelings in perfect alignment, one of the last moments in which this would ever occur.

Some weeks after that, MacHale recovered the ability to walk without crutches, and then he was gone, finally driven away by Lee's whims and her nattering.

Thirteen years later, Miles would break his left tibia and fibula playing college football and find himself bedridden for too long and slowed by a cast for even longer, a total of six idle weeks during which he thought he might scratch out his eyeballs from boredom. When the cast came off, he would feel as though he'd been fired from a cannon, an unstoppable projectile who ran instead of walked whenever possible and, through this experience, would finally come to understand why, after surviving all those years with Lee, his father nonetheless could not survive a single solitary second with her post-crutches.

And so when MacHale's letter, five dense handwritten pages addressed *To my firstborn on his 21st birthday* arrived—only a few weeks late—to confirm the projectile theory, Miles would find that he felt satisfied with this explanation. Not that he had ever felt particularly otherwise.

But in the immediate, MacHale's abrupt exit ripped a hole in their little house in Northeast, all its inhabitants left at Lee's mercy. What outcome could MacHale possibly have foreseen but pandemonium? Before anything else, there was Lee's unilaterally scrapping Ella and Pearl, the very good names MacHale had chosen for his daughters-to-be, replacing them with absurdities she'd dreamed up through God only knew what nutty numerology. There was an intolerable glut of visitors, relatives of Lee's come out of the woodwork to rock the babies and distract Miles and Theo from their grief with nonsensical questions about school. There were foods served that MacHale never would have tolerated, the

delicious staples replaced with eggplant and tofu and loaves of bread with
pea-sized seeds in them.

There was the unceremonious discarding of the double bass, which
MacHale had said he would come back for but which instead became
the property of a disadvantaged District high school's music department.
MacHale's left-behind shirts and pants, the ones he wore to gigs, a spare
collection of twenty or so all-black garments, were swept from the master closet and sent to the Salvation Army. MacHale's Copper Pony went
down the toilet and the bottles into the trash can, leaving the bar cart
empty. For a short time they lived as if in a sanitarium, every word anyone spoke echoing disconcertingly off the bare walls.

It did not last. Soon enough Lee filled the closet with more clothes
of her own. The extra space seemed to give her the feeling that she could
now acquire as many impractical garments as she wanted, new things
from department stores and the leftover inventory from the consignment
shop. Bolts of cloth found all over the place, wrapped around her body
in ridiculous ways but still drawing street whistles that burned her sons'
ears. She began wearing her turquoise Afro pick again, sometimes in her
hair, sometimes tied to a length of cord and worn above her cleavage as a
statement necklace. She spray-painted the bar cart magenta and gold and
filled the top half with the priciest of each kind of spirit, the bottom with
bottles of wine brought to the house by her consignment shop employees
and other friends when they visited.

She collected stacks of papers that nearly reached the ceilings. Recipes
torn from health magazines; drawings the girls did that she could not
bear to throw away; Miles's and Theo's schoolwork, which miraculously
had not lapsed. When mail arrived bearing MacHale's name, she quickly
spirited it away, envelopes and all, to places unseen, sometimes returning the most boring contents—old invoices, typewritten correspondence
from the city—to her stacks of papers. Lee's treatment of MacHale's more
personal mail infuriated Miles: sometimes he'd see the scraps of ripped-
up letters in the trash can and find himself consumed with thoughts of
vengeance, wanting to take scissors to her precious clothes, wondering
how she'd like finding the silken garments shredded similarly.

Once, Lee opened a check from MacHale and laughed aloud as she
crumpled it into a ball before Miles's horrified eyes. *If I threw this on the*

ground, it would bounce right through the ceiling, she said with a cackle, dropping it into the pocket of her carnelian skirt.

There was no more jazz; she played terrible music on the tape player and then on the CD player, and cheered the children through their homework with that imbecilic tambourine. *Look what I found!* she crowed one day, and to Miles's horror she pulled from her satchel two sets of hand cymbals to give to her daughters. Their small hands barely fit into the straps, but they screamed with happiness anyway, filling the room with noise.

She gave MacHale's entire vinyl collection to a man she met at work, and for the first time in a while Miles and Theo had something to talk about.

She gave Daddy's records to that guy, said Miles, barging into Theo's room and finding him there with his head in a textbook. *I think they might be dating or something.*

Theo lifted his head, looking sick. *Oh, that's nasty,* he said.

A silence hung between them. After a time, Miles cleared his throat. *Do you ever,* he asked carefully, *think about that one time when Daddy sent us with her to Safeway?*

And then bought us the Nintendo.

Yeah.

Yeah.

Miles had decided immediately upon receipt of MacHale's only letter to him that he would neither mention nor show it to Theo. It went on for five pages and did not once mention MacHale's younger son, nor either of his daughters. The return address, to which Miles sent multiple over-eager replies, had turned over to another renter mere days earlier, with no hints as to where MacHale might have gone. Anyway, the letter itself was more than good enough, and even the revelation of seeing MacHale's quirky handwriting up close was an unexpected joy. Whatever unease he had felt seeing it inked on Theo's arm just now was repaired by knowing its less-than-honorable origins. Miles sat a little taller now, reassured that his was the only letter. Not that Theo hadn't deserved one of his own, of course.

Their exit loomed. "Will Lauren and I see you again soon, then?" asked Miles, flicking on his turn signal.

"Don't know," said Theo.

Miles thought of Mariolive, who by Lauren's report was holding on to her shithead college boyfriend even though she should know better by now, all those letters after her name. Maybe they'd be hitting Safeway again soon, for her.

Into the shabby, wire-crossed neighborhood he steered the car. Beside him, Theo was silent but alert, scanning the boxy little houses of Lee's neighbors, his phone for once inert in his pocket.

The grass was freshly cut, a touch that struck Miles as the work of a much craftier adversary than all the sloppy past boyfriends. A dog, chained to Lee's wrought-iron fence and unsurprisingly not wolf-sized, slept under Mister Signet Ring's black sedan. Its collar was turquoise and spattered with glitter, and seemed to have sprouted a number of multi-colored feathers.

They retrieved the cardboard boxes from the trunk and walked shoulder to shoulder up the walkway, Theo hunching just the tiniest, barely perceptible bit, which Miles appreciated. A hideous summer foliage wreath hung from the front door, and the faintest four-on-the-floor seemed to pulse through a downstairs window.

Both brothers lifted their fists. Theo dropped his, and Miles knocked.

Lee opened the door, a fuchsia scarf tied around her silver-and-copper hair. The synthesized sounds of disco music flooded out into the front yard, rousing the dog. Shades of excitement and then concern passed over her expressive face in an instant. "Boys?"

Behind her, sitting on the couch in veritable purple jeans, the *Post* spread out before him, his ringed little finger keeping time against the edge of the newspaper, sat Mister Signet Ring himself, looking at the brothers with only mild curiosity.

"You," said Theo, maintaining eye contact with the boyfriend as he stepped around his mother, while Miles began the work of containing her in the foyer. "We need to talk to you."

Bird of Paradise

Evening fell and up came the automated glow of the citronella torches. Cassandra had noticed them as she first stepped into her boss's backyard, a dozen earthen obelisks discreetly lining the patio and the outer reaches of the lawn, and registered them as a particularly un-Jon-like aspect of his Takoma Park home. Difficult to imagine the university president—who dressed each day as if for a press conference, fleurs-de-lis flashing at his jacket cuffs and the school colors shining in the satiny threads of one bow tie from his bottomless reserve—strutting into a Lowe's in search of these garden lights that looked like mud sculptures. Now, though, the darkness-activated torches turned majestic, their steely basins emanating scent and showy little flames. *This* was Jon: drama, spectacle, pomp and circumstance, and so forth. Presidential!

However, while the torches gave off a warmly flattering aura, performing small mercies on the zits and crow's-feet of the faces in the assembled crowd, they didn't provide nearly enough light if one happened to be looking for someone, which Cassandra was. "Sorry, just a minute," she told the group clustered around her. She touched the arm of the person before her—some young hanger-on from Student Affairs—and the seas parted; she pushed through.

She needed her nieces for a photo, quickly. They'd only just been here, gathered with the crowd on the patio to hear Jon's end-of-evening remarks, and then seemed to disperse as Cassandra was swept up in toasts and congratulations. She thought now that she saw one by the koi pond, a high-piled puff of hair above a shadowed young face, a lissome body in black. She headed that way, gathering the skirt of her dress in one hand and clutching her glass of Opus One in the other, careful, so careful not to trip.

"Beautiful dress," murmured a woman named Janet as their shoulders grazed each other in passing. Janet would start the upcoming semester as the new dean of diversity and inclusion, once Cassandra ascended to the role of provost. Passing Cassandra the name of her favorite fashion rental service had been Janet's first act of solidarity with her predecessor.

"A little birdie helped me find it," said Cassandra, winking, and hustled past.

For Jon, for this, Cassandra had chosen a dress called the Zofia by a designer well outside her ken, a magenta cocktail number with a plume of shirring for a shoulder strap. She had done so, understanding that it would draw even more than the usual share of Michelle Obama comparisons so many of her colleagues seemed dead set on making, suggestive as it was of last year's inaugural ballgown. That was all right; one could see that as a sort of compliment. The Zofia had been a nod to Jon's preference for sartorial regality. Cassandra had had her hairstylist put in a bronze rinse and take off an extra inch to dilute the Michelle-ness of the overall look, and—it was all fine. But the structure of the dress, its constrictive boning and the flare of tulle at the hip, made hurrying difficult. Especially now that night had fallen. And by the time she reached the koi pond, the phantom niece had disappeared behind a wall of party guests.

Of the eightyish guests, Cassandra supposed that half—including Jon, hence the party, the heavy hors d'oeuvres, the unending cases of upper-midlist French wines—were sincerely happy for her appointment. Twenty-eight or so had openly backed Neil Margolis, the other apparent front-runner. Another nine were utterly goddamn inscrutable, their faces sealed in neutrality all evening as they burbled their congratulations and clinked Cassandra's wineglass. Fine. They had their own aspirational reasons. But of course it left her to twist in the winds of uncertainty, both tonight and once they were all back in the hallowed halls.

And so—operating on such a slim margin of confirmed support—how grateful she had been all evening for the true agnostics! The catering staffers passing bacon-wrapped scallops on trays. Jon's cleaning ladies, two lithe brown figures clad in black, clandestinely collecting dropped napkins and left-behind plastic flatware, sweeping them into the wide mouth of a garbage bag for what Cassandra suspected must be double overtime. The photographer, someone's earnest nephew, wielding a gifted Nikon DSLR. When one needed a break from the bullshit—and one often did—one could reach for a scallop or duck into a dim corner and supplant university small talk with, for example, a comment about the mosquitoes that despite the citronella seemed sent straight from hell to swarm Jon's backyard. God, the relief of it, these few blessed souls present who truly didn't care one way or the other.

Except that now the photographer, worried about the dying light and the party guests' accelerating drunkenness, was beginning to reckon with a preordained list of hoped-for shots, photos that would likely punctuate the next university bulletin and perhaps a local culture magazine or two. Half an hour earlier, he had accosted Cassandra by the fruit display. *Dr. Collins, could we get one of you with your family?*

Family. When Jon had put this thing together, he'd floated a possible date by her, and she in turn floated the date by her husband during their bi-nightly phone call.

"I don't know, Sandy," Charles had said after a moment, not concealing his distraction or the clattering of his fingers on a keyboard. Down in Atlanta, he was sorting out the details of an acquisition turned nasty, managing trips up to DC only as absolutely necessary. "This is instead of the other thing?"

He meant the official do that would take place once the semester ended, a gargantuan gala the likes of which Jon was famous for. Tuxes and gowns. "In addition to," Cassandra clarified, though she understood already that this was the groundwork for a *no*. "This is a more intimate gathering at Jon's house. You could wear a sport jacket. It's not a big show."

Charles huffed a little at that.

"Not a big donor show," Cassandra clarified, cradling the phone between her ear and shoulder as she parted the curtains and peered down at the cacophonous Saturday nighters below. The window in the living room of her condominium overlooked the corner of Eighteenth and M, a triangle of bars and restaurants. On weekends after dark, the block teemed with under-thirties, interns from the Hill and students of nearby institutions, their dance music throbbing from the windows. Cassandra let her eyes wander over the crowd without focusing on any particular tearaway, careful as always not to positively identify some drunken student from her university.

"I don't know, Sandy," Charles said again, this time in a tone that effectively ended the conversation. "The other thing, though, I'll be there, absolutely. Spit-shined and suited up."

It wasn't such a disappointment. The handful of times she'd gotten Jon and Charles in a room together, Cassandra had found herself physically disoriented, as if the hemispheres of her brain had switched sides without warning.

Her daughter, Cecilia, didn't answer the phone. This stung but didn't surprise Cassandra. Compiling recent data, she realized there was, at any given moment, a better than 65 percent chance that Cecilia wasn't speaking to her.

Her son, Cyrus, answered midway through the second ring. Though she'd meant to launch right into the question of the garden party, first she couldn't stop herself from bitching for a full fifteen minutes about Cecilia, to Cy's gentle clucks of validation. His patience persisted even as noise swelled behind him, collegiate debauchery not unlike what went on outside Cassandra's window, and finally Cassandra forced herself to come to her point: "Anyway—could you get here for the party, by any chance? On the tenth?"

"I have a dance final," said Cy, not without tenderness. "But you know I would, if not."

She did know, and after they hung up she sat motionless for a minute or two, picturing her dismay as a small gray stone, turning it over in her mind, painting it a bright white with wide, forceful brushstrokes of gratitude. She took a few deep breaths, and then she called her sister Lela.

"Can I bring somebody?" asked Lela. Of course.

"No," said Cassandra. "Bring who?"

"I'm seeing someone," said Lela.

"I know," said Cassandra. "But—"

"You don't know. This isn't that guy. This one's name is Irving and he's been saying he wants to meet you."

"This isn't the time for that, though," said Cassandra, pinching the bridge of her nose. "For this, just family is best."

Lela exhaled theatrically. "Worrying we'll make you look bad," she murmured, as if to herself. "You already have the job, don't you?"

"Listen, Lee," said Cassandra. "It's a yes or a no. I'll get you a ride from Southeast if you need one. Jon always has good wine."

Lela gave a dry laugh. *"Jon always has good wine.* You know what, looks like my calendar just opened right up."

"Yes or no, Lela?"

"Didn't I just say I'll be there?"

Though she was alone, Cassandra gave a firm, victorious nod. "All right, well, good," she said. "Thank you."

"It's outdoors?"

An image flashed unbidden into Cassandra's mind: her voluptuous sister striding into Jon's backyard in a minidress, a thin layer of spandex barely covering her ample, middle-aged behind. Flirting with the men of Jon's administration and maybe even Jon himself, parading crassly around in front of him like an underdressed flamingo. "You know," she said, tripping over the words a bit, "a colleague of mine gave me the name of one of those places where you rent a designer dress for a night."

Lela said nothing, but maybe snorted once or twice.

"My treat," said Cassandra.

Lela snorted once more. "I just checked my calendar again," she said. "And guess what?"

Cassandra sighed.

"I'm busy after all, you stuck-up motherfucker," said Lela, and hung up.

Cassandra had wandered into the kitchen, where she now fixed herself a much-needed rum-and-Coke. As always, she shut her eyes and thought of her father's face, lifting the glass heavenward before she tipped it toward her mouth. The first sip was a little moonbeam of ecstasy.

By the time she reached her bedroom, she'd downed a third of the drink and was ready to call her other sister. Felice still lived in their childhood home in Atlantic City and was crazy as a bedbug, rattling around doing God knew what, but she had never called Cassandra a *stuck-up motherfucker.* Standing at her bathroom mirror, daubing Lancôme Visionnaire onto the delicate skin around her eyes, Cassandra rehearsed her words and then dialed the landline number with determined fingers—

Nothing. The number in her contacts list had been disconnected, again. When had that happened? But that was something to worry about another day.

She climbed into bed and opened her MacBook. The university emails practically spilled into her lap; for every brief note of congratulations, there were at least two more messages generating action items she'd need to tend to before the term ended. *Inward and down*: her new credo. If it was Jon's role to look *up and out*, conveying the university's strengths and ideals to the larger world, Cassandra was now charged with upholding the same within the orbit of the school itself. And doing so with the indefatigable excellence for which she hoped and believed she'd been selected.

Among the emails, here was a recent one from Jon: *Graduation season—caterers in high demand. I made my deposit for the 10th, sincerely hope this is OK. Looking forward to backyard twirls with your lovely family. Best, J.*

Cassandra leaned back against her headboard. Not for the first time, nor for the last time, she felt a stab of fresh, palpable grief for her late sister, Suzette. Some therapist along the way—lo, these twelve years—had cautioned against reactions exactly like this one: it was important not to romanticize the lost sibling, unfairly attributing to her the ability to provide precisely whatever was missing from the present scenario. In other words, you couldn't say, *Suzette would have handled Jon's garden party perfectly.* No matter how true it might seem. No matter how readily you might imagine Suzette gliding among the party guests, all perfect diction and uncontroversial cultural references. *Michelle Obama, yes, exactly!* she might say, laughing politely, casting a look in Cassandra's direction to clarify that allegiances lay intact.

But how could you avoid it? Suzette would have been fifty-one by now, gracefully cresting menopause, wearing a dress that downplayed the shapely rear end she shared with her eldest sister. No one would look at Suzette and think, *Well, is* that *a Collins ass?* and cast an appraising look in Cassandra's direction. Nor would they seize upon any aspect of Suzette's careful speech and project its implications onto Cassandra. She wouldn't need to be coached, as Lela originally had, not to mispronounce Cassandra's new job title: *pro-boast.* Her prettiness would be a boon, her softspoken manners a fine endorsement.

Suzette, Suzette, Suzette. Cassandra collected herself, and then took another sip of her rum-and-Coke. She fished her cell phone out from beneath the cushions lining her headboard.

It had come to this. Suzette had left behind two daughters, passable surrogates who lived in a nearby suburb with their father. Cassandra called the elder, her niece Bellamy, who with Suzette-like primness accepted the invitation on behalf of herself and her younger sister, Aubrey. "It sounds nice," said Bellamy.

"There's a dress code," Cassandra thought to say. "I'll send something for each of you to wear."

"Okay, Auntie," said Bellamy. "Thanks so much."

Finally, the twins, Lela's daughters. As she dialed Mariolive, the more accessible of the two, Cassandra considered how she might leverage the outcome of the call. The twins could be, to varying degrees, as slippery and uncooperative as their mother. There was a mitigating factor, though: Cassandra had gotten each of them accepted to the university, where they were now sophomores, on merit-based scholarships; moreover, she paid the bulk of their remaining tuition. They lived together in an apartment just off campus, supplemented their scholarship and work-study hours with Cassandra's periodic infusions. Assuming Lela hadn't gotten to them first—

"Hi, Auntie," said Mariolive.

"Mark your calendar," said Cassandra. "On the tenth, I'd like the both of you to come to a party at President Elledge's house."

"Okay," said Mariolive.

"Okay?" said Cassandra.

Mariolive said something to her sister, Caprice, who seemed to be hovering nearby.

"There's a dress code," said Cassandra.

"Okay . . . ?" said Mariolive.

"I'll send something for you to wear," said Cassandra.

"Okay," said Mariolive.

Well then. Easier than expected. They hung up, and Cassandra texted her four nieces—Suzette's daughters, and Lela's—the details about the party. Lela had two sons a few years older than the twins, and Cassandra considered contacting them as well, but it began to make the whole thing seem unwieldy and complicated, and would they really be willing anyway? And, honestly, perhaps owing to the rum-and-Coke, she began to doze right there in front of her laptop, and so she never got around to inviting them.

It was Caprice she thought she'd seen by the koi pond. Both of the twins had snatched their hair into buns for the party, tall piles of curls greased into submission. *Shit*, Cassandra had thought as she sat in her C-Class in front of the twins' U Street apartment building three hours earlier, waiting for them to emerge. She should have sent salon money.

But there were bigger problems than that, as she'd realized immediately when the girls had pranced out of the lobby. Mariolive was wearing one of the dresses Cassandra'd had shipped—a sweetheart-necked thing in cornflower blue, perfect for drawing the eye up toward her heart-shaped face—but Caprice, who should have been wearing the same thing in coral, was in another dress entirely, something strappy, skintight, and black. "That other dress didn't fit right," she said when Cassandra asked en route. It reeked of bullshit, but what could be done now? One could only be thankful for her youth, her smooth, unblemished legs, the fact that she was a few weeks shy of twenty—unlike her mother, Lela, who seethed at home.

A few yards from the koi pond, Cassandra was waylaid by Jon's wife, an egret of a woman named Brigid. "Cassandra," droned Brigid, pressing a fresh glass of Opus One into her hand. The light of the Pisa torches had turned Brigid halfway pretty, smoothing the angles of her features and reconstituting her shapeless beige caftan into something elegantly bohemian.

"Hello, Brigid," said Cassandra, and sipped the wine.

"Your dress is just to die for," said Brigid.

Cassandra's mind flopped like a fish on land. "So is your . . . *home*," she said finally, and meant it. "The interior—I got a look when I passed through a little while ago. So lovely. I love the Craftsman accents. Those high ceilings!"

Brigid's grin widened. "These Stickley monstrosities," she said with a dismissive wave of her hand. "If you only knew how Jon *begged*."

"So lovely," said Cassandra again.

"Really nice when the kids were young," said Brigid. "You know, all the alcoves and shelves. Ours used to entertain themselves for *hours* in the little rooms. They still do, really, when they're home."

She gave another wave of her hand and Cassandra followed the gesture, casting her eyes up toward the dormer perched on the sloping roof of the house. "Speaking of," Cassandra said, and pointed. "I didn't realize your son was home."

The kid's name was Boyd. He had Jon's affable, freckled face under a cap of amber-colored hair, an air of understandable if unwarranted confidence as he strode around the campus. A lanky senior, he'd hung around on the patio long enough to hear his father's remarks this evening, and had circulated briefly among the guests. As he should have! Half the faculty, Cassandra included, had taken part in seeing to his timely graduation despite his grades, his general inattention to section requirements.

(Neil Margolis, as hard-nosed as his reputation, had flunked the kid in a sociology class a few semesters back. It was the sort of thing one wouldn't necessarily hear about, a single failing grade in an out-of-major elective, until the giver of the grade was one's direct rival for an administrative appointment.)

Now, up in the dormer window, Boyd seemed to be gazing over the party with vague interest, peeling himself free of his jacket. Brigid squinted. "Oh, there he is," she said in a voice Cassandra thought she recognized, one that seemed to tell a familiar tale of filial noncompliance. "He told me he'd be right back for pictures, and that was twenty minutes ago."

At another time, they might have commiserated over it. But now—

"Of course," pivoted Brigid, "I just *knew* you would win out over that other one, old What's-his-name."

"Neil Margolis?"

"Him! Because, you know—not that it comes down to what Jon wants in this case, but—if you only knew how Jon *rooted* for you." Brigid leaned in closer. "It really means a lot to him, having you in the role. Which isn't to say that Neil wouldn't have been just wonderful—but having you there, it'll be such a nice thing all around. For Jon and for the school."

"If you'll excuse me, Brigid," said Cassandra carefully, and charged ahead.

She'd spotted another of her nieces, seventeen-year-old Aubrey this time, at one of the drink stations, being poured a glass of generic chardonnay.

"Aubrey," she called as she trotted toward the girl.

Aubrey froze, a deer in headlights in wedge sandals.

"Listen," said Cassandra, catching her breath. "Your sister, your cousins—have you seen them?"

"Uh," said Aubrey, fumbling with her wineglass.

"Just drink it," said Cassandra impatiently. "Don't tell your father I let you."

Aubrey swigged at length and then said, "Bellamy's in the bathroom. Not sure about the twins."

For Aubrey, whose slender frame could be shimmied into just about anything, Cassandra had chosen a sweet little A-line dress in a demure shade of plum. Up close, she saw now that the child had removed the modesty panel from the front—it must have taken a good deal of unstitching—and shoved in a set of cutlets, giving herself what was for a Collins woman a really rather impressive display of cleavage.

Cassandra reached out and gave the collar of her niece's dress a hard upward tug.

"*Hey*," said Aubrey, frowning, and dodged away, spilling a little of her wine.

"Stay right here," said Cassandra. "We need to get a family photo."

Aubrey sucked her teeth and gave her shoulders a little shake, undoing Cassandra's modification.

Cassandra turned away and stalked toward the house, her eyes rolling heavenward. Grief for Suzette—so quickly it came on, always—prickled like perspiration on her skin.

"Dr. Collins!" thundered a voice near the back door to Jon's basement, and Cassandra stopped. Here was a trio of male deans, vociferous Neil Margolis supporters, all grinning broadly at her.

With effort, she unclenched her face and managed a smile.

"*Strelitzia reginae*," said Dean Giry, gesturing toward Cassandra. His teeth flashed in the torchlight.

"Oh?" said Cassandra, waiting.

"The bird of paradise plant," elaborated Dean Giry. "Queenly, tropical, *exotic*."

"Oh," said Cassandra, and fiddled with the strap of the Zofia.

"You look lovely," said Dean Schoenfeld, closing a hand around hers, and leaning in to peck her cheek. With a quick sniff, Cassandra realized the men's glasses, like hers, contained Opus One from Jon's private stash.

"Big things in store," said Dean Denning, raising his white eyebrows. "When they send out the campus bulletins"—and here he pantomimed opening an invisible pamphlet, turning it to the page on which Cassandra's face beamed alongside Jon's, the vice president's, the other deans'—"they'll say, *Wait, I didn't realize I'd subscribed to a fashion magazine!*"

The men chortled. Cassandra produced something that was at least half a laugh.

"If we haven't already said, *congratulations*," said Dean Schoenfeld. "Jon is obviously just delighted to have you in the role. Just delighted."

"He really did lobby hard on your behalf," added Dean Giry. "He so wanted to see you next to him in that office."

As though it had all come down to what Jon wanted, and not to a year's worth of rigorous selection procedures; Cassandra appearing bright-eyed at every fundraiser, building positive relations even with faculty members like these—

But there behind them, emerging from the bathroom, was her eldest niece, Bellamy. "Thank you, gentlemen," said Cassandra, smiling widely at them as she pushed ahead. Excellence, indefatigableness. *Inward and down.*

Bellamy, thank God for her, beautiful, compliant Bellamy. *Truly* Suzette's daughter, down to her tasteful mauve pedicure. She had worn the dress Cassandra'd had shipped, modest olive green jersey covering all the right parts of her neat body. Without being asked, she'd had her hair freshly styled, thick, soft waves brushing her shoulders. Her makeup was perfect. She regarded her aunt amiably as Cassandra got close, hitching up the hem of the Zofia.

"I need you to help me," said Cassandra, closing a hand around Bellamy's. "The photographer wants a picture. I've got your sister standing over there by the drinks table. Do you know where the twins are?"

"Mariolive has been sitting in your car for the last ten minutes," said Bellamy. "But I haven't seen Caprice since it started getting dark. Why don't you text her?"

There was no judgment in her tone, no generational disdain that Cassandra could make out—and she would know it, as she dealt with it daily on campus, most often from students whose common sense would fit into a thimble with space left over—but Cassandra's face burned with embarrassment anyway. "Go wait with Aubrey," she told Bellamy, and watched as the child walked off.

Of course, this, too, had been a trait of Suzette's: an irritating practicality that cut through everything in a way that could come off as unfeeling. But at least the child had dressed properly.

She texted Caprice as she hustled through the crowd, around the sprawling Stickley house. *Where are you? Meet us on the patio for a photo.*

There again was Jon's son, Boyd, in the dormer window, still staring passively over the crowd. She wondered why he didn't come and rejoin the party; ordinarily, he had his father's boisterous extrovertedness, always turning up at faculty events to snag free snacks, in the loudest school paraphernalia. It was rumored that he sometimes subbed for the university mascot, donning the hot, furry outfit to strut across the football field in a showy but anonymous display of school spirit. It was a sort of loyalism Cassandra had never quite come to grips with; surely the kid was in fact too cool for that kind of silliness, and yet he did these things without apparent irony, which to some extent, Cassandra understood, evinced an even more fundamental suavity. Sort of the way Jon seemed to draw some of his legendary social confidence from the very threads of his bespoke suits and bow ties, which in most other contexts would be considered a bit much, at best.

Boyd's photo was all over every campus bulletin; he could even be seen on the peripheries of some of the faculty photos that lined the hallowed halls. No wonder the kid thought he owned the school.

Cassandra marched down Jon's driveway and up the block toward her parked C-Class, where indeed she saw Mariolive curled up in the passenger seat, bare knees to her chin. The waste of it—Mariolive in her sweet blue dress, one of only two of Cassandra's nieces to wear what she'd been asked, and here she sat hiding in the car.

As Cassandra reached for the door handle, she saw that her niece was crying, little rivulets of drugstore eyeliner streaming down her cheeks. Cassandra sighed heavily before opening the door. "Mariolive?"

Mariolive swiped at her nose, leaving her upper lip gleaming with moisture. "Auntie, hi," she said. "I'm sorry, I—" She faltered and fell silent, breathing slowly, sniffling every so often.

You had to feel sorry for the child, having grown up with a mother like Lela. All this beauty, the smarts brimming from her shining little face, and no clue what to do with any of it. Wouldn't a face like that look perfect on display in the campus bulletin? It was why Cassandra never felt particular resentment, peeling the checks from her checkbook when it came time to pay the twins' tuition balances; why she'd labored over her search for the dress Mariolive now wore, this layer of protection against the critical eye of the world, of the school. Wordlessly, Cassandra wrapped an arm around the girl's shoulders.

"I just get so stressed out," said Mariolive after a moment. "At things like this."

Cassandra took the opportunity to smooth the curls around her high-piled bun. "You're doing fine," she told Mariolive. "You're doing just fine."

"There you are, Dr. Collins," said the photographer. "I need to be leaving soon. Do we have everyone?"

"Three out of four," said Cassandra, gesturing to indicate Bellamy, Aubrey, and Mariolive, who sat perched on the stone wall along the patio. Three nice-looking girls in a tricolor rainbow of jewel tones, only one dress altered, their makeup freshened, heads ducked together. Cassandra had draped a shawl across Aubrey's décolletage; Mariolive had composed herself with a practiced and frankly remarkable swiftness. One of the girls murmured something and the others giggled, Mariolive's bun bobbing overhead. "Still looking for the other one," added Cassandra, checking her phone.

Nothing from Caprice, and now another ten minutes had passed. She would try calling. She moved away from the noisy drinks table, the chattering crowd clustered nearby; she kept wandering until she found quiet in the grassy valley near the Japanese maple, and dialed.

No answer. She tried again, and then sent another text.

"Taking a break from your own party?" boomed a voice nearby, clarion and familiar, an affable laugh around its edges. Cassandra tensed and turned. Jon's cuff links, pearlescent abalone squares, glinted in the flickering torchlight. Jon held an open bottle of Opus One, from which he topped off her half-full glass.

"Not exactly," she said, and flashed him her widest, most reassuring grin. *A break, surely not, never,* she hoped her face said.

"Cheers!" said Jon, tapping her glass with his own. "What a nice night. I hope you've enjoyed yourself."

"A very nice night," echoed Cassandra. "I feel so welcomed."

"You look fabulous." Jon gestured broadly in her direction. "Our very own Michelle Obama."

Here it was—and it was, finally, a relief. His eyes stayed north of the shirring at her clavicle. The hours she had spent trawling Janet's website recommendation for a dress that promised to in absolutely no way whatsoever cling to her behind! Eliminating option after option, this one too short, that one ruled out by the eye-catching trickle of sequins down the backside. More than once she'd regretted her outfits on campus, even the suits she'd sent through two rounds of tailoring; and if Jon snuck a peek every so often, could it really be called his fault?

The Zofia, though, clung nowhere; it flared in a sexlessly floral way, all visual interest that piqued without titillating.

And, of course, Cassandra understood that this—along with the reports she would file, the faculty pep talks she would deliver, the oversight she would administer with competence that never edged into stridency— was the unwritten duty she was stepping into. To amplify the brand Jon had built. To wear magenta silk shirring that made sense of his shining cuff links, which might otherwise seem a bit much. To validate and fortify him as he worked his magic, up and out. Nothing more and nothing less than that.

And yet, of course, if they lingered here in the grass too long, there would be no shortage of eyewitness gossips, twenty-eight or more, ready to swear they had seen President Elledge unabashedly flirting with the new provost at what should rightfully have been a celebration of Neil Margolis's appointment.

Cassandra began to move back toward the patio. "I'm missing one of my nieces," she said by way of a segue. "Any ideas?"

Jon fell into step beside her, lighting a hand briefly on the small of her back, and scanned the crowd. "What should I be looking for?" he asked.

She pointed toward the patio, indicating Mariolive. "The one who looks just like that one, but in black."

"Aren't they gorgeous, by the way," boomed Jon, projecting this last for her nieces' benefit; the girls straightened, smiling shyly. He extended the bottle of Opus One. "Anyone care to try?"

Cassandra held back, her eyes still roaming the crowd, rigorously avoiding the photographer's glare of mounting impatience. The torches threw light across the assembled faces, none of them Caprice's.

She checked her phone: a text from her son, Cyrus, who thought this might be the night of that party and hoped she was enjoying herself; another from her sister Lela, passing along a joke from reality TV as if to say that all was well. Nothing from Caprice.

Cassandra downed the rest of her wine, wandering a bit, and finally set the glass on a table.

"Ma'am," said a soft voice at her side, and Cassandra turned. It was one of Jon's cleaning ladies, the one who earlier had sympathized with Cassandra about the seemingly citronella-impervious mosquitoes. "Were you looking for your nieces?" Even in the dark Cassandra could see the funny look in the other woman's eye. By instinct she leaned in, as if preparing for the woman to whisper into her ear.

Instead, the woman lifted an index finger and pointed, oh-so-discreet a gesture, and again by instinct Cassandra affected the same discretion, looking without seeming to look. Following the woman's small motion, she lifted her eyes to the dormer window two stories above, where Boyd Elledge had shifted a bit but still sat moving very little, his gaze glassy and fixed on a wall somewhere inside. Something, a dark shadow, seemed to flicker before him.

Cassandra squinted, and as her vision adjusted her heart clenched with longing for her dead sister, or for anyone on whom she might later unload the minutiae of this night, its small triumphs and failures, without fear of judgment or name-calling.

Right up there where anyone could see, if they happened to look: a puff of dark hair—a high-piled bun—bobbing up and down in the bottom-most pane of the Craftsman-style window.

The Gatekeepers

Janet and Blair had almost made it out of the supermarket when Blair gasped and announced she had to double back for, of all things, a packet of vegan cheese substitute. She had been gone for all of three minutes, leaving Janet to watch over their purchases, when who should breeze through the sliding-glass doors but Stephanie fucking Simmons in exercise pants. Janet's heart lurched at the sight of her old friend, the very person she'd hoped to avoid as she hustled Blair out of the house an hour earlier for this errand, knowing full well her chances were low: in more than twenty years as neighbors, and especially in the decade since their nests had emptied, Janet and Stephanie had done their shopping with unplanned but near-perfect synchronicity. Janet's running into Stephanie on a Saturday morning was all but guaranteed, hard as she'd hoped otherwise.

"Hello!" said Stephanie, pushing her shades up the slope of her forehead. She had a basket over one elbow and the unhurried look of someone embarking on a casual, just-a-few-things-I've-run-out-of sort of grocery trip, because why shouldn't she? Christmas was a whole three weeks off; only a total fool would already be out buying the makings of elaborate holiday cooking. Only an idiot who'd let herself be bullied into playing second fiddle to someone else's late-December travel plans.

"Hi, honey," said Janet, receiving the cheek peck Stephanie offered her. She tried to use her body to obscure the segregated contents of her shopping cart: Blair's canvas bags of fresh produce at one end, her own processed and dairy foods in paper bags at the other, a plump wrapped turkey playing sentry between them. Of course, it didn't work; Stephanie seemed to be looking right past her, directly into the cart, taking inventory. "Just grabbing a couple of things," added Janet anyway. "You coming from spin class?" Immediately, she regretted prolonging the conversation;

somewhere behind her back, Blair was probably halfway through the express lane by now.

"I quit last week," said Stephanie. "That teacher was like a barking Chihuahua. Got on my damn nerves. I've started running in the neighborhood, though! Once, as of today." She laughed and loosed her hair from its high post-workout ponytail. It fell in smooth waves around her shoulders, freshly pressed and colored, not even a hint of silver at the roots. There had been some question about whether she could pull off chestnut highlights at her age and with her in-between skin tone, but overall it worked, the whole effect coming together in a late-career Pam Grier sort of way.

At a better time, and in a better mood, Janet might have brought forth a compliment. Now, though, from somewhere nearby came Blair's voice floating out above the noise of the aisles, a sharp soprano loudly declining a bag. "Well, good for you," said Janet to Stephanie, desperately, and moved to give the cart a suggestive little push. "I'll see you—"

But then here was a hand on her arm and a *whoosh* of citrus-scented air to herald Blair's return. As Stephanie watched, her coiffed head tilted ever so slightly to one side, Blair dropped the Daiya mozzarella shreds into the open mouth of a canvas bag and her wallet into the empty child seat of the grocery cart. "Found it!" she said to Janet; and then, to Stephanie, "Hi!"

Earlier in the week, there had been an incident at the university where Janet worked, reports of student protests turning violent, necessitating shelter-in-place tactics in Janet's building and the ones adjacent. It had happened at five minutes to three, just before Janet's scheduled appointment with a student who had been raising hell because of Janet's teaching style and late-work policies. The sort of young man who, like so many of them did these days, felt that the problem with his grades reflected the faculty's failures to tailor the fabric of the university—of academia itself—to *him*. Janet had dreaded the meeting for days, had spent the hours of this particular day praying that God would send an ice storm or something like it through the city to spare her from yet another of these conversations with yet another of these entitled kids; and then, with five minutes to go: the shelter-in-place mandate. A well-timed miracle that had apparently gotten the best of the student's pervasive laziness. Even after the lockdown had lifted, and the threat had been defused by

3:05, the kid had simply emailed a discouraged two-word cancellation: *Never mind.*

Was it too much to hope that something like that might happen now? Not an act of violence or a natural disaster, necessarily, but—surely God's imagination was better than Janet's—some unexpected escape valve to spare Janet from having to reintroduce her curious neighbor to her out-of-town guest. Stephanie and her constant hurry, her cell phone that never seemed to stop buzzing—where was the sudden urgent call?

But it seemed that Janet's luck for the week had run out. "Hello!" returned Stephanie. She turned her big berry-lipsticked smile on Blair and then back on Janet, pushed a hand through her chestnut waves. "You have a shopping buddy."

"I do. You remember Blair, my—" Janet started, and faltered. It was like searching a drawer for a lost object in the dark; her mind's fingertips grazed various options—*son's girlfriend, granddaughter's mother*—but, with the term they really wanted not there, couldn't do much other than push this clutter aside. The moment stretched and yawned wide open.

"I'm William's partner," said Blair. She offered Stephanie her hand, bitten-down fingernails and all. "You're Janet's neighbor, right? The other *gatekeeper*. We met before—it must have been a few years ago, when William and I were last out here?"

"That's right," said Stephanie, her smile brightening with recognition. She took the younger woman's hand in her manicured one and gave it one firm little pump. "I *thought* I saw Will's car pull in this morning. Of course we've met before. How's that baby of yours? I was wondering when you'd bring her back for a visit."

Blair laughed. "Caswell is fantastic. Just awesome. And *so* not a baby. *Kindergarten*, can you believe it? Her daddy took her to the aquarium today so Janet and I could get some cooking done."

"Some serious cooking, it looks like."

"Ha! Right. We're calling it our Casual, Not-Quite-Vegan Christmas before Christmas dinner."

"*They're* calling it that," cut in Janet, startling herself. The other women looked her way, a little glint in Stephanie's eye suggesting she'd caught the bitter edge to Janet's words. Janet straightened herself, adjusted the strap of her purse. "Because, you know. December ninth isn't *really* Christmas."

Blair rolled her eyes skyward and gave an exaggerated little sigh. *"December ninth isn't Christmas,"* she echoed mechanically, around a laugh. To Stephanie: "We'll be in Paris for Christmas itself." She reached into the cart and began plucking out canvas bags, hauling them one by one over her solid shoulders. Her fingers were deft, altogether avoiding the turkey and Janet's paper bags as though they posed a contamination risk; and when the Daiya Mozza packet slithered out onto the supermarket floor, she did a full-bodied arabesque to retrieve it. Tossed it with a flourish, letting it spin twice in the air before catching it in her upturned palm.

Stephanie stared, mystified. "Paris for Christmas," she repeated finally. "Isn't *that* a fancy trip for Miss Caswell. Do you have family there?"

"No blood family," said Blair. "But we'll crash with some very good friends of mine for the first few days. The rest of the time, we're at the mercy of some hotel that's barely in our price range. William's never been, and he was hard to convince, but I was determined! Do you know"—and here she leaned in, actually pressed a hand to Stephanie's wrist—"that he didn't even have a valid passport when we got together?"

A fist clenched, hard, in the pit of Janet's stomach. It was another of those moments that unfurled into an eternity, leaving Janet plenty of time to absorb its grotesque details: the fraudulent mozzarella on display in Blair's outstretched hand, the headless turkey spreadeagled in the cart, the millimeter-widening of Stephanie's eyes at Blair's theatrical disclosure. At least one and maybe both of Stephanie's children, Janet remembered, had studied abroad in college.

"Caswell's had hers since her second birthday," Blair went on.

"Well!" said Stephanie, and gave her mane another broad fingercomb. "You know, I'd better start shopping." She gave Janet a long look and then a small smile. "You ladies enjoy your cooking. Blair, it was so nice to see you again!"

On the way to Janet's Acura, Blair wanted refreshers on details she'd forgotten since Will's and her last visit years back. For how long had Janet and Stephanie known each other? What was it they had all chatted about together on Janet's lawn, Caswell still small enough to have slept through all the cooing, the stroke of Stephanie's admiring hand?

The fist in Janet's stomach made it difficult, but she managed answers. She told Blair—as they loaded the vegan groceries into the back seat of the car and the others into the trunk—that she'd moved into the house directly opposite Stephanie's when their children were still in grade school, their husbands still in the picture. They had playfully called themselves *the gatekeepers* because of the way their mirror-image houses were situated. The channel between the two homes was the only road into the cul-de-sac beyond, so that between them they could see nearly all the neighborhood comings and goings—each other's especially.

It was a phone call from Stephanie, in fact, that had tipped Janet off to Will's first and only episode of high school truancy; and Janet who had warned Stephanie when she spotted loose shingles to be addressed on the other woman's rooftop. They'd exchanged waves from car windows as they took turns driving out of the neighborhood before dawn—Stephanie off to her corporate high-rise, Janet to the sprawling university downtown. In fact, only two years earlier, it had been Stephanie who'd hosted a little affair on her back porch to toast the announcement of Janet's hard-won deanship—a small but thoughtful gathering with delicious wines and cheeses.

Janet started to remind Blair about the wine-and-cheese thing, but remembered just in time that Will had declined her invitation, emailing his regrets. Possibly Blair had never even known about it. So Janet found a few other threads to share from the two-decade tapestry of memories, and then she shut the trunk with a bang. In the car, it took her three tries to insert the key fully into the ignition.

"Good God," murmured Blair after a time, as Janet steered the Acura through the parking lot and out onto the main street. "I couldn't stand to live under that kind of constant surveillance. I think you've just named the reason William and I won't be moving out to the suburbs anytime soon."

After that it was silent, blessedly so, until the drive was nearly over. Turning onto the street at the end of which Janet's cul-de-sac lay nestled, they passed—for the second time that morning—the corner playground where a dozen young families ran and climbed and laughed, not a soul among them yet in mind of Christmas.

"They could've skipped the aquarium thing altogether," Blair said brightly, for the second time that morning. "Cas would have been just as happy on that playground."

But of course it had been Blair herself to shoot down this very idea, presented hours earlier by Janet, seconded hopefully by a Will still exhausted from the road trip into town. The aquarium was nearly an hour's drive away; the playground within sneezing distance of Janet's front door. Regardless, Blair had practically shoved them down the driveway toward Will's car, peppering her goodbyes with unending instructions. *William, don't forget her snacks. Check the ingredients first if you're going to buy anything from the cafeteria. William, her coat isn't zipped all the way up. Nothing from the gift shop, William.* And then finally, as Will fiddled with the car seat, she'd turned momentarily sunny, waving her arms over her head to get Caswell's attention. *Hey, Cas*, she'd called out. *See ya, kid! Wang Chung! Enjoy the fishies!*

Janet had watched from the doorway, the exchange stirring in her the uneasiness that would settle in and stay with her through the rest of Christmas before Christmas. What in the world was *Wang Chung*? She knew Blair had spent most of her twenties in Beijing, teaching English to native Mandarin speakers, and early on there had been ambitious talk of raising Caswell bilingual—maybe this was that? Caswell, seeming to understand, had thrown back a graceless wave of her own, her solid little torso vibrating with anticipation. Blair had her carrying her own things in a backpack, one almost half her body's size; she'd nearly dropped the damn thing, hopping and waving.

Wang Chung. Janet had cast her eyes up to the facade of the house across the street, not seeing Stephanie behind any of its great windows; grateful that even if she was watching from somewhere over there, she could hear none of it. Could see only Will—lanky, clean-shaven Will—helping into the car a child whose looks and build were nothing like his. Pushing aside her wild feathers of uncombed hair so he didn't accidentally trap them in the car seat buckles.

"Well, no one who knows better bothers with the Eiffel Tower," Blair was saying, sending a sweet potato across the gleaming blade of a mandoline. "Definitely not at Christmastime. It's a cesspool and a tourist trap."

"Oh," said Janet. She had lost track of how many spoonfuls of flour she'd stirred into the roux thickening on the stovetop. To be on the safe side, she added two more, then another splash of milk, and resumed her quick-wristed whisking. "Well, that's news to me. Will's father and I loved it. But that was back in the eighties."

Blair pulled a brand-new casserole dish out of a canvas bag and set it on the counter, began laying slices of sweet potato across the bottom without rinsing it first. "There are other spots to see the city from," she said. "We'll go to Montmartre and climb the hill, or maybe do the Montparnasse observation deck if Cas is interested, and then she and Will can at least *look* at the Eiffel Tower."

"*If she's interested*," repeated Janet. "How would she know if she's interested?"

Blair reached back into her bag, frowning, and produced a can of organic tomato paste. "How would she know if she's interested?"

"She's a little kid, and she's never been to Paris. How would she know—well, why wouldn't you just take her there, if *you* think she should see it?"

Janet thought Blair gave a little snort, but maybe it was just a bubble in the tomato paste, an unappetizing little fart escaping as she layered it, viscous and red, across the mat of raw sweet potatoes. "She's five, she's human, she has opinions. We're not in the business of forcing her into experiences she doesn't want."

"Well, all right," said Janet. She took the roux off the burner and poured in the hand-shredded Gruyère, overturned the bag of sharp cheddar on top of that.

Blair went on: "She enjoys the experience more fully, anyway, if she chooses it herself. If it's something she really wants to do."

Janet gave the cheese a good mix, covering the shreds with sauce, and let the spoon fall hard into the bowl. "All right," she said again, and turned to head out into the garage. "Getting some butter," she added, pointing.

There *were* a few extra sticks in the outdoor refrigerator, and Janet *would* need one of them to finish off the crumble dish she'd prepared the night before, Will's favorite; but mostly what she needed was a few moments of brisk December air. Outside, she shut the house door behind her and hit the button to send the garage door rolling to the ceiling. Fingers of cold slipped in and curled around her face. She thought of her student, the one who'd canceled that week, and what he'd written in one of his bitter emails: *My parents aren't paying this school for you to tell me I'm wrong about everything.* Which had baffled her, really, because—his inflammatory characterization aside—wasn't that essentially *exactly* what they were paying for?

Across the street, Stephanie's car was pulling in, her morning shopping and whatever other errands completed. Janet watched as the other
woman climbed out of the driver's seat, pulled her hair carefully up
into a protective knot, and began unloading items: her leather purse,
her shopping bags, a weighty rectangular object wrapped in tape and
brown paper. A family portrait, Janet remembered; one of the fancy
posed ones—evidently back from professional framing. Stephanie had
mentioned it a few weeks earlier. She'd paid for the shoot, of course, but
to their credit her children and grandchildren had cooperated, and it had
turned out well, everybody smiling and wearing something that looked
all right, though not the matching cabled sweaters Stephanie had first
requested. Janet supposed Stephanie would hang it before the children
came for Normal Christmas, all those days from now.

She wondered, with a start, whether Stephanie could see the makings
of Blair's *sweet potato lasagna*, as she'd called that vegan mess in the casserole dish, or the many kitchen implements Blair had insisted on bringing
from home or purchasing new at the grocery store, in perfect duplication
with the contents of Janet's well-stocked cabinets. But no. Both kitch-
ens, Janet's and Stephanie's, faced the homes' respective backyards; only
later, when the finished foods were carried out into the dining room,
Will and Caswell assembled around Janet's dressed-up walnut table,
might Stephanie catch a peek of Nearly Vegan and Whatever-the-Hell-
Else Christmas before Christmas. Caswell in a T-shirt and unmatching
leggings because why should a little kid be forced into fancy clothes to
spend time with family? So Blair had said.

With a sigh, Janet hit the button to close the garage door and let herself back into the kitchen.

"I'll use the upper and you use the lower?" asked Blair, gesturing to
indicate the ovens.

"Whichever," said Janet. She watched her hands, found her post,
began pouring cooked macaroni into the integrated cheese sauce.

"Great," said Blair, and began jabbing at the row of buttons up top.
"I cleaned the upper one out a little bit."

Janet checked the oven clock: noon, or very nearly so. "I'm opening some wine," she announced. On her way to the basement, she issued a command—*Jazz, please*—to the automated speaker Will had sent
her last Christmas, silencing the faint strains of what Blair had called

new-wave British pop. The friendly computer chose a bebop station playing Christmas staples; Janet nodded in moderate satisfaction. Enough standing around at opposite ends of the kitchen like they had sticks up their rears.

In the basement, she chose a cabernet franc that she liked very much and figured wouldn't suffer from lack of breathing time. Back upstairs—and now it *was* noon—she made a beeline for her glass with the little cluster of gold flecks along the stem, a gift from Will on some past Mother's Day, the only one like it in the house. She had the corkscrew in hand, inches from the bottle, when she remembered her manners.

"Blair?" she said. "Can I pour you a glass?"

Blair looked over, her hands full of Daiya Mozza. "I'll take one," she said quickly. "Please."

The wine, and the buoyant Christmas music, helped considerably. Finally, time moved like it had someplace to go. Blair moved on to start her brussels sprouts dish on the stovetop; Janet gave the turkey its final lemon-herb bath and started the Crock-Pot. The macaroni, bubbling in the lower oven, filled the room with the playful aromas of nutmeg and sharp cheeses.

"Hope they're having fun," said Blair after a time. "Caswell couldn't wait to see the fishies."

"Will's father and I used to take him," said Janet. "They had those eels in the tank on the floor that kids could touch—not sure if they do that anymore—and he went *bananas* over those eels. He loved them. But then there was the room where one whole wall was a shark tank—the sharks with all those teeth, like you would see in cartoons—and he went bananas over that, too, but in a bad way. He was sure one of those sharks was going to swim right through the glass and have a little-boy snack." She took a sip of her wine and closed her eyes, remembering: Will with his back pressed up against his daddy's legs, pearlescent little tears in the corners of his big cocoa eyes.

"Wow," said Blair.

"He got used to them later," added Janet, thinking of an older Will striding toward the tank on longer, more confident legs. "He probably doesn't even remember how scared he was at first."

"He was terrified of the sharks," said Blair slowly, "but you took him back to the aquarium anyway?"

Janet, topping off Blair's glass and then her own, didn't answer. It
seemed like a question undeserving of a response. Over the years, there
had of course been countless invitations to the aquarium—from the Boy
Scouts, the church youth group, the other university professors with kids
around Will's age. Even considering all the times they'd declined—Will's
homework or sporting events or playdates getting in the way—there must
still have been dozens of visits, most of them overall positive. Delightful,
even. Out loud, she said, "Pardon my reach," and knelt by Blair's waist to
check the progress of the dishes in the lower oven.

"Why didn't he go with you to Paris?" asked Blair from above. "When
you and your husband went in the eighties."

Janet took her time checking the dishes, testing the springiness of
the macaroni with a careful finger. When she straightened up, she took
another swallow of wine before answering. "That was before Will was
born," she said finally, and set down her glass to begin the work of gathering up the dirty dishes, the no-longer-needed ingredients. "We went for
our first anniversary. It was my husband's favorite city."

"But then you never took William?"

With her back to the other woman, Janet flung open a cabinet and
returned the salt, the pepper, both types of paprika to the spice rack.
"There wasn't a chance, after that," she said. "Will came, and then we
spent the next twenty years on Will." She added, charitably, "You know
how it is when they're little."

Although, Caswell's clothes and hair looking as they had that morning, maybe Blair *didn't* know; maybe she'd be shocked to learn that some
people invested hours each week even on basic child-grooming rituals so the neighbors and the schoolteachers wouldn't talk. Will's father
had faithfully broken out the clippers at seven-day intervals to shape the
fleece at Will's nape and temples, a process involving much squirming,
endless distractions, cajoling that turned gentler or firmer depending on
how the child cooperated. All in the name of sending him out into the
world each day with the look of a kid you might ask to join your debate
team, and not one you'd worry would break into your car. Caswell, as far
as Janet could tell, hadn't seen a comb since her last visit years ago.

Janet had reached the bottom of her glass again. "When you're done
with the stovetop," she said, pouring herself a refill, "I need to finish
Will's crumble."

"Mm," said Blair, giving the skillet a little shake.

"Take your time," said Janet. "I'll go make sure all the beds are ready." Sidestepping the stovetop area, its woodsy smells of sprouts and balsamic, she took her wineglass and headed for the stairs that led to the second floor.

She'd put Will and Blair in the guest bedroom, Caswell in Will's old room. In the latter, Caswell's things lay scattered across the carpet: the toys that had occupied her on the long car trip, the garments she'd tried on and rejected before the aquarium. Janet set her wineglass on Will's dresser and started folding. Surely there was a theory at work— that children should control their own environments, or that a tidy room mattered less than Caswell's free exercise of sartorial choice—but a generation earlier, a different theory had reigned over this same bedroom, and the result had been a child who'd kept his surroundings as neat as if he'd been paid to keep them that way. Whose teachers had praised him, highly and often, for the meticulous state of his cubby, his workspace, his physical person.

Janet's student, the complainer, had come to class twice that semester in low-hanging sweatpants and what she'd been sure was an undershirt, his dark-blond underarm fuzz caked with crumbs of deodorant. *THAT,* she'd have told Will, had he been he there to tell, *is what we couldn't have from you.* Thinking of the idlers who loitered just off campus dressed exactly that way, who could have been Will but weren't Will, no parents to insist they stay in school, keep their hair cut close.

Even in neater piles, Caswell's clothes looked ratty and smelled well traveled under the residue of her mother's tart handmade soaps. Involuntarily, Janet cast a look through what had once been Will's window, across the street and into what had once been the Simmons boy's. Some ten years ago, Stephanie had all but turned the room into a home gym; before that, though, it had been a hurricane of posters and unwashed laundry, the other boy lacking Will's instilled fastidiousness.

But—Janet took a sip of wine, remembering—it had been a conscious decision of Stephanie's, letting the mess slide. You had to pick your battles with children. Stephanie's son, her baby, had given his parents fits for years, the daily struggle sending shoots of silver through Stephanie's hair long before her fortieth birthday. If Will had tried his hand at truancy once, the Simmons boy's attempts had been downright chronic for a while. Janet had lost count of the number of times she'd seen his be-leaguered parents standing watch in the morning as he descended the front steps and shuffled his way onto a school bus. Neither of them head-ing back into the house until the bus was all the way down the street, rounding the corner to, they fervently hoped, actually deliver him to school. That the child had earned his diploma on time, had matricu-lated to college, a good college, would be called a *miracle* if it hadn't in-volved years and years of backbreaking work. A full-time job for two. And if the Simmons boy hadn't ever learned to pick up after himself—well, he hadn't landed himself in jail, either. On the morning of one of his graduations, Janet had taken care to high-five his mother on the lawn, just as they'd done over Will's a few years earlier.

Wang Chung. Each year, the school had sent its eighth-grade class to France at the culmination of its multiculturalism unit, two hundred bur-geoning teenagers under the care of a handful of chaperones hardly a few years older. First Janet and then Stephanie had summarily declined to submit permission slips for their respective sons, Janet kept awake by nightmares of Will being mistaken for a Parisian gypsy and locked in some juvenile detention center an entire ocean away. It was the sort of thing that happened constantly, brown people the world over answering for one another's crimes; and earlier that same year, she and Will's father had endured a bitter battle with the school over Will's suspension just for standing *near* a fistfight on the basketball court. Gentle, cautious Will! Forgive her if she hadn't entrusted his international well-being to the same clutch of perky teachers who'd allowed *that* to happen. Anyway, he did Model UN on Tuesdays after school, met with a language tutor on weekends. Not the same as seeing the Musée d'Orsay up close, maybe, but certainly safer.

She and Will's father had withstood their son's begging and brief, in-dignant outburst, the short-lived hunger strike that followed, his last-ditch plaintive tears. When he'd had to do a little bit of supplementary homework to make up for what he'd missed in France, Janet herself had gathered the needed library books and coached him through it, reward-ing his patience with Bullets tickets.

So they hadn't gotten around to taking him there. Even without leav-ing the continent, they'd produced a wonderful kid, both feet on the ground, unimpeachable manners, respect for his elders. He had shown affection freely to his parents and grandparents, offering hugs without being asked, none of the false shyness Caswell had shown on her arrival this weekend.

But Blair had been all over the world. To Beijing, to London, to Paris—enough times, apparently, to consider herself among those who would know better than to bother with the Eiffel Tower. And to Reykjavík, her ancestral homeland on one parent's side, where she'd been dazzled by the turquoise fjords she must have mentioned a dozen times at Janet's and her first meeting.

You've never heard someone use the word fjord *so many times in one sitting,* Janet would have said to Stephanie afterward, had she felt like talking about it.

She smoothed down the sheets encasing Will's old twin bed, pulling hard at the corners to get them crisp. His old AfriKids pillowcase was deeply wrinkled; she gave it a tug and then a punch, squarely to the middle. That helped, actually, so she did it again.

Several punches later, Will's pillow beaten into submission, she descended the stairs, wineglass in hand. Her cheeks flushed with exertion, and feeling emboldened by the wine, she thought she might find it in herself to say something about the state of Caswell's borrowed room; at the very least, she could ask for compliance with the house rules. Kids cleaned up after themselves here, whether or not it was what they *wanted to do.*

But of course, Will already knew that, just as he knew the corner playground was a perfectly fine place to pass a morning; that five-year-old children didn't get to set their own travel itineraries; that a little girl should have a little girl's name, rather than some fanciful unisex creation of her mother's; and that a little girl also deserved a single-family home in the suburbs, parents who cared enough to marry each other, all things he and the Simmons children had had at costs that he—and Blair—could barely imagine.

By the time she reached the bottom of the stairs, her wineglass empty, she knew she wouldn't say anything about the clothes after all. The visit was scheduled to last only two days, and there probably wouldn't be another for a while. Caswell would be a completely different child by the next one. Maybe the children in Montparnasse would have taught her to pick up after herself.

"They'll be back at three," said Blair, holding up her phone.

"Wonderful," said Janet. "May I use the stovetop yet?"

"Um, sure," said Blair, and removed the empty skillet from the front burner. "For the crumble you were talking about?"

"Just to brown the butter," said Janet, reaching for her smallest saucepan, the sticks still cold from the outside refrigerator. "There's not much else to it, after that."

"Okay," said Blair. She was quiet for a moment, refilling her canvas bags with the remnants of her groceries. Then she cleared her throat. "Well, what if you skipped the crumble?"

Janet frowned. "Why would I do that?"

"It's just that it's a lot to go through for something most of us won't eat. Too much butter for Caswell."

Janet's frown deepened. "But Will would want it." Will at twelve, shoveling seconds onto his plate; at twenty, road-tripping home from college for the holidays and sniffing the air for the scent of nutmeg the second he walked in, even before saying hello.

"Maybe not. He'll have turkey and some of your macaroni—he's been talking about it for days—but he's otherwise doing pretty well lately, staying the course."

"So he's vegan now."

Blair laughed, a little dryly. "Sort of. Lightly so, with coaching. He's the *casual, not-quite-vegan* component of Casual, Not-Quite-Vegan Christmas before Christmas."

Janet had pulled two half sticks of butter out of the box; now she slid them back inside, wordlessly returned her saucepan to the cabinet. "All right," she said after a moment. "No crumble."

Blair hesitated. "Maybe you could serve just the berries themselves with a little brown sugar," she said with forced brightness. "I know we'd love that!"

In her glittering turquoise eyes was a look Janet knew too well from her own maternal repertoire, the same practiced cheer she'd shone on Will to sell a Bullets game as a stand-in for the missed trip to France.

"Maybe," she said lightly. "That's a good idea." She pinched shut the box of butter sticks with a chilled thumb and forefinger. Then: "Blair," she said, just as lightly.

"Yeah?"

The fist in the pit of her stomach had unclenched itself, its fingers unwinding themselves up toward her throat. "I'm getting tired," she croaked, shaping the words into an apology, a guilty admission. She held out the box of butter. "Would you take this to the garage and put it back into the outside fridge? Since we're not using it after all."

"Sure!" said Blair, taking the box, the word ringing with victory.

"And while you're out there," added Janet, her voice tight around the fingers in her throat, "we need the leaf for the dining room table."

"For just the four of us?"

Janet managed a nod and a smile. "All the food. The turkey and all the casserole dishes, so we don't have to keep coming back into the kitchen."

"Okay. Where's the leaf?"

Janet described its location, indicating that Blair should check the wall behind her late husband's old Lexus. "It's propped up on its side between some other things. Be careful back there."

"Okay," said Blair, and spun on her heel. She let herself out into the garage. Janet heard the door to the outdoor refrigerator open and then quickly close.

Janet turned her attention back to the state of the kitchen. Blair had reclaimed all her personal dishes and put away some of the others, had shoved the cork back into the half-full bottle. Janet lifted the bottle and gave it a swirl, watching the ruby-colored liquid dance behind the glass. On the granite countertop, Blair's wineglass remained nearly full. Janet wondered whether she'd had better in Montparnasse.

After a time, Blair came back into the kitchen, carrying the wooden leaf under her arm. "Found it," she said quietly.

"Great. If you put it in the dining room, we can let Will insert it when he gets home."

Blair started for the dining room, then stopped at the doorway. "You keep a crib in your garage?" she asked casually, over one shoulder.

Janet forced a frown. "A crib . . . ?"

"There's one behind that other car in the garage."

"Ah," said Janet, as if remembering.

"It must not be William's. It looks new. Just dusty."

"No," said Janet. "We gave his away decades ago."

"So what's that one for?"

Janet gave an ambiguous little gesture: half shrug, half dismissive wave. "There was a sale at a baby store going out of business," she said. "It was five or six years ago. Stephanie Simmons across the street and I both impulse-bought them, thinking we might eventually need them for grandchildren who'd be around a lot." She paused and reached for a carton of berries, began rinsing them in preparation for their changed destiny. "You learn to adjust," she said, almost to the berries.

Blair's pale eyes darkened. The arithmetic needed was quick; *five or six years ago* put the purchase just before Caswell's birth. "Oh," she said, and kept walking.

When Janet finished rinsing the berries, it was five minutes to three; punctual Will, rarely a minute later than he said he'd be, must have already turned off the highway by now. She walked into the foyer and looked out at Stephanie Simmons's house, trying to locate her friend behind one of its many windows. There was movement west of the front door, in the playroom–turned–TV room, where Stephanie sometimes fell asleep on the same couch on which Janet had once seen the Simmons daughter climbing on top of the no-good boy they'd spent the next two years prying her off of.

That made Janet chuckle, remembering, but only because she knew it had turned out all right: They'd rid the daughter of that particular boy and fended off similar threats for long enough to see the daughter through the rest of her fast-assed adolescence. She'd made it to college and then medical school, married a nice man, had babies. Unlike Janet, Stephanie *did* have occasional reasons to use the crib she'd bought at the sale those years back. The little ones called her *Nana*.

Behind her, Janet heard Blair ascend the stairs, calling out that she wanted to change out of her cooking clothes. There were five minutes, maybe more if Will happened to hit a snag in the neighborhood traffic. Janet saw that Stephanie was watching a home-shopping show, the sort of idle programming she'd have on in the background while doing her laundry. She was perched on one of her nice armchairs and Janet felt the irresistible urge to slump into the other one. She wondered whether Stephanie might like to split the last of the cabernet franc, whether they could polish it off in the five or more minutes it might take Will and Caswell to make it home for dinner.

She let herself out the front door and was hit with another memory: Last Christmas, Normal Christmas, on her way out to dinner with a few colleagues from the university, Janet had watched the Simmons boy—a man now, slighter than Will and more sharply dressed—arrive in a cab, then climb Stephanie's front steps with his fingers laced through those of another young man Janet had never seen. She'd watched them share a kiss under Stephanie's mistletoe-adorned porch light, their lips and hands parting just before the front door opened.

There was something she had always wondered. Had Stephanie been home on the day of Janet and Blair's surprise first meeting? If so, had she spied something similar in the moments just before Janet answered the doorbell? Maybe she had watched Will and Blair hold hands up the walkway, watched them kiss on the porch, watched Will stare adoringly into Blair's fjord-colored eyes as they waited to be let inside. Maybe Stephanie had noticed Blair's eclectic hand-me-down maternity frock—had known for seconds or minutes before Janet had about the coming baby that was to be Caswell. But just as Janet hadn't said boo about the Simmons boy and his boyfriend, then or afterward, Stephanie hadn't breathed a word about Will's new family, either. Hadn't asked till she'd been told.

Janet thought of Stephanie in the supermarket this morning, her hair freshly laid, her manner as relaxed as a woman's could be only when her children were off in their corners of Elsewhere, presumably doing exactly what they were supposed to be doing. What they'd been raised to do. Whereas in years past, still in the throes of raising teenagers, still anticipating the loss of her husband to his persistent mistress, Stephanie had—rather regularly—appeared at the supermarket looking like a different person altogether, a stressed and haggard person, an inch of silvery new growth at her temples.

Janet giggled at that—mentally overlaying the beaten-down Stephanie of past supermarket trips onto the carefree glory of this morning's Stephanie. Wasn't it a little funny that, two weeks or so from now, Normal Christmas descending upon them like an anvil, it would be the stressed, haggard Stephanie—the one anxious about her children and in need of a touch-up—out doing the shopping, while Janet relaxed and watched home shopping, Vegan Christmas blessedly behind her?

Janet's giggle bloomed into a bubbling laugh. She was tipsy and the bottle made a funny sloshing sound in her hand. By the time she reached the opposite driveway, she was laughing aloud to herself. Stephanie's front door opened several beats before Janet had made it up the front steps; Stephanie, when she moved aside for Janet to enter and took the bottle from her hand, was laughing too. "*Caswell's had hers since her second birthday,*" mimicked Stephanie, just that; it was all she could manage before she lost her breath. They wasted at least two of the five precious minutes that way, both of them doubled over in the foyer, laughing without speaking, as Janet felt—firmly and suddenly—they'd earned the right to do.

Rule Number One

Always have your shoes reheeled before they really need it. Don't wait till they wear down to the noisy, clicking nubs and turn cacophonous on hard surfaces. Go at the very first sign of rubber erosion, while the last reheel job still looks practically new. Forget about cheating, hoping to stick to places with carpet. There are surprise hard surfaces everywhere, such as every elevator and public bathroom on the planet, and unless you plan ahead, you'll be caught at all the worst times. So it's worth planning ahead, worth what it costs you in cobblers' fees.

Why? Because it seems like a little thing, but it's exactly the kind of little thing that distinguishes a person who has her life in order from one who's about to fall right off the edge. A person wobbling around on clicking heels probably has all sorts of issues she's not tending to. And maybe you do, too, but the last thing you need is to walk around broadcasting that to people two blocks away.

Said my mother. This was when she was telling me everything she could think to tell me right as it occurred to her. For this, she came into my room after she'd already tucked me in for bed, showing me a tiny dent in the coal-black heel of one of her work pumps. You see this? she said. This little dent? Tomorrow I'm taking these to get the heels redone. Let me tell you about rule number one.

Another day, she found me at the kitchen table, practicing my cursive letters, and invited me to touch the sleeve of one of her nice coats. This, what you're touching, is called suede, she said, pressing it to the side of my face. What I want to tell you about suede, she said, is that it doesn't belong in the rain. Rain ruins suede. It'll make it ugly. Okay?

Okay, I said. I have to practice my cursive.

Another day still, she grabbed my collar just before I climbed out of the Volvo for school. Let's listen to this song, she said, turning up the volume on the car radio. It was the Four Tops, one of them singing about feeling like the hand sewn into his girlfriend's glove. About wanting to kiss the ground she walked on. My mother sang along with the song, moving her lips but not making any noise. She pressed her forehead to mine and then pulled it away. This man is singing to a woman he loves, she said. What do you think about that?

I don't know, I said. I don't like when boys talk about kissing. I don't really like this song.

Okay, said my mother. Just remember it for later. Rule number one is you don't want to have anything to do with any boy who wouldn't sing about you that way. Don't go near him unless he would kiss the ground you walk on.

For those last few months, she did that all the time, dropping one tiny lesson after another into my head like marbles. She could find me anywhere in the house. Let me teach you how to iron, she said, clutching the iron in her fist, as I crouched with my sister behind the dollhouse in the playroom.

Once, I heard her do it to Daddy. Micah, let me talk to you, she said, in exactly the same voice she had used earlier that day to tell me about smoothing down my baby hairs with a toothbrush. She was holding the necklace he'd bought me that week, a series of bright blue pony beads on a length of yarn. When you buy one of the girls a necklace, she said, you have to buy them both a necklace.

He was eating his breakfast, a plate of scrambled eggs, and his fork paused over the eggs in freeze-frame as he stared at her. I bought it because Bellamy loves little necklaces, he said. I just saw it out somewhere and I thought of her.

I know, said my mother. But there are two of them. That means you have to buy two necklaces.

Aubrey is four, said Daddy. She couldn't care less.

That doesn't mean you don't buy her a necklace, said my mother. Maybe it means you buy her the necklace, and show it to her, and tell her that when she's a big girl like Bellamy, you'll let her start wearing it. You either give her the necklace or give her something to look forward to. As she said this, she shook the beads a little bit, like dice.

Daddy set his fork down on the table, still with pieces of egg attached to it. You're upset, he said. Aubrey is little. You put a necklace on her and she pulls the damn thing off in two seconds.

You need to listen to me, said my mother, a little loudly, leaning forward. If you give her a necklace and she throws it right in your face, then that's the situation and you deal with it. But rule number one is if you have two daughters, you buy two necklaces, whether they're four or thirty-four. I am *right* about this, and it's something I don't want you messing up.

Suze, said Daddy. Susie girl. He pulled her close. He'd stayed seated as she stood over him with the necklace, so that when he put his arms around her, his face smushed into the fabric of her A-line dress. I never saw him kiss the ground, but I could almost imagine him doing it.

I mean it, Micah, said my mother. She'd made her voice soft again.

I don't remember making any noise, but they both looked over right then to see me watching wide-eyed from the playroom, my sister kicking and then biting the backs of my legs to recapture my attention. Before that, it had been months since either of them had used adult words in front of us, or even spoke in anything but the sweetest tones, like characters on after-school sitcoms.

Well, all right, said my mother, nodding me over. She opened her fist and dropped the necklace into my outstretched hand. It's yours. Enjoy.

There were rules for everything, each one singularly important. Marbles falling ever faster, *plunk, plunk, plunk.* I started writing them down in my birthday journal, taking every chance to work on my cursive.

There were rules for school: Try your best. Always do the extra credit. Stay after class to ask questions, even if you got it the first time.

Rules for company: Mop the foyer beforehand. It's all right if your guests dirty it up with their outside shoes, but the floor should sparkle right up until that happens. Serve yourself last in your own house. Keep the powder room clean at all times, just in case someone drops by. Always have a bed made up with good linens on it for guests.

But wait a minute, I said when she told me that one. What if someone drops by and you don't have the bed made?

Well, that's what I'm telling you, she said. You just make sure you do. But on that subject, don't *you* ever drop in on anyone like that. I guess we could call that rule number two.

Rules for the body: Drugstore lotion is good enough for arms and legs, but you need Vaseline or cocoa butter for your heels. Heels are just different that way. Brush your teeth like this. Your hair like that. And others that didn't make sense at the time, but would a few years later, when I was more woman than girl.

Rules that didn't fit into any other category, that got their own pages in my journal.

Try to make people feel good about being around you. Happy. Comfortable. Unafraid. It'll make your life easier.

Always look out for your sister. Always, always look out for your sister. She won't always want you to, but do it anyway, even then. Especially then.

Keep a few plants around the house. Also a good bottle of brown liquor.

At the end, she started repeating herself.

You already said that, I reminded her when she told me yet again about the heels. I climbed onto the sofa beside her and showed her where I'd written it in my composition book; she traced the words with her narrow finger and smiled at me.

What a good listener, she said. And your handwriting is excellent now.

Why don't you tell Aubrey? I asked her.

Tell Aubrey what? About the heels?

Yeah, I said. You've already told me that one, but you never told her.

She sighed heavily and let out a little laugh, both at the same time. Because look at her, she said.

We both looked down at the carpet, where Aubrey was watching TV upside down, lying on her back with her dress hiked up and her Ninja Turtles panties showing. She was muttering to herself around the thumb she still sucked despite months' worth of my mother's valiant efforts to break her of the habit. Wearing a ruffled sock on one foot and a Stride Rite sandal on the other.

You tell me, said my mother. Does she look like the kind of person who's going to care a lot about that sort of thing? But maybe you can tell me for her, later, whenever she learns how to wear two shoes that match in the first place.

Not all of it made sense at the time, but I had always been good at following directions.

The very last one was about Linda Ronstadt. She came on the radio and sang a song that sounded like crying, saying she'd done everything she could think of to try to trick some man into being her boyfriend. My mother asked me to turn up the volume and shushed me through the whole thing, lifting an eyebrow each time the caterwauling reached a climax.

Yuck, I said after it was over.

Yuck indeed, said my mother. Remember when I told you to wait for a man who'll kiss the ground you walk on? That's so you never have to sound like this. Crying about a man who doesn't want you is worse than walking around with your buttons in the wrong holes.

Worse than clickety-clackety shoes? I asked.

You're damn right, said my mother, rubbing my shoulder. I think you've got it.

At Aubrey's college graduation, I sat cringing as she tottered across the stage on rubber heels that had somehow reached two different degrees of erosion. How many times had I reminded her in the weeks beforehand? My heart lurched with each step she took, even as Daddy and I clapped and hollered our encouragement. All her friends too. Tottering and clicking around and getting too drunk in their caps and gowns at the reception, broadcasting their dysfunction to the whole campus. As the afternoon wore on, my sister sank a heel between the slats of a sewer grate and toppled over with a braying laugh, treating everyone watching to a flash of her fuchsia thong.

I knelt down to help her up, but she reached instead for the arm of the broad-shouldered boy she'd been flirting with all day. He got her to her feet and then walked away, tossing back a look like you'd give a square of used tissue.

For the next few years, I just did the reheeling for her. Every few months I would visit her hurricane of an apartment and take an armful of shoes with me when I left, returning them a few days later with new heels. It took a huge bite out of the tiny paycheck from my first clerkship, but I did it anyway.

Sometimes the cobbler would tell me they were too far gone, that she'd been walking on the nubs too long and that he'd have to use markers to color on the illusion of material that had worn down. When that happened, I just threw the shoes away.

You're such a bitch, Aubrey said, scowling, when one day I handed her a bag of shoes minus her favorite pair of dirt-cheap pleather boots, destroyed beyond repair.

Rule number one, I told her.

I was going to take those to Atlantic City this summer, she whined. Nobody but you cares about that kind of shit, anyway.

Rioja

Cecilia was asking Cole to repeat all the names yet again. She'd bought a notebook at a rest stop that was now behind them on the interstate, and as he began the run-through for the third time, he realized she was drawing and scribbling, constructing what his peripheral vision told him was a family tree. Her Tupperware containers full of green beans, the fancy wine with its neck tied up in ribbons, stood cradled on the floor between her leather boots. The rental car swallowed the highway beneath it too swiftly.

"So your aunt Pearline, the one whose house we're going to, that's the one you call Peach," said Cecilia, pointing somewhere on the page.

"Yeah," said Cole.

"But I should call her Mrs. So-and-So?"

"Ms. Chatwell. She kept her maiden name."

Cecilia made a note on the page. "Her son is Anthony, the one you grew up with, like brothers. Married, new baby."

"Yeah," said Cole, his hands tightening around the steering wheel.

"And your dad's first cousins will be there, too, and their kids, and in a couple cases also grandkids."

"Right."

Cecilia waved her hand, with its gleaming chrome-colored fingernails, over the tree she'd drawn. "Starting a generation before Peach and your dad, all the adults are college educated. Everyone has advanced degrees too. This one over here, she's the third Black Ivy League PhD in the country."

"She's dead, though," said Cole, scanning highway signs for the exit that would let them bypass District holiday traffic, eventually delivering them to Peach's suburb, just west of the city. "She won't be at dinner or anything."

"Right, no," said Cecilia. "Just for my reference." She ran a hand through her hair, meticulously blown out and hanging to her rib cage. She'd spent hours on it, straightening one tiny section at a time till it was smooth as silk. "Anyway," she said, shifting a little behind her seat belt. She cupped a hand over a corner of the tree; it glided from one area to the next as she spoke: "Peach and all these ones live down here in Washington. These ones over here came out from Cincinnati. This little group, these are the vegetarians. These ones love red wine and will hopefully like the Rioja I got. These ones don't drink anything but Scotch. These ones are the ones who started the game night tradition. Right?" She had the notebook tilted in his direction, her face turned expectantly toward his.

"I'm driving. I can't look right now," he said, impressed and annoyed by the accuracy of her memory, constricted by the flowery scent that filled the car, the arresting grip of her prettiness. He narrowly managed to avoid inserting the word *fucking*, twice. "What are you doing, anyway? Why are you cataloging my relatives?" Other than the omission of a particular uncle who hadn't finished high school, caught up with heroin and quick to make fatherless babies and therefore lopped off like a gangrenous limb, Cecilia had gotten the family tree exactly right. And leaving him out wasn't her fault, really.

"I just want to be sure," said Cecilia, her tone rising a bit. "I want to feel prepared and have things to make conversation about so I don't have to follow you around all evening like an effing duckling. Is that a problem?" She shut the notebook and fiddled with her seat belt again, situating it between the full peaks of her breasts.

"I don't think you need to worry about having a full dossier on every person at dinner," said Cole, keeping his tone even. "I already told you: just be yourself, be polite, don't mention anything off-limits, don't be like Madison. I told you about Madison?"

"You told me," said Cecilia. "I won't, of course."

Some Thanksgivings back, Cole's cousin Anthony had brought home a girl, Madison, sweet and pretty but dumb as a brick, which everyone had realized even before family game night. Saying the most airheaded things for hours, mispronouncing words, getting so far under Peach's skin that Cole had worried his aunt might burst a blood vessel. And then the game, trivia-related, had required Madison to name some reasonable number of US presidents within two minutes; she'd gotten as far as the four most recent, plus Washington and Lincoln and one of the Roosevelts, and then she'd run out. Couldn't produce another one to save her life. A girl named Madison. Peach barely able to be civil after that. *I hope the pussy is good*, Cole had said to Anthony privately, an elbow to his cousin's rib cage. *Because I have serious questions about the rest.* But Cecilia would never, of course. She was a vast repository of random knowledge, her brain richly associative and hungry for details that somehow she managed to retain even after so many wild nights in the East Village.

"It's too bad I won't meet your parents," she said now.

"Another time," said Cole. For years, his parents had spent Thanksgivings with his mother's family out west. Once—only once—Cole had experimentally spent his Thanksgiving with his half-siblings and his father's first two wives, the first Linda and the second Linda, who had formed a sort of two-woman sorority down south, where Cole Senior had ended an entire phase of his life before Cole's had even begun. The Lindas were plenty kind, but it was a strange, stilted, confusing Thanksgiving; he'd gone back to Peach's every year thereafter.

"Goddamn it," continued Cecilia, slapping a palm to her forehead, the noise startling Cole into nearly rear-ending the car in front of them. "I should have brought Scotch."

"What the fuck, Cee," said Cole, easing off the brake.

"Sorry. I just mean because I got the Rioja, I made the beans with and without bacon. I did something special for everyone but the Scotch faction."

Their exit appeared; Cole followed it with both hands on the wheel. "You're already walking in with two Tupperware containers and a bottle of wine. You're saying you think you need a *fourth* gift?"

"I can't believe this," said Cecilia, studying her face in the passenger-seat mirror, fingering her cheek. "For the first time in literally ten years, a fucking zit."

"You don't need Scotch," said Cole. "There will be Scotch there."

"But," said Cecilia.

"The thing is," said Cole, "you don't need to walk in with a hundred different dishes and everyone's favorite drink made to order. I would focus on game night. It's a big deal with us." They were coasting down a smaller road now, past palatial houses with lawns like football fields.

Cecilia laughed throatily, her breasts bouncing under the fabric of her tunic. "*Wear this, don't wear that. Slay everybody in some as-yet-undetermined board game. Bring wine to be polite, but don't bring Scotch, because it'll seem like you're trying too hard.* To be honest," she said, "to be totally honest, I almost wonder if you're pulling a Cannady Shuffle on me."

Cole tensed, the hairs on his arms standing erect. "A what now," he said, steering the car into Peach's neighborhood, large Victorian houses rolling past.

Cecilia cleared her throat, readjusted her seat belt. "I guess I haven't told you this one," she said. "From when I was dating Gavin Cannady."

Cole made a wrong turn, realized it, threw the car into reverse.

"Toward the end," continued Cecilia, "he invites me to some family wedding, a cousin or something, way far away from New York. I forget where. We went to a lot of weddings."

"Uh-huh," said Cole, refraining from saying anything else. Gavin Cannady's was the lap Cecilia had been sitting on at Cole's and her first meeting, at a bar in the East Village, her beautiful face red with laughter, a waiting bump of coke conspicuous on the tip of her finger.

"So we go to this wedding, and he tells me on the way that I need to learn the Cannady Shuffle. Some line dance everyone in his family does at every big event, like the Electric Slide or the Wobble but their own thing they've made up. He says it's a big fucking deal to them, that all the Cannadys know the steps but they're kind of hard to figure out, and that this is sort of the last test on the agenda. If I can figure this out—this is what Gavin tells me, as we're on the way to this wedding—then he'll know he can marry me."

"Uh-huh," said Cole, trying to push thoughts of Gavin Cannady, his broad, charming smile, out of mind. "Is there a punch line here?"

"Yes," said Cecilia. "So by the time we get to this wedding, I figure Gavin is going to propose regardless, and that this is just his cute little way to do it. I mean, at this point we've been together four years. Any other outcome would be ridiculous. So throughout the reception I'm watching all the Cannadys, trying to figure out the steps to the Cannady Shuffle. They're all going to the right and then the left, and then backward and forward, just like it's the Electric Slide, but to me it sure fucking looks like every single Cannady is doing something different."

"Really."

"And Cannadys are standing up and sitting down, and I'm watching like a hawk, trying to get it, but I can't get a handle on it for even one rotation. The dance is totally different depending on whether you're looking at this or that Cannady, and if you ask they just laugh at you. And even when I watch Gavin for five minutes straight, I can't catch on, because apparently there are thirty thousand steps that never seem to repeat. But I figure Gavin must have a ring in his pocket regardless, so I just play along. I keep watching. I try to imitate Gavin's cousins. I do my best for literally hours, till finally I tell Gavin my feet are killing me and I give up."

Cole saw the house, wide and handsome, with golden bricks and a gorgeously manicured lawn.

"And of course I assume that if Gavin has a ring in his pocket, it won't matter whether or not I can do the Cannady Shuffle. So as the night is winding down, I tell him I guess I failed the test because I can't figure it out, and then he tells me—he's laughing this whole time—that the Cannady Shuffle doesn't exist. It's literally just everyone doing anything they want to, within that right-left-backward-forward framework. It's a joke they play to troll non-Cannadys who come to Cannady events, and then they all entertain themselves watching you try your best to learn the—nonexistent!—steps."

Cole was silent, resentful that the specter of Gavin Cannady had joined them on this trip down I-95. Had he been in the car this whole time, lurking in Cecilia's thoughts of meeting another man's family?

"And then of course you already know whether he wound up proposing after all that."

"We're here," said Cole. "Remember everything we talked about, please."

"I do," said Cecilia, already unbuckling herself as they coasted to a stop behind a car Cole recognized as his cousin Anthony's. "I won't bring up any of that stuff."

Cole had tried to keep the list short, but as Thanksgiving approached it had expanded significantly beyond the obvious do-not-mentions. He hoped Cecilia would not bring up, unnecessarily, that they'd met in the cave of a bar in which Cole had found it easiest to score women like her; or that he'd pried her, over six difficult months, from her stormy entanglement with another man. Hoped she'd be discreet about her recent

move to Brooklyn, into Cole's trim studio apartment, reflecting desperation on both of their parts: Gavin Cannady seemed unlikely to track her
all the way from Manhattan. He'd asked her to omit her white father—
"I don't mean pretend he doesn't exist, just don't make a giant proclama-
tion about him like you always do"—and to cover the sankofa adinkra
tattoo on her forearm, to be careful with mentions of her brother, who
worked as a drag queen in the East Village, and . . . on it went. This was
only Cole's second time bringing a woman for Peach's inspection.

They exited the rental car together, Cecilia cradling her gifts in her
arms. Noise from the house, relatives' voices rising and falling, met them
halfway up the driveway. "Do I look okay?" asked Cecilia.

Cole considered the hang of her loose tunic, the black fabric skimming her long legs, the supple leather of her boots. She'd worn her good
jewelry, not the usual clunky Lucite stuff but the real 14-karat pieces:
diamond studs in her ears, a tasteful opal-and-diamond necklace at her
collarbone. "You look good," he said.

The front door opened before they could knock, laughter spilling out
onto the driveway. There stood Peach, soft and smiling, various cousins
peeking around to see who'd shown up now. "There you are," she said,
as if Cole and Cecilia were returning from a trip to the corner store. She
wrapped an arm around Cole's waist and stood on her toes to peck his
cheek. "Looking just like Cole Senior," she added, as she always did.

"Happy Thanksgiving, Peach," said Cole, warmed by her familiar
powdery smell, her soft laugh lines. He felt Cecilia inch closer to him
from behind.

"Introduce us," said Peach, gently.

"Peach, this is Cecilia Heaven," recited Cole. "Cee, this is my father's
sister, Pearline Chatwell."

"Aren't you just gorgeous," said Peach, reaching up to touch Cecilia's
shoulder. "You're making this old lady feel awfully petite!"

"I've heard so much about you," returned Cecilia. "This is—really—
such a pleasure, for us to finally meet!" She handed over the Rioja, gestured to indicate the Tupperware. "Cole said you said I could bring a
veggie."

"Aren't we lucky," said Peach, considering the wine, impressed. "Cole
Senior will be sorry he missed this."

Inside, the gauntlet of introductions seemed to go on forever, relatives looking Cecilia up and down, exclaiming over her height, her loveliness, the presentation of her thoughtfully prepared green beans. Peach pressed a glass of wine into Cecilia's hand, and Cole watched, alert, as she fielded questions, giving the wine occasional, thoughtful sniffs.

"Do you live somewhere in New York?" asked a cousin from out west.

"We live in Brooklyn," said Cecilia. "A studio in Williamsburg," she added before Cole could stop her. Cole took the glass of wine Peach now handed him, took a few deep gulps.

"Where did you and Cole meet?" asked someone else, Anthony's wife who wasn't Madison, the new baby squirming in her arms.

"A dive bar!" said Cecilia, laughing.

Cole left the foyer and found his cousin Anthony on a remote sofa in a room off the kitchen, enjoying a momentary break from the family. "Good to see you, man," said Cole, lifting the bottom of his wineglass to meet Anthony's. "Cute baby."

"Pretty girl," said Anthony by way of reciprocation. "Great tits. She ready for trivia? Know her US presidents?"

"Think so," said Cole. "We'll find out soon, if not. How's fatherhood?"

"Ridiculous. Defies explanation. Both better and worse than you'd think."

"Peach happy?" asked Cole, watching through the kitchen doorway as his aunt collected the baby from some visiting cousin, bounced and stroked it, kissed its little heart-shaped face.

"Happy as fuck. Shitting herself with happiness. You'd think she'd never seen one before. Outside my comprehension, really."

"Mine too," said Cole, watching as Peach found a set of arms into which to deposit the baby again, covered its face with kisses before buzzing toward the dual ovens. Aromas of meats and roasting vegetables and the unexpected tang of citrus floated out from the kitchen. Cecilia appeared at Peach's side, offering help.

"How's Cole Senior?" asked Anthony, but broke off when his wife appeared in the doorway.

"Diaper," she said, tapping the tip of her nose with a finger. She spun on her heel.

Anthony got to his feet. "I'll be back," he said to Cole. "You say hi to the olds yet? They're in the living room."

Cole followed Anthony through the kitchen toward the living room,

parting the group of women hovering around the oven, Cecilia's fingertips grazing his shoulder as he passed. In the living room, Cole Senior's
elderly DC cousins sat in their usual tableau with the stereo up too loud.
"Good to see you, good to see all of you," said Cole, yelling a little over
the pounding piano jazz. Hugs, greetings, Cousin Rose-Lee planting the
imprint of her lips on his cheek.

"You brought a woman with you!" said Cousin John.

"I did," said Cole. "Cecilia."

"Friend, girlfriend, fiancée?" asked Cousin Rose-Lee.

"Girlfriend."

"I saw her in the foyer. What a beautiful girl. Looks a little like your
mama, really."

"Does she have college?" Cousin Heck wanted to know. The others
leaned in for the answer.

"College and business school. She runs marketing and curriculum de-
velopment for a standardized-test prep company."

"A what?" asked Cousin Rose-Lee.

"Sort of like teaching," said Cole, reaching for the volume knob on
the stereo. The cousins nodded, impressed.

As if they'd summoned her, in came Cecilia, her sleeves pushed up
to reveal the black heart-shaped symbol on her forearm. The wine in her
full glass wobbled as she slid onto the couch beside Cole. "Hello, everyone!" she said. "Warm in here. Are we listening to Bill Evans? I like it."

"We were just talking about you," said Cousin Rose-Lee. "About what
a pretty, smart girl you are. Have you met Cole's mama? You look like her."

"I haven't yet," said Cecilia, sliding a hand behind Cole's shoulder. "I
hope to soon. I hear she and Cole Senior spend Thanksgivings out west.
I know she spends three months a year out there without him, and that
he joins up with her for Thanksgiving."

"Have you met the Lindas? And Cole Junior's sisters and brothers
down south?"

"No, unfortunately. But I love that everyone gets along so well, that
they're so kind to Cole."

"Beautiful necklace," said Cousin Rose-Lee, pointing.

"Thank you! It's a family heirloom."

"That's an interesting tattoo," said Cousin John.

Cole let out a long breath.

"The symbol for sankofa," Cousin John continued. "For *go back and get it*. West African." He nodded, approving.

Cole felt a current of happiness pass through Cecilia's fingertips. "Yes, exactly," she said, nodding. "Not many people know it. I get asked a lot whether I made it up myself, when of course it's the opposite. I'm hugely passionate about the idea of roots, about people staying connected to where they come from. I love that we're here right now, that I'm meeting all these people Cole loves so much." Her fingers, warm and soft, tickled Cole's close-shaven scalp.

"Are you close to your parents?" asked Cousin Rose-Lee.

"Not physically close—they're in Atlanta—but we talk and visit all the time." Before Cole could comment, Cecilia had her cell phone out of her pocket and was showing the rapt trio a recent picture: the sharply dressed black woman, the impossibly proportioned white man, their willowy offspring laughing between them in miniskirts. "This was on my brother's birthday last month."

"Your brother!" said Cousin Rose-Lee, studying the picture. "My, my."

"Will we have you back for Christmas?" asked Cousin Heck. "We'll have Cole Senior and that wife of his here then."

Cole stiffened. By Christmas, Cecilia would certainly be showing, no tunic able to hide the changes in her figure since he'd first undressed her at her apartment in the East Village. Since the days when she'd been scarce as a thousand-dollar bill, climbing into bed with him only when Gavin Cannady had to travel.

"I hope so," said Cecilia. "I really hope so."

Here, thankfully, was Peach at the door, clanging a spoon against a copper pan, as she always did. "Attention, relatives: Soup's on! Everyone get moving so we have plenty of time for family game night before the lovebirds have to get back on the road." She shot a wink at Cole and Cecilia and trotted off to clang her pan in other rooms, rousing other family members. Slow movement began, Cole and Cecilia offering arms to the elderly cousins, Cousin Rose-Lee lacing her fingers through Cecilia's as they made their way to the dinner table.

"That's my seat, honey," said Peach gently when Cecilia tried to lower herself into a chair at the center of the long, rectangular dining table now covered with steaming dishes of food. Cecilia flushed, covering her mouth with one hand.

"Down here," said Cole, guiding her by the elbow to a pair of seats in the corner, near the Scotch faction, who were all too full of mirth to pay attention to much other than the clanking of glasses and their own in-jokes.

"How embarrassing," said Cecilia softly, as they settled into their seats. "I like it, though. She's the matriarch! Why shouldn't she have a spot that's always hers? A seat right in the middle, where she can see everybody?"

"Right," said Cole, refilling his wineglass. The Rioja was deep and oaky, worth the ridiculous price Cecilia had paid.

"I guess that'll be me someday," continued Cecilia dreamily.

Peach's husband stood and announced grace; heads bowed, Cecilia pulling Cole's left hand into her lap. As Uncle Allen unspooled his lengthy prayer, mentioning each person present by name, as he always did, Cecilia lifted Cole's hand and pressed his palm against the firm curve of her belly, guiding it silently across the fabric of her tunic until he felt a cottonball-soft tap from within. On the other side, some member of the Scotch faction kneaded Cole's right hand roughly, making him wince. "Amen," said Uncle Allen, finally. Cole did his best not to yank both hands back too quickly.

"Amen," echoed the crowd, heads lifting.

Plates were passed; food was spooned out in heaps; everyone exclaimed over the menu, Cecilia's delicious beans, the debut of baked fish with bright oranges and limes; Peach poured the last swallow of Rioja into her own glass and uncorked another bottle. "Delicious Rioja," she called from mid-table, raising her glass in Cecilia's direction. "Do I taste viura grapes?"

"You should," Cecilia called back over the din of flatware on dinner plates. "It's a Rioja alta, a lot more tempranillo than grenache."

"It's a beautiful choice. Hard to find!"

"I guess that's why it's so expensive," murmured Cole.

"I'm glad you're enjoying it!" said Cecilia, brightly. She lifted her own glass, still full, and gave it a delicate, wistful sniff.

Peach had meant it when she told those who asked that she could handle the cleanup herself, that they should get on the road before dark; but various insistent helpers—her husband, her daughter-in-law, cousins still a bit too unsteady to start the drive—lingered in the kitchen anyway, bumping into one another in their efforts to scrub and dry dishes. So Peach stole away to the living room, settled with her glass of wine on the sofa, Bill Evans still merrily tickling the ivories. Her feet ached.

She needed to call her brother Cole and his wife out west, the expected Thanksgiving-day formality of wishing them a happy holiday and reporting on how their son seemed to be doing, this Cecilia he'd brought to dinner. She stalled, though, spinning the stem of the wineglass between her fingers, and finally she called the Lindas first, knowing they would be together at the first Linda's condominium in Dallas. She had loved them dearly, both of her brother's first two wives, their lovely faces and bright laughter. Her brother Cole had always hankered for pretty women with sweet dispositions.

Where they'd gone wrong was in their outsize need, the way they'd both—years apart from each other—hung desperately on his arm at holiday dinners, vulnerable as caught prey. Peach had told them, the first Linda and then the second Linda, that her brother Cole was afflicted with a certain repulsion for what seemed too available. That they might stay pretty for decades, but that it wouldn't matter to this hungry Chatwell man who only wanted to chase. *You ought to at least find a hobby*, she remembered telling the second Linda. *Be out of the house every so often.* Already too late by then, a third child heavy in that Linda's belly, her need too great.

Where they'd gone right, though, was that they both were named Linda. Because of course there is no word for the wives that come first, and Peach wanted Cole Junior to think on them with reverence. They were good to her brother; they deserved a title.

The Lindas answered the phone immediately and said they were well, dining on pork loin that the first Linda had marinated in soy sauce and ginger slices, a recipe Peach said she'd like to try. She told them she'd used their baked fish recipe, with delicious results and to compliments from the family. They congratulated her on her first grandbaby—between them, the Lindas themselves had eight—and thanked her again for recommending the show they'd been enjoying together on Netflix for a few weeks now. Not asking about her brother Cole, as they never did. What could you say about women like that? The salt of the earth. She hung up feeling refreshed, restored from a day full of trials.

Then it was time to call her brother and his wife, and they answered after many rings. "Peach," said Cole, his voice deep and sonorous as a bassoon.

"Happy Thanksgiving, Peach!" echoed the wife, whose name wasn't Linda. "Tell us everything. Tell us about the girl."

Peach liked her brother's wife; she was smart and well-mannered, had her act together, never a hair out of place. Loved her, really. Hadn't Peach been the one, after all, to pull aside this third wife, the non-Linda, and whisper to her the one piece of marital advice that seemed to have worked? *Make yourself scarce*, she'd said in a corner, that first Christmas right after they'd married. *Even when you're in the same place, wander a little so he has to come and find you.* Watching, impressed, as not-Linda seemed to actually understand that by instinct and pulled it off impressively, always inches from her husband's reaching fingertips. Nodding her approval when not-Linda left home for stretches of weeks or months at a time, sometimes going where she'd said she would and other times just checking in to a hotel or even sleeping in one of Peach's guest rooms. Making herself scarce so that the Coles, Senior and Junior, couldn't get enough of her when she came back. She was a good woman, really, though God knew she couldn't cook and didn't know the first thing about wine, or jazz.

"I'm just so curious about this Cecilia," not-Linda was saying.

Peach cleared her throat, shoving certain thoughts out of the way. Her brother Cole's contentment hummed its way over three thousand miles of phone wire. "She was a nice girl," she said finally. "She brought green beans and an amazing wine."

"She was pretty? Tall? Cole Junior mentioned that she's tall."

"As tall as he is, really," confirmed Peach, and took a sip of her wine. "Slender too." Not so slender, though, that Peach hadn't caught a glimpse of a certain roundness in Cecilia's silhouette as the girl stood by the oven receiving serving dishes, her tunic clinging to the fullness of her lower abdomen. Which might have been intentional on Cecilia's part, really, in the same vein as how after a whole evening spent pretending to nurse the same glass of Rioja, she'd finally just poured the wine down the drain, throwing a wink Peach's way.

"And Cole Junior seems to like her?"

"That's certainly the implication," said Peach. Though if he did, how did you explain his listlessly wandering the house all evening, frankly avoiding her, the most evasive Cole Junior she'd ever known? This nephew who, as a boy, had run up to each relative in turn, bubbling over with affection. Who just last year had been radiant, loving, happy to be among family, away from the coldness of New York. And how did you explain the thing Cole Junior had done after dinner tonight, steering the family away from Trivial Pursuit—surely in Cecilia's wheelhouse, such a smart girl—and insisting on Pictionary instead, leading to that great unpleasantness, Cecilia's tears in the kitchen later? Cole Junior wearing that sullen look, unreadable like Peach's other brother, the one who hadn't been to a Thanksgiving in years. The two of them, Cole Junior and Cecilia, leaving just after dessert, not touching each other.

"I'm glad," said not-Linda, as Peach's brother Cole grunted his vague agreement. "I'm so glad. You know, he really doesn't bring women around us much."

Peach, pretending to continue listening, propped her tired feet on the ottoman and thought of how she'd gotten Cecilia's phone number, using the pretense of wanting to correspond later about the green beans recipe; how easy it would be to just send a text message. But what would she say? The longer not-Linda prattled on, the more drafts Peach considered and scrapped. And anyway, texting a stranger? Albeit a friendly one, one who wanted to be included and liked. Cecilia had her people, her good-looking mother and expensively dressed father, her brother, who seemed open-minded, if nothing else. Surely that lot could help Cecilia with her situation or help her find her way out of it entirely. Peach couldn't, shouldn't, intrude. Instead she'd call her brother Cole one day in six months, playing innocent, revealing nothing when he said he didn't know what Cole Junior was up to, hadn't heard much about Cecilia in a while.

"Well, thank you," said not-Linda. "We're so glad Cole Junior has you while we're away."

"I'm glad Cole Senior has you, Melanie," returned Peach automatically, as she always did. "We'll see you two at Christmas."

La Belle Hottentote

With the party just getting started, the new provost's nieces are already bored to death. They are also desperately uncomfortable in their dresses, the ones Aunt Cassandra chose for them and the one she didn't. They gather in the shade of what they're told is a 150-year-old ash tree, next to a koi pond with a burbling waterfall. The university president's backyard, full of such rich absurdities, reminds each of them of a Maggiano's-like restaurant they all went to once for a family birthday, but since none of them can remember the name of it, they don't bring it up.

They have been given access to wine via the drinks stations throughout the lawn, their mostly underage statuses immaterial under the lofty circumstances. They tug discreetly at bra straps and wedgies whenever no one is looking, though it seems like someone always is.

Aubrey, who at seventeen is really too young to be here, snarls, "I hate this!" and slurps from her glass of chardonnay.

"Well, get comfortable," says Caprice. "You see that?" She points to catering staffers forming a conspicuous line on one edge of the lawn, each holding a tray of slender champagne flutes. "I'll bet you anything there's about to be toasts. Eons and eons of toasts."

Aubrey pretends to kill herself. The others look away: exasperated, embarrassed, and, as before, *bored*.

"Project Be-Cee is just getting started," adds Caprice.

Project Be-Cee is what they're calling their mandatory presence here at this godforsaken gathering of sixty-year-olds in knee-length gowns and ascots. Aunt Cassandra couldn't get her own daughter, their cousin Cecilia, to spare an evening for this—on principle, Cee doesn't leave Brooklyn on weekends, and anyway is probably too busy doing drugs in a bar with a two-block line or something—and so they have been called

in to pinch-hit. They are here to *be Cee*, or the version of Cee who has
time for her mother's bougie aspirations.

To varying degrees, the nieces respect Aunt Cassandra and want to
be good surrogates. Also, when it comes to Aunt Cassandra, they share a
general feeling of indebtedness, its origins and expressions different but
deep for each. Like the Maggiano's thing, this goes unspoken. But they
all agree the assigned dresses were a bit of a slap in the face.

Even Bellamy, who understands the importance of dressing for the
occasion, is rather salty about the outfit Aunt Cassandra chose for her.
Olive green, a color with all the sex appeal of army fatigues. Poofy,
dowdy sleeves and an empire waist that instantly impregnates her short-
ish torso. When it arrived in the mail last week, Bellamy allowed herself
a few minutes to sulk, then resolved to try to see in it whatever her aunt
saw, since of course Aunt Cassandra's taste is normally unimpeachable.
Here is where she landed: Aunt Cassandra trusts her, the eldest niece,
to set a solid public example—which means perfect elocution and absolutely no cleavage.

To that end: "Let's not complain so much," she says to the others, lifting her chin. "All *we* have to do is sit here. Can you imagine if you had to
spend this whole night, you know—"

"Kissing ass like Aunt Cassandra?" finishes Caprice, gesturing. In another corner of the yard, Aunt Cassandra, wearing a dress like an ex-
ploded raspberry, flits from person to person, university faculty and
geriatric donors, receiving their congratulations with supplicating head
bobs. The sight fills all the nieces with an unnameable shame.

"That's not what I was going to say," says Bellamy after a moment.

"Okay, but ew," says Caprice. She does an unflattering imitation, tip-
ping prayer hands at each of them in turn. Bellamy, then Mariolive, then
Aubrey. Aubrey laughs and pats Caprice's head.

"No, she's good at this," says Bellamy. "She's doing it exactly right.
This is how it works."

"This?" says Caprice.

They watch as Aunt Cassandra stops before the university president,
a loud white man wearing an even louder paisley bow tie and blinding
white cuff links. As she pushes a hip out to one side, dips her head so he
can whisper something into her ear, and rewards him with a long laugh.

They barely recognize the behavior: In general, Aunt Cassandra does not do mirth or even show her teeth when she smiles. Their whole lives, they can count on one hand the number of times they've seen her wear a color other than navy.

"I mean, this is pathetic," says Caprice. "She's practically sucking his dick. She already has the job, doesn't she?"

Bellamy narrows her eyes at Caprice. "Oh?" she says. "And you're just a paragon of dignity, I guess?"

Of the four of them, only Caprice has gone rogue, eschewing the frock Aunt Cassandra sent her—girly, modest, pink—and wearing instead a slutty black bandage dress she already had in her closet. It's so short she can't bend over; it took her five minutes to perch on the stone edge of the koi pond without flashing everybody.

"Maybe try covering up your whole pussy in public," says Bellamy, turning away. "Then feel free to comment on what other people are doing."

Aubrey stops laughing and Caprice scowls. Bellamy can be such a goddamn killjoy. Though at a seasoned twenty-one, and with her own bougie future practically sewn up already—having finished college a year early, she's headed to law school in the fall—she probably knows what she's talking about. Rumor has it she sweet-talked herself into a partial tuition scholarship at a reception for admitted students, an affair the others imagine as similar to this one. Stuffy and unsexy. Like Bellamy.

"You guys are embarrassing," Bellamy continues. "Do you literally not know that rule number one is to laugh at your boss's bad jokes?"

"Tuh," says Caprice. "Do *you* literally not know we have a Black POTUS? And I don't have a boss, so, no."

She knows as she says it that it's a stupid, pathetic response. Of course she doesn't have a boss; she doesn't have a *job*. Even with her excellent GPA, the social sciences department wasn't exactly coughing up leads. Aside from work-study hours, which will consume the better part of each day all summer, she's got no plans to make any money for the next three months. Despite desperately needing some. She applied at Sephora and Borders and a little mom-and-pop bakery in her neighborhood near campus; no bites. She is beginning to worry that she gives off the odors of both desperation and disorderliness, or that she should have at least worn nicer outfits to the interviews, but it is not clear to her what business-casual attire has to do with her ability to stack mascara and eyeshadow or alphabetize novels by author.

In any event, she can wear whatever she wants to the campus library, but the prospect of having to call Aunt Cassandra midsummer to pay her Comcast bill looms ominously. And her own mother has only this to say about it: *You're twenty, right? I don't give grown folks money anymore.*

Meanwhile, Bellamy will be doing lawyer-lite work at some big DC firm, practice for her illustrious future, at three times the minimum wage and wearing ruffly blouses from LOFT. You can't help but hate her for it a little.

Truthfully, Caprice knows she could stand to rejigger her paradigm, to learn something. And so then Bellamy's little shrug, which reduces the discussion to the insignificance of elevator small talk—as if she can't *possibly* waste any more time trying to convince the likes of her jobless cousin—is quietly infuriating. A little storm brews in Caprice's gut.

"Hey," says Aubrey, and does a little jig-in-place on the grass. "I thought rule number one was to get our shoes reheeled before this party."

"That too," says Bellamy. "And don't you wish you had?"

She points at the soil around the stone koi pond, which is pockmarked where the exposed metal of Aubrey's heels has attacked it over and over for the past hour. "Oops," says Aubrey.

Bellamy sips her wine and tosses back her hair, which has been flat-ironed so meticulously it looks like a wig, even in the heat. In this way, she has really taken the *be Cee* charge to heart. Cecilia gets her hair genes mostly from her father, a big, aggressive blond guy to whom all the nieces have privately likened the university president. Uncle Charles is not here; like his children, he's found reasons to be hundreds of miles away from this celebration of his wife's ascent. But he isn't *not* here. Because of the president.

Each of them has had the thought that Aunt Cassandra must have actually sought out men like this to shape the corners of her structured life. Formidable white men with vast cuff link collections. To varying degrees, they consider that this might not be a matter of accident or coincidence. But until Bellamy says what she says next, they'd always assumed it was at most some sort of subliminal affinity.

Bellamy says: "Aunt Cassandra is the smartest person in this whole yard, let alone in the family. You see if *she's* not the president of this shitty school in a couple years. Grandma Opal played this same game and wound up with a jazz club."

The others stare at her, not quite comprehending. "Wait—huh?" says Aubrey finally, giving voice to their collective confusion. Why are they talking about Grandma Opal, who's been dead forever?

Bellamy smirks a little. "The jazz club," she says. "The one that sent our moms to college. You really think they bought it with bar tips?"

The others are silent, chastened, though they still can't figure out what this has to do with anything. In fact, that's *exactly* what each of them has always thought, as it's the bedrock of the family lore. Atlantic City, the late 1960s: their grandparents, a good-looking couple with a passel of dutiful daughters, worked Kentucky Avenue nightclubs in the lush years before the casinos opened, squirreling away money until they could afford their own little hole-in-the-wall bebop spot just off Kentucky. And what of it?

Bellamy laughs dryly. "You'd have to be pretty naive—I mean really painfully *stupid*—to take that at face value. Have you ever tipped a bartender? How many White Russians do you think it takes to—? Well, you wouldn't know, I guess."

The others seethe quietly. She's right, of course; they have no idea what a club costs, no concept of the pay structure for nightlife workers. Certainly no clue how the two correlate. But what exactly is her point?

"My point," says Bellamy, "is where do you think they got the down payment for Little Suzette's? Grandma Opal *kissed ass*"—finger quotes around this phrase—"and made a friend, that's where."

Because they have nothing better to do, they scoot in closer and let her paint the picture. Their grandmother, youngish and pretty, all wide, dewy eyes and plump lips and that dimple in her chin, her hips swishing back and forth as she carried drinks on trays. Their grandfather, stuck slicing lemons behind the bar. Both of them working at one busy place Friday through Sunday, and at a sleeker, sleepier spot the other four nights of the week.

Even with legal segregation over by almost a decade, Opal would still have considered it rather an event to serve a cocktail to a well-dressed white patron like the one who started showing up for all her shifts at both places. He liked her for her figure, curvy but trim; and for her modest cotton dresses, which contrasted so sharply with the nothing the go-gos wore just a few feet away. The way she left something to the imagination. He joked about her churchy uniforms, all while peeling the cotton from her body with his ice-colored eyes.

He'd order a single drink and then tip her for ten. At the close of a long week, he'd slip another fifty into the waistband of her skirt. What could she do? She had children at home, lots of them, including the big-brained Cassandra, who'd need expensive schooling one day.

And it was more than money; sometimes he brought her gifts, little practicalities and occasional treasures she could fold into her life without her husband's notice. Chocolates, little cushions to put in the heels of her shoes. Silk scarves you could mistake for the ones from the Black-owned boutiques but that actually came from the expensive wing of Macy's. The rich-looking little opal-and-diamond necklace you never saw her without in the now-faded photographs—

"Hold up," said Caprice. "No. Granddaddy gave her that necklace."

Bellamy frowns at her. "No. This man did."

"My mom told me," says Caprice, stressing the second word ever so slightly. "He gave that to her for her birthday one year."

"That's what I heard too," says Aubrey helpfully. She feels wild, saying it. Rarely does she contradict Bellamy in matters of fact; and especially not here, in discussing the belongings of a person only Bellamy among them ever even met. But Aubrey *has* heard the story, and seen the necklace, which now belongs to their cousin Cecilia.

"Where did you get this info, anyway?" presses Caprice.

Bellamy stares off toward the party. "I just listen better than you all," she says. "Trust me on this. They've shuffled the details a little over the years to make the whole thing more pro-Granddaddy. A better story. But it was this other guy who gave her the opal necklace."

"But Granddaddy—"

"I know. You're right, Granddaddy gave her *a* necklace, later. One that wasn't as nice. She took a chance that he wouldn't notice a difference—you know how men never notice anything—and started wearing the other one as though it was Granddaddy's gift. Like, *Oh honey, look at me wearing the necklace you gave me! I got it cleaned so it would sparkle more!* And he never caught on. We're talking fourteen-karat gold versus costume jewelry, but he had no clue."

Each of them thinks of the men she knows, and this holds water.

"So anyway, back to the guy. First it was little stuff, then the necklace, and then he writes her a check for—well, for a lot. Enough to get them started."

Caprice sucks her teeth. "Sometimes I think you're full of shit," she says. "*Often* I think that."

"Whatever," says Bellamy. "You can believe they did it one tip at a time, dollar bills in a mason jar. But anybody who says that's what happened is a liar."

"Hey guys," says a voice behind them.

They turn and here is Boyd Elledge, son of the university president, coming around the koi pond. Their collective posture straightens as if they were all marionettes attached to the same rod, and it had just been ever so subtly yanked. Boyd is Adonis-like in his Banana Republic chinos, his champagne-colored hair brushed forward in a tasteful Caesar.

"Having fun?" he says.

They mumble affirmatives; Caprice tugs at the hem of her skirt.

Boyd holds out a bottle of orange wine. He makes particular eye contact with Mariolive. "MO, you want some?" Before she can answer, his gaze broadens to include the others. "Anybody want?"

They all nod in unison and watch as he produces an instrument from his pocket, plunges it into the cork. Twist, twist, twist, and *pull*. He does the last bit with his teeth, which are neat and white. He knows somehow to fill their glasses in age order: Bellamy's, then Mariolive's, Caprice's, and Aubrey's. He pours heavily, leaving only a swallow in the bottle, which he downs.

"Okay, well," he says, and starts on his way.

"Thanks," says Bellamy.

"Thanks," say the others, embarrassed they didn't think of it on their own.

"No problem," Boyd calls over his shoulder. "Oh, and actually? I think there's about to be toasts or something. See you in maybe a couple minutes?"

When he's safely out of sight, Aubrey fans herself dramatically, first her face and then her crotch, and the others laugh. It's mostly for show; she's agnostic on boys generally, and so far the ones who've caught her attention have been more melanin-endowed, less slickly attired. Black and brown gamer types. But she likes the surprised reaction she gets from her sister and cousins; it goads her to try a rather daring line. "Speaking of sucking dick!" she says. Bellamy elbows her; *Too far*, the gesture means.

For the first time in a long time, Mariolive clears her throat and speaks: "We took Psych 202 together. Boyd and me."

The others fall totally pin-drop silent. With Mariolive, you have to.

"It was actually kind of weird," Mariolive continues. "The class was mostly sophomores. He was the only senior. I think maybe he needed a credit? But anyway, we studied together a few times."

"Studied?" says Caprice. "Or"—she gyrates subtly—"*studied*?"

Mariolive glares at her sister. "Studied," she says firmly. "Like with books, in the library. But I did start thinking there was, you know, maybe a little bit more to it."

"Okay, well," says Caprice. "Congratulations. I guess any day they'll name a building after you on campus. Did he just call you *MO*, by the way?"

A flush creeps up from Mariolive's sweetheart neckline. "Forget I mentioned it," she says.

"You have to admit that's really another level of brownnosing," presses Caprice. "Throwing it at the president's kid. You can't possibly need the study help. You trying to get your tuition waived or something? First dibs on housing? *MO*?"

"Shut up," says Mariolive softly. "He's actually pretty nice."

Bellamy and Aubrey exchange a quick look, through which passes the resolve to stay out of it. The twins are rising juniors at the university where Aunt Cassandra will be provost, and where Boyd's father is president. Bellamy has wisely steered clear of the school for her own higher learning, and Aubrey won't apply in the coming year. All this— Aunt Cassandra's appointment, this irritating so-called party, Boyd's attention—likely means more to the twins.

Also, Mariolive is as fragile as a soap bubble, which gets old, in all honesty. She stands now and sips at her strange-colored wine. "Looks like it's time," she says, and starts for the Elledges' patio, where the guests are gathering, without waiting to see whether anyone else does the same.

"Welp," says Caprice. "Project Be-Cee, part deux." She turns sideways and slides off the wall, trails her twin at a cool twenty feet.

Aubrey gives Bellamy a look of desperation. "Okay," she says. "But do we really have to? We could just go get in your car and . . . ?"

"Sh," says Bellamy, and strokes her sister's hair. "Come on, let's get down there."

President Elledge, resplendent in the school colors, with his cuff links flashing and a backyard full of listeners in his thrall, rambles at length *about* Aunt Cassandra, giving the impression that at any moment he'll turn over the figurative mic and let her say a word or two about her new position; but then he just keeps talking, and talking, and talking:

"If I tried to list everything Cassandra has done for us, all her myriad wonders and achievements, we'd be here all night. You will just have to take my word for it that this brilliant being you see before you—"

Aunt Cassandra hides a smile behind her fingers, which are freshly manicured, the nails painted to match her dress.

"—has had a hand in countless initiatives that will shape and color the tapestry that is our institution's future. Cassandra is a woman of elegance and *vision*. And I know you all look forward to learning exactly how she plans to execute that vision."

Be Cee. The nieces straighten, ready to applaud louder than anyone else, expecting that finally President Elledge will duck into a shadow and let Aunt Cassandra tell the gathered audience exactly how she plans to execute her such-and-such. Instead, he just keeps talking: about her brilliance, her team spirit, her respect for the university's rich history and mounting reputation.

Each of them notices how every time he throws a look in her direction, acknowledging her presence even as he invites her to remain quiet, his eyes find their way down one side of her dress and up the other. They watch as she weathers his gaze, shifting just perceptibly as her feet get tired from standing, her posture nonetheless putting theirs to shame. It weirds them out—she's so *old*, after all, Jesus Christ—but it also worms its way into their respective hippocampi.

Boyd, who's been roaming the backyard with leonine indifference this whole time, stops behind the twins and whispers something into Mariolive's ear.

The others watch, and—because it now seems well settled that Aunt Cassandra won't be saying anything whatsoever—their attentions attach to this small interaction. They watch the flush creep up Mariolive's neck and the tremble in her hands, which she quickly slides into the pockets of her modest skirt.

Finally, *finally*, President Elledge says something in a tone of finality, and everyone lifts their champagne flutes. Aunt Cassandra exchanges cheek kisses with him and then walks over and toasts her nieces in the classiest way, just barely touching her glass to theirs. Bellamy's, then Mariolive's, Caprice's, and Aubrey's. Then she disappears, off to schmooze some more, and the crowd disperses.

Feeling strangely deflated, the nieces drift back to their staked-out area near the koi pond and perch along the edge.

"Welp," says Caprice. "At least now this shit's almost over."

"Seems like it," says Bellamy. "Do you two need a ride to the Metro?" She's addressing the twins, who rode in from DC with Aunt Cassandra, but only Caprice is listening; Mariolive is watching as Boyd chats with his dad down on the patio, both of them laughing heartily. The others watch her watch him.

"So what'd he say to you just now during the toast?" asks Aubrey.

Caprice smirks. "Yeah, *MO*, what'd he say?"

Mariolive blushes. "He said, *Nice dress.*" She looks down and smooths the flared jersey skirt around her legs. "He's into, like—well, I don't know. This sort of stuff." She sweeps her hand across her torso to indicate her modest dress, its sweetheart neckline and darted waist.

"Right," says Caprice. "A dress your aunt picked for you that's too ugly to wear to Easter Sunday. He could barely conceal his boner, I'm sure."

Mariolive's blush deepens. She glares at her sister. "Fuck off," she says. "Fuck. *Off.* I'm going to sit in Aunt Cassandra's car."

She wobbles to her feet—this is more wine than she's ever had in a single evening—and wanders falteringly back toward the patio, weaving between the other guests and giving the Elledge men a wide berth.

They watch her go, losing sight of her when she reaches the densest part of the crowd near the large house. Sympathy stabs at Bellamy and Aubrey, who have always found their cousin's moody shyness disquieting.

Caprice dismisses her twin with an eye roll and turns back to the others. "I'm right, aren't I?" she says.

"You don't know what you're talking about," says Bellamy.

"*You* don't," retorts Caprice. "First of all, you're entirely wrong about that necklace thing. Half the time I think you're just making stuff up, but we listen anyway because you're—"

She waves a hand to indicate Bellamy's general visage.

She continues, "I don't know where you got this thing about some weird white benefactor, but it's not true. The seventies were the seventies, not the eighteen hundreds. My mom has told me the whole story about that necklace, and you're just wrong. You don't know *anything*. Granddaddy bought the necklace, and they saved up the money for the club. Nobody gave them fucking shit. Especially not if all Grandma Opal did was parade around in church dresses. Men don't work that way."

"The necklace, is it even that expensive?" muses Aubrey. "I mean, Cecilia just sort of, you know."

She gestures to indicate the careless way Cee styles the piece in question, layering it with chunky plastic chains and polyurethane scraps.

"Don't go by that," says Bellamy. "Cee doesn't care about looking expensive."

"She doesn't have to," says Caprice. "If you have anything else going for you, you don't have to."

Bellamy huffs and sets her chin on the shelf of her fist.

Aubrey, interpreting the gesture to mean her older sister has shut down and won't be responding further, shrugs and slips away for more wine.

As soon as she's gone, though, Bellamy gives Caprice an elbow shove that's not entirely playful. "*You* don't know anything," she growls. "And you didn't even have the decency to wear the dress you were supposed to, on Aunt Cassandra's big day. You look like a—a fucking—"

"Ho," supplies Caprice.

"That's not what I was going to—"

"Strumpet," says Caprice, pulling the term from last semester's Shakespeare seminar. "Libidinous harlot."

Bellamy stares.

"Coochie on legs." Now Caprice is doing her best to defuse the moment or at least make her cousin laugh. She pulls again, this time from a sociology unit on nineteenth-century propaganda. "Hottentot Venus. *La belle hottentote.*"

This last one breaks Bellamy. She lets out an involuntary laugh, a noise loud enough to draw the attention of a nearby cluster of liberal arts professors in shirtdresses. She mouths the word *sorry* and then, once they've turned away, leans in close to whisper her reply into Caprice's ear: "Hottentot Venus who shops at the Guess outlet."

Caprice socks her, none too gently, in the upper arm. It's a cymbal crash, a wave breaking against a pier. All the remaining hostility dribbles out in their blooming laughter, and for a moment Caprice actually rests her head on Bellamy's shoulder. They are, both of them, moist from the humidity of the encroaching summer and lightheaded from the wine, from starving themselves in preparation for this stupid party.

Finally, Bellamy pulls away. "I have to pee," she announces, rising.

Caprice stands too. "Away, thee, to the water closet," she says. Her tongue twists around the words. She watches as her cousin walks off toward the big bajillion-dollar house, squeezing her butt so the non-stretch fabric of her dress swishes only minimally around her careful strides. Bellamy is a bitch, thinks Caprice, but a benign one. A saditty suck-up, like Caprice's mother has always said. And definitely, *definitely* mistaken about the origins of their grandparents' club. Men don't just go around doling out heirlooms in exchange for chaste smiles and cocktails. Not in the same universe in which Caprice herself, with near-perfect grades, can't score a summer job.

This thought pisses her off all over again, actually. By the time she's back in the thick of the party, she's back to sulking, wanting Bellamy to be wrong but worrying she isn't. There is a Black president, and her grandparents were hardworking and handsome; she's seen the photos. And yet.

Evening falls and lights come up in a ring around the yard. As Caprice wanders, hoping for nothing except to avoid the only professor who gave her a B, she spots Boyd Elledge standing on his own and lets his eye catch hers. He's got a fresh bottle of wine in hand. His forehead glows lightly with perspiration. He extends the bottle toward her, and she finds her most gracious smile. As she approaches, she resists the urge to tug at the hem of her dress.

Mote

They would only be in the house on Ashburn Street for six or nine months, a year at absolute most, and so although Merritt knew she should make a point of meeting the neighbors, she put it off for two weeks after the move-in. She had begun to specialize in putting things off; these days she was leaden as an anchor, and Ashburn Street was the ocean floor. Screw the reverse welcome wagon, the hours of tweaking snickerdoodle recipes until she hit on one with just the right blend of nutmeg and friendliness. She was in no mood to put on a sundress.

"Should you maybe . . . ?" tried Anthony on their first morning in the house, knotting his tie in the rising September sunlight, falling silent when Merritt shot a foot out from beneath the sheets and toward the crotch of his slim-fit trousers. He dodged it and gave the bed a wide berth as he broke for the door, the stairwell, the wide world outside. His wingtips beat out a judgmental tattoo on the pavement below: *Fuckup, fuckup, fuckup.* It was Monday, and as a non-fuckup, he had places to be, small miracles to conduct. It was time to chitchat with strangers in transit. To excel at his job, even the parts he disliked or had to teach himself on the fly. His faltering suggestion—that Merritt get up and *do* something—drove her deeper into the plush cocoon of pillows around her.

That first day and each of the next thirteen, she waited until his footfalls faded and then begrudgingly made herself *do* things. She rattled around the house performing small unpacking tasks that stabbed at her temporal lobes but kept the creeping nihilism at bay. On the main floor, where her parents hadn't laid carpet, even a small sigh echoed thunderously. She trawled Amazon and ordered rugs.

Their accumulated furniture had jam-packed the overpriced city apartment they'd left behind, giving it a cozy *Breakfast at Tiffany's* vibe, but here in her parents' single-family house it looked sparse and doll-housey and stupid. Merritt hated it, all of it, even the little birch curio table she'd bought in rosier times, trotting into Pier 1 Imports and plunking down the blessed extra she'd saved from a first paycheck, customizing it by adding a little faux ruby finial as a drawer pull. Formerly one of her prized possessions, it now looked like something you'd relegate to step stool status before finally putting it out with the trash. Scuffed and dwarfish, it looked like what it was: an impulse buy chosen by a twenty-something Pinterest disciple with no real understanding of life or decor.

She stuck it in the kitchen and stacked it with cookbooks. Then, another day, she moved it to the foyer, where it would greet theoretical visitors with an array of framed photos, its ruby handle twinkling in the sunlight. Still another day, she carried it up to the master bedroom and tucked her bullet-shaped vibrator into one of its drawers.

When she caught herself moving it for a fourth time, she recognized her behavior for what it was, fucking lunacy, and forced herself out into the neighborhood.

Just as she'd figured and feared, Ashburn Street was largely the same place it had been twenty years earlier. The houses were compact and crisp, timeless golden brick trimmed with power-washed shutters. The homeowners' association allowed some pizzazz in front-door colors, and they sparkled like a string of multicolored jewels: crimson, salmon, pearl.

Merritt's parents had bought their house in the eighties, at a price that now seemed unimaginable. They had since moved to a different house upcounty, but still meticulously maintained this one to earn rental income—or so they had until Merritt's great comeuppance, a for-cause firing so harsh it had obliterated any chance she'd had of being hired someplace similar anytime soon. There had followed a great valley of difficulty. A generation earlier, Anthony's up-and-comer's salary could have supported a family of four; now, for their little unit of two, it was either rent or student-loan payments, but not both. They fell short three months in a row, downgrading to cheap toilet paper.

And so they had had to go to her parents. The shameful slinking-back, the sheepish begging: *That thing you always said, about how I could move back to the house on Ashburn Street if I needed to? So . . . did you really mean that?*

Of course they had. When the current tenant's lease expired, Merritt's parents were only too happy to welcome their only daughter and son-in-law back into the family home. The circumstances worried them, but they rallied, summoning false cheer over the phone as they worked out logistics.

Won't it be nice to have more space? said her mother, conspiratorial. *You know, square footage is the secret to a happy marriage!*

This is nothing to be ashamed of, said her father, jubilant. *Think of all the money you'll save on rent once you find a new job. This is how generational wealth is* built!

Generational wealth. Sure it was—forgoing paying tenants to shelter a jobless fuckup. On moving day, she'd sobbed bitterly as Anthony and a buddy carried the birch curio table out of the apartment and down to the blanket-lined rental truck.

And now here they were, and again it was Monday.

She drifted toward the intersection of Ashburn and Greer, where on move-in day she'd noticed evidence of another Black family, but that turned out to have been a miscue: a Haitian nanny looking after the sandy-haired children of the couple who'd bought the sprawling corner house. The nanny barely returned her hello.

Shrugging off her disappointment, Merritt turned onto Greer Lane, where the homes doubled in size. Benzes and BMWs stood in the driveways or coasted toward the distant city. Luxe marble fountains burbled on lawns you had to resist the urge to spit on. She walked west along the Greer semicircle, and there at number 303 was Lucy Shealy, watering a persimmon tree.

It had been twenty years, but the recognition was mutual and immediate. "Oh my God," said Lucy. "Merritt Scott? It's really you!"

Lucy still had her cascade of amber hair, but now that they were old enough to run for president, she had chopped it to a respectable shoulder length. Her twinkling eyes remained the color of Jacuzzi water. In the old days, a bit of prepubescent chub had portended a future weight problem, but it had not materialized; she was long and trim aside from a mild postpartum doughiness where her top met her jeggings. Her changeable little-girl face was now a beautiful woman's, her rosebud mouth babbling disclaimers about the infant sleeping behind 303's upstairs windows. She was closing in for a hug.

Merritt was self-conscious. Having waited out the last of sundress weather, she had draped herself instead in leggings and a tunic and a sweater—black and black and more black. She had spent two hours meticulously straightening her hair for God only knew what reason; it hung lifeless around her face. She searched her memory for her most recent shower. In the mirror she had felt broody and complex, but now before her old neighbor she felt like a low-budget Halloween witch.

Still, it was nice to see Lucy after all this time. Shocking, but nice. She heard herself answering in kind: "Lucy Shealy. It's really *you*!" Their torsos met, Lucy's arms mussing Merritt's scorched lengths of hair. She had quite a grip.

"Tell me about her," said Anthony over Japanese takeout. "You were friends?" He was being kind, Monday being the day he and his coworkers gathered each week in his boss's office to receive praise for the excellent work they were doing; and when he then gathered his own team in *his* office to pay the compliments forward. On Mondays he came home buoyant, with takeout, and did his best to make Merritt smile.

"Good friends," said Merritt. "We used to play at each other's houses *all* the time. And we got on and off at the same bus stop, so we told everyone we were sisters." She speared a blocky hunk of tuna roll with her chopstick and studied it, remembering. Two awkward little girls in the flannel and vests of the early nineties, hefting bulging L.L. Bean backpacks toward the corner of Ashburn and Greer. A smile tugged at the corners of her mouth.

"Sisters," repeated Anthony, a twinkle in his eye. They'd looked up Lucy online, finding her slick and winter-pink in a professional photo from the corporate job she'd left to have the baby. He pursed his lips in a performative O and whistled a string of familiar notes: *Ebony and i-vo-ry* . . .

"Shush." Merritt kicked him lightly in the shin. "You know what I mean. Friends. Sister-friends. Joined at the hip. Little-girl stuff."

"I get it," he said. "That's nice, to reconnect with her. She's home for now? With the baby?"

Merritt's brain fired a neon warning flare, having caught the shift in his tone, the measured casualness of the question. "Home with the baby," she affirmed tightly.

"Well, great," he said. "Great." He cleared his throat and shifted his weight. He was gearing up, she saw, to launch into the *should you maybe*s of the day, starting with some innocuous comment about their dinner accommodations. They ate perched on stools before the kitchen sink. *Should you maybe finish setting up the kitchen?* he was probably going to say. It had been her project for the day, but she'd met quick defeat: their Formica dinette was too collegiate, all wrong for the cavernous dining space her parents had added to the house in recent years. He was going to say that it was okay if she hadn't readied herself to tackle job applications just yet, but maybe she could at least do something to spruce up the dinette—or, better yet, maybe she *should* be starting to think about job applications, since eating on stools at the sink, like anything less than ideal, was tolerable enough if temporary. And then he would say that her catching up with Lucy was *great, great*, but Lucy had a baby—which, of course, Merritt did not—and priorities of her own, and meanwhile Merritt's priorities would eventually have to include job applications—

"The other sushi place is better," said Merritt a little wildly, cutting him off before he could start. As he sputtered a bit, she showed him the pink-and-white hunk on the tip of her chopstick. "This place uses zero nori and barely any tuna. I mean, what the hell."

"Oh. Sorry."

"No big deal," said Merritt, rising. "Just, next time, let's use the other place."

What sucked, what really rankled, was that in fact both sushi places were excellent, their fish generously portioned, but now she had to make a show of not eating the rest and of letting the remainder fall into the sparkly blue Ikea trash can that looked all wrong against her parents' stainless-steel kitchen appliances.

A few days later, another weekday (though Merritt wasn't sure which), Lucy came strolling up Ashburn Street from the east, the baby tied to her torso.

Merritt watched from the window in the spare bedroom they'd designated as an office. She was finding there were details she'd forgotten about the neighborhood, such as that Greer Lane wrapped all the way around and rejoined Ashburn Street at the other end, though you had to walk a foot-trampled path and duck aggressive brambles to take advantage. The sight of Lucy approaching, brushing dogwood leaves from the shoulders of her sweater, reminded Merritt instantly: It was the quicker route. It was how they'd traveled between each other's yards back in the old days.

At the door, Lucy was flushed but smiling. Under her arm was a bottle of Rondel, icy-necked and deep pink. "Hey there! Wondered if you'd like to chat for a bit, finish catching up?"

Merritt's anchor heart lifted a little. "Yeah, come on in," she said, pushing out the words before she had time to feel self-conscious about her grubby True Religions, the kitchen that still looked like an almighty shitstorm. Or what Anthony would say—that she was supposed to be applying to jobs. An unfinished application blazed from the screen of the laptop balanced on her forearm; she slapped the machine closed and stepped aside, taking the Rondel as Lucy entered for the first time in twenty years.

They covered lots of ground quickly, falling into a sisterly shorthand as they exchanged briefings. Many of the beats were symmetrical. They'd parted ways in high school, when Merritt's parents moved upcounty. Then off to their respective universities, good ones; meaty, impressive degrees. Merritt's historically Black sorority and Lucy's functionally white one. Cutthroat internships in cities full of educated singles.

Lucy had lots of good hookup stories punctuated with party drugs and names Merritt recognized. In college, she'd fucked the cutest guy from their middle school; a few years later, a well-preserved New Kid on the Block.

Merritt hadn't done anything like that, but she recounted her own history as juicily as possible, imagining an earlier version of herself—the sixteen-year-old virgin Lucy had last known—gawking in disbelief.

She made Lucy laugh a lot, the sound a sultry tremolo. The wobbly dinette chairs creaked on the hardwood.

Lucy wasn't actually Lucy Shealy anymore; she was Lucy S. Something-Else, having married a Joey Something-Else a decade earlier. Also, the baby was her third child; there were two others in school. From the pictures she pulled up on her phone, it was evident Joey's genes had bested hers three times over. The children had the sleek dark hair of otters, espresso-chip eyes. On Thursdays—it turned out this was a

Thursday—Joey picked up the older kids from school and took them to dinner with his parents, who hated Lucy for her failure to genuflect properly. That was more than fine with Lucy. It meant Thursday was her oasis of solitude, just her and the baby from sunup to late evening. Nobody demanding the parmesan picked out of their alphabet pasta by hand.

"What about you guys?" asked Lucy. "No kids, looks like."

"Nah," said Merritt. Another swallow of the rosé and she found herself telling the rest. The closest they'd come was an abortion she'd had a few years back, weeks before their wedding. Anthony came from a family of gossipy churchfolk; he and Merritt had stared at each other over the little blue plus sign, telepathically working out the plan to stay in their good graces. It was early enough to do it with pills, each cashing in a single vacation day. Anyway, Merritt wasn't much of a kid person. A few weeks later, clutching her peonies under the summer sun, she'd felt only relief.

"Well put," said Lucy, nodding solemnly. "They're real life-ruiners." She winked and gave the baby's back a pat.

"Tell that to Anthony," said Merritt. "Sometimes he wonders what if. Just every so often." She cleared her throat and returned to a thread from earlier in the conversation. "So you left your job?"

"Had to," said Lucy. "Once we were outnumbered. But I had a good run!"

From the way Lucy lifted her glass, punctuating this answer with a long chug of Rondel, Merritt understood that they weren't going to get into it—but according to LinkedIn Lucy had been hot shit, a high-ranking marketing dynamo at one of the largest regional retailers of women's workout apparel. The sort of thing no eleven-year-old would name as her dream job, but that many working women between thirty-five and forty-four would kill for. It was obvious how she'd risen to the top that fast. You could see the jets of intensity behind her eyes, the controlled intelligence in her posture. She was nothing like the millions of friends Merritt had lost to motherhood, who couldn't string together two sentences without lapsing into banalities about cesareans and sleep training.

"How are your parents?" asked Lucy.

"Fine. They live up north. Not even a half hour away." Merritt paused. Emboldened by the wine and the camaraderie, she added, "They're letting us stay here for free until, you know. I find something else and we can go back to renting. Yours?"

"Both gone," said Lucy. "Five years, three years."

"Oh, sorry," said Merritt. Trying to locate a memory of the elder Shealys' faces, her mind settled instead on an image of Lucy from fifth grade—pudgy, wearing a hand-sewn dress in colors that put one in mind of dusty mantelpieces. The Shealys were old parents by the standards of the time, close to retirement age, which back then had meant small but noticeable missteps. Sending their kid to school in the starkly wrong clothes, spouting inscrutable film references. Merritt supposed their deaths might have been normal, timely ones. It seemed okay to add, then, "I guess that means the house is yours."

"Yep. We were looking to buy around then anyway. I would have picked something downtown, but, you know." Lucy gave her glass a swirl. "*So mote it be*," she added, and leaned back to take a long swallow. The baby emitted a little bleat at the change of balance, but slept on.

"*Mote*," said Anthony. "The fuck does that mean?"

Merritt stopped what she was doing—measuring an overhead length of wall, trying to center a picture frame—and cocked her head to the side, thinking. "It's like—it's just what you say," she said. Weakly, she knew. "When you want something to happen. *So mote it be.* It's like *amen*." She wasn't sure how she knew this; consumed with trying to remember, she lost her balance and dropped the nail, the hammer, the frame. They clattered to the floor and Anthony leaped aside, gripped her waist to steady her. "Sorry," she said, frustrated. Her head was foggy, Rondeled. "I just—can we finish this later?"

"Yeah," grunted Anthony. He knelt to reach under the sofa, fished out the dropped nail. "Later. Fine. *So mote it be.*"

They had to have Merritt's parents over for dinner. It was one of the unspoken terms of the arrangement. Anthony had printed a coq au vin recipe from his work computer and spent a whole Sunday afternoon chopping vegetables. Merritt uncorked a Beaujolais.

Stepping into the dining room: "It looks nice!" said her mother, though it didn't. "I like the airiness."

Plates had to be served at the stovetop; the dinette table was just barely large enough to seat four. The women sat sidesaddle on the chairs. "Cozy!" said her father.

As they ate, Anthony gushed praise for the house, the wood-nestled neighborhood. He chattered about work, his invigorating new commute, the small victories of the past week. He hopped up and down replenishing the bread basket, spooning wine sauce over his in-laws' bowls.

Merritt sipped her Beaujolais and dissociated, fixing her gaze somewhere between her parents' heads. Flavorless lardons burst between her clenched molars.

Her mother was elegant and coiffed as always, a ruby teardrop at her clavicle. The proof of forty years of successful marriage.

Her father was dapper in his oiled brogues, self-actualized enough to laugh at Anthony's jokes without reservation, a homeowner twice over.

In the old days, her parents had sat together in this dining room, albeit at a grander table made of real wood, to pay the bills by hand. Her paycheck plus his, a chunk carved out for the mortgage, another for the utilities, the rest into savings. Often they had let Merritt lick the stamps.

"Merritt?" Her mother, phone in hand. "Want to see?"

Merritt forced herself to refocus. "See what?"

Anthony, en route to the dishwasher, paused to heave a deep, showy sigh.

Merritt leaned in to look at what her mother was showing her. "Oh!" It was a picture she must have snapped at home, of a faded Polaroid on display in an old-school photo album. "Me and Lucy!" They were elevenish, Merritt's hair in box braids, their heads tilted sideways in parallel sassiness. A crumb-sized black crystal twinkled in the cartilage of each girl's upper ear.

"I found this!" said her mother, turning the phone to show Anthony. "When you told me you'd been seeing her around, I went and dug up the album. I had forgotten how much *time* you two used to spend together."

"I had too," said Merritt, zooming in. Her preteen self looked ecstatic. They had *begged* their parents for those cartilage piercings, because some girl a grade ahead had gotten one, and it had taken Merritt a perfect report card to earn permission. Her mother had chaperoned, turning the girls loose in a now-defunct mall. Merritt remembered how they'd forgotten their age and newfound maturity, galloping on sandaled feet toward the Piercing Pagoda they knew was tucked behind the food court.

Lucy had gone first, swearing it didn't hurt *at all*; when of course it did, Merritt had felt not betrayed but simply impressed.

The site of Merritt's piercing had gotten infected a few weeks later, her body unceremoniously rejecting the cheap little stud. *Ping!*—it had fallen from her ear in the middle of their accelerated math class, striking the tiled floor and rolling into the void beneath Lucy's neighboring desk. Never to be seen again. A ferocious crumb-sized wound had remained for weeks in the cartilage of Merritt's upper ear.

"They were like *this*," said her mother to Anthony, locking two fingers together at the knuckles. "Did *nothing* without each other. This was the same school year they actually got suspended, both of them."

"Can you believe that?" added her father merrily, an elbow to Merritt's ribs. "Honor roll every quarter, Sixth Grade Student of the Year—and then we get this call on a winter day. *Come pick up your daughter. She was naughty, naughty, naughty!* Ha!"

"I can't even remember what they did," mused her mother. "But if you ask me"—and here she leaned in, stage-whispering behind a manicured hand—"whatever it was, it was Lucy's fault!"

"Ah," said Anthony, looking at Merritt. "I see."

Merritt realized she was rubbing the ancient indentation in her upper ear and redirected that hand toward the bottle of red. She had forgotten all of this. "Wild," she said, pouring.

In the morning, she was supposed to be finishing a job application, she was supposed to be organizing their books, she was supposed to be searching the moving boxes for the Tupperware they'd been unable to find the night before. But she'd had too much wine, opening a second bottle as motivation to deal with the dinner dishes, and the air wafting through the open bedroom window was muggy and Mondayish. She covered her face with a pillow and went back to sleep.

Anthony texted from work. *BFD?*

Breakfast for dinner. It had been one of her specialties back in the apartment. Cornmeal pancakes, the batter made from scratch; a frittata conjured up from this and that and farmers market gorgonzola. But who knew if there was a farmers market this far out in the suburbs, and she found the local Safeway uninspiring.

She checked the fridge. Leftover coq au vin sealed awkwardly in zip-lock bags, and very little else.

She texted back: *Takeout?* It was Monday, after all (wasn't it?). It seemed cruel, his making her ask, surely realizing how her throat would fill with bilious inadequacy as she sent the message.

She left her phone beside her laptop and wandered out onto Ashburn Street. A sharp-edged wind licked her face, nudging her eastward. She found herself making for Greer, spotted Lucy on the glider bench on the front porch of 303, the baby in her arms. Rocking, rocking, rocking.

Merritt draped herself over the porch railing, whispering in case the baby was near sleep. "Can I bitch about my husband?"

Lucy leaned forward, blue eyes widening. "I wish you would," she whispered back, scooting over. The persimmon tree trembled in the autumn wind.

Her mother dropped by midweek with gifts. "Just a few things I thought you could use for the house!" she said brightly, setting an armful of retail bags in the foyer. "I noticed you were still working on fixing things up around here . . . ?"

"Well—we'll only be here for like a year or two." Merritt watched her unload picture hangers, crisp hand towels, curtain rods, and velvet valances like the ones in the house upcounty. "Anyway, thanks," she said. "Isn't it Wednesday? Aren't you working today?"

A crease appeared between her mother's eyebrows. "It's Thursday, silly," she said. "And I'm *obviously* teleworking. Can't you tell?" She winked.

"Right," said Merritt. It was one of the perks, of course, of a long and steady career, of striding into an office exuding straight-backed confidence, as her mother had done for decades. Merritt's feet felt leaden, anchored to the floorboards.

"Last thing," said her mother. She reached into the bottom of the final bag and produced a volleyball-sized pumpkin, bright and orange, its stem curled cartoonishly.

"Oh, right," said Merritt. Halloween, just around the corner. Lucy's kids were going as characters from a Pixar movie Merritt hadn't heard of. She sat the pumpkin on her birch curio table. Its waxy skin reflected in the translucent ruby drawer handle.

"I still have your witch hat at home, if you need it."

"That's okay."

"We remembered what it was, by the way!" Her mother tapped her shoulder emphatically. "Your dad and I—we remembered why you got suspended in sixth grade. They claimed you were bullying other kids, you and Lucy. A boy from your class and a girl from another one. We actually had to keep you home for a week. It was totally trumped-up and ridiculous, of course. You? You'd never bully *anyone*."

This struck the flimsiest of chords. Merritt grasped for a relevant memory and located a contender: recess in their last year of recesses, Lucy in one of her weird outfits, rage blazing behind the blue of her eyes as they huddled together beneath a canopy of oaks at the edge of the playground. *We need to get back at him*, Lucy had said, nodding in the direction of a boy on the four square grid. In a time of great antagonism, an incessant crossfire of pubescent teasing, his taunts had particularly rankled because he was . . . well, *hot* was still a few years off—college— but *cute*, certainly, with a fringe of eyelashes that could be seen from space.

And the girl . . . Merritt recalled a flaxen-haired seventh grader— she of the original cartilage piercing—being sort of a bitch on the bus. Name-calling and taunting sixth graders for being sixth graders, flashing teeth free of orthodontia, flipping her waist-length braided ponytail hither and thither. *Maybe* targeting Lucy on occasion. It rang a bell.

What had they done to warrant suspension? Merritt couldn't remember and actually wasn't even sure *they* had done anything. Those were the days of accelerated math and other sources of tantalizing validation, her first of many campaigns for the honor roll. And after-school activities: violin, a kids' cooking club. She was busy, always busy. Mostly, she thought she had kept Lucy company, working on homework while Lucy enacted whatever girlish revenge constituted *bullying*.

"Well, speak of the devil," murmured her mother. Gathering her things to leave, she'd paused to look out the window. Merritt peeked around her shoulder and there was Lucy, pushing a stroller up the driveway. A bottle of Rondel peeked out from beneath the carriage.

Back in their overpriced apartment, Anthony and Merritt had argued infrequently, and only over matters of territory—like when someone had piled sweaters in the other's designated closet space. On Ashburn Street, there was a surplus of space, fourteen rooms in total from the top floor to the bottom; what was there to argue about?

And yet Anthony had chosen to plant himself in the kitchen, mere yards from where Merritt and Lucy sat talking, browsing the sparse contents of the fridge, and—Merritt could feel it—spoiling for a fight. He didn't even make his usual beeline for the bedroom to change out of his work suit. His posture was charged with antagonism. He wanted Lucy to leave, and he was being a dick about it. Reaching into the fridge to pick up objects, sticks of butter and condiment jars, and then setting them back down roughly, producing enough noise to interrupt the conversation. Over and over.

Lucy didn't seem to care, even when a particularly loud slam woke the baby. "Totally, I remember," she said, lifting her voice over the infant's pitiful wail. "That girl's name was Alexandra. You don't remember her?"

Merritt didn't remember much, but maybe it was because Anthony— glowering in the corner, making a huge show of not being able to find anything to eat—was consuming too much of her Rondel-addled brain space. Her eyes darted back and forth between Lucy and Anthony, her mind lighting on the image of the person Lucy was calling *Alexandra*.

"We *hated* her. Remember?"

Merritt didn't, but she believed it. In those days, it hadn't taken much. She, Merritt, had resented anyone who bested her along any metric. A classmate with higher grades or a girl who better exemplified their homogenous middle school's Prussian beauty standard—as they nearly all did. She remembered little about Alexandra, but she remembered the white-gold braid. A neat, slim stream whose terminus hung in her lap when she sat hunched on the bus, painting her nails, being pretty.

Lucy got to her feet and swayed back and forth with the baby pressed to her shoulder. "She made fun of my clothes. She made fun of your hair. She absolutely sucked! The bitch to end all bitches. I can't believe you don't remember that."

And then Merritt sort of did. "Did we do a—did we do something to her?" The words dribbled out, the memory half-formed. She saw them, hunkering unsupervised in Lucy's basement with the geriatric Shealys pacing the kitchen overhead. "Lucy, what did we do?"

A smile spread across Lucy's face, her rosy lips twisting upward at the corners. "You cut off part of her braid," she said. "Waiting for the buses.

The same week I stole Nick's world studies notes and made him flunk the midterm."

The counter was piled high with persimmons, a gift from Lucy's garden. A stoic, slow-blooming little fruit. Anthony pushed them aside, found bread and peanut butter and the only clean knife in the kitchen. He pulled out a plate and began slathering with painstaking slowness. "Cut off some girl's hair," he muttered from the corner.

"She was so nasty to us," continued Lucy, "and then this one day she was sitting on the little brick wall in front of the bus lines and you just sort of crouched behind and, *schwick*. We hid it in my backpack."

"But we got caught?"

"Well, some administrator found Nick's spiral in my desk, and then a note you had passed me in class that day, about how you always wished you had hair like Alexandra's. Proof positive." Lucy paused and took a sip of her drink, seeming to savor the memory. "We got suspended. Both of us, for a week. And it was Halloween! So, like, twenty-five years ago this week. We weren't even allowed to trick-or-treat."

A murky memory had assembled itself in Merritt's mind, but with critical pieces missing. A note? Her preteen longing for white-girl hair had been, she thought, her secret shame. The sort of thing she'd have committed to her diary. She didn't remember confiding so directly in Lucy about that. What would such a note even have said?

Nor did she remember the makeshift haircut itself, which seemed like the sort of thing one *would* remember. The weight of the scissors, the feel of release as the hair separated from its owner's head. A physically passive person, she could count on one hand the number of times she'd had contentious contact with a peer in childhood. How could this one—this *assault*—have slipped her mind?

But she *did* remember the week of her suspension, her parents departing for their respective offices each day at dawn after warning her to stay put and work on her at-home studies. She, gangly, elevenish, had sat obediently in her room until their footfalls faded—and then, off like a shot, reckless in her hurry and leaving the front door unlocked, she'd raced through the dogwoods to enter Greer Lane from the east, finding Lucy waiting behind the open basement door. Lucy's parents were indiscriminate bibliophiles, and the basement was lined with wooden shelves, the volumes of Faulkner and Tolkien warping in the October damp.

There would sit Lucy amid the books, tween-plump and munching Thin Mints, a glint in her blue eyes, a tabletop-sized tome in her lap. Black text springing starkly from the yellowed pages.

Merritt reached for the bottle of Rondel. "This is bizarre," she said. "I have no memory whatsoever of cutting off what's-her-face's braid. But I remember getting in trouble for it. And I remember hanging out at your house, and you had this giant book."

"From the university library," said Lucy. "*A Guide to Spells and Incantations.*"

"And you had the . . . the piece of braid, in your basement. And Nick's world studies notes." Could that be right? A hank of woven hair, limp like a dead snake, gathered with elastics.

Lucy's baby had gone quiet. Lucy crossed the room to retrieve the stroller she'd parked near the fridge. Anthony stepped sideways, giving her a wide berth. Lucy lowered the baby into the stroller and adjusted the little canopy, bathing the interior in darkness. She turned to Anthony, ignoring his body language, and let forth a husky little laugh. "Get this," she said to Anthony. "I got this book out of the library, on modern paganism"—Anthony's shoulders shuddered slightly—"and so while we were suspended, we tried like hell to make one of the spells work."

"A binding spell," said Merritt. Remembering was like the cracking of an egg. They'd found it in the book, the very first section: *Basic binding spells.* It was vivid, suddenly. Two little girls drawing chalk circles on the hardwood floor of Lucy's basement, setting their findings in the center: a disembodied bit of braid, a red Mead spiral filled with Nick's notes on the Renaissance.

Lucy had a gleam in her eye and was still addressing Anthony as though he wasn't visibly leaning away from her, cramming the remainder of his sandwich into his mouth. "You take something the person cares about very deeply," she said, rubbing her hands together.

"Like part of a ponytail she spent ten years growing," supplied Merritt.

"Right. Or like Nick's totally fucking incredible, perfectly thorough world studies notes for the first half of the semester. And you put it in a so-called *magic circle*, chalk, or salt if you have it. We didn't, because my parents were upstairs in the kitchen. And then you say some words, and *bam*, they're bound."

"Bound?" Anthony said around a mouthful of peanut butter. Fumbling to fill a glass with water.

"Stuck in place. You can use it for lots of reasons, but it's perfect for bullies. Can't fuck with you anymore."

Anthony took a few long sips. "So did it work?"

Lucy laughed and returned to her seat next to Merritt. "Like hell," she said. "We had to go back to school the next Monday and it was rabbit season." She crooked her fingers, raised them to her temples: bunny ears. "Plus, Nick got to retake the midterm, and it turned out Alexandra was Claudia freaking Schiffer with a proper haircut. Disasters across the board." She reached for the bottle "However, I *did* fuck Nick at a frat party in college, ninety million years later, if that counts for anything. And I beat him out for a job later. He wound up working for his dad's restaurant like five miles away from here."

"Well," said Merritt. "I never saw Alexandra again. So I guess that's a wash."

Lucy drew up her legs and laid them across Merritt's lap. "She works for the DMV. Had kids, got fat." She lifted her glass.

Merritt, moving almost involuntarily, clinked Lucy's glass with her own. "Amen to that," she said.

They were late to Anthony's work thing, catered Thai chicken skewers and an open (wine) bar at the office, because Merritt hadn't gotten around to unpacking the box of her party dresses. Technically, they were supposed to be *in costume* anyway; Merritt vaguely remembered having been offered a witch hat (by whom? Lucy?), but she went with leggings and a tunic and a sweater, all black, supposing it was better just to blend in.

Anthony, in a Jackie Robinson jersey, tried to introduce her to the members of his team. Young people with plastic plates in hand and uncomplicated, tipsy faces, sure they were getting away with something as they got drunk on the company's dime. Everyone turning their dutiful interest to Merritt. *What do you do for a living?* The trillion-dollar question, everyone's favorite conversation-starter in this godforsaken city. She managed with a bit of temporal finesse, telling them what she had *done* before her comeuppance, to impressed nods and other forms of approval. She pivoted the conversation back to Anthony, deftly and repeatedly.

A young woman named Loulou, her keen face amplified by an enormous Diana Ross wig, touched Anthony's arm as she babbled compliments. *The best boss I've ever had! He works soooo hard!*

Anthony's boss pulled them aside and offered them hearty shots of Macallan Scotch from his private desk stash.

And then it all began to fall apart. First Merritt forgot her way to the marble-esque lavatory, not once but twice, and Anthony lost his patience as he led her there for the second time. She had once been able to hold her liquor, in case she'd forgotten. Shouldn't she maybe slow down?

Then Loulou, grafting herself onto them once again, made a joke Merritt didn't understand. Anthony dealt with the awkwardness badly, repeating it twice verbatim without further context, adding to Merritt's mounting frustration.

Then Merritt had to pee again and intentionally got lost in her solo search for the bathroom, holing herself up in the building lobby instead. Her feet hurt in her heavy boots. She texted Lucy: *Help! Anthony's work party sucks. Am feeling like a failure among the gainfully employed. And there's this irritating fangirl named Loulou.* But it was Halloween; she realized after sending the message that Lucy and Joey were on a snail's-pace journey along Greer Lane, trailing tiny Pixar characters.

She passed out briefly on a stool in the lobby and half awakened a few minutes later to find Jackie Robinson propping her up at the front door, gruffly summoning the valet.

At home, Jackie became Anthony again and there was some half-hearted fumbling in bed. His kisses were rough and dispassionate, Merritt's painfully uncontrolled; finally, Anthony made his decree—*I'm going to sleep*—and immediately fulfilled that promise. He snored, as he did only when he was pissed off.

Merritt tumbled out of bed and went looking for her vibrator. She knew it was still housed inside the birch curio table, which finally she had moved from the master bedroom into the main-floor hallway. Banging her elbows and shins on absolutely every-fucking-thing, she felt her way down the stairs in the dark. Muscle memory led her to the place where she'd finally set up the table, and she confirmed its location by ramming it with her knee. "Fuck," she muttered, and reached for the drawer handle. The sensation in her palm screamed and simmered, an arpeggio of pain. "Fuck!" she said again.

She pulled her phone from the deep pocket of her pajama pants and turned on the flashlight. The curio table was without its bespoke handle. The faux ruby finial was gone; the sharp edges of the underlying screw glinted in the glow of her phone's flashlight.

II

The November sunlight glowed persimmon-colored in the window. Anthony had tried a persimmon once, at a Japanese coworker's wedding. The thing looked like an underripe beefsteak tomato and tasted like a gummy bear.

Merritt stirred beside him in bed, still asleep. She was rumpled and irritatingly beautiful, her shoulder-length hair imprisoned in a silk bonnet. She looked like a younger, less-assured version of her mother, frowning in her sleep. She snored lightly, as she always did in the suburban aridity.

Anthony showered and then dressed in the dark, fuming. On moving day, they'd had a whole discussion about setting up standing lamps in the walk-in closet. It was one of about twenty things Merritt had promised to do with her rafts of unstructured time, and it hadn't gotten done.

Back in their old apartment, they had always brushed their teeth simultaneously at the his-and-hers sinks and snuck touches as they dressed together in his-and-hers suits they'd had tailored in Chinatown. On Ashburn Street, he had been asked not to make too much noise if she was still knocked out when he descended the stairs and headed out to work.

He gave the front door a hard tug and experienced a nasty little current of satisfaction at the loudness, then an aftershock of guilt. The guilt settled in his throat—or was it the start of a November cold?—and stayed with him all day.

From the driver's seat of his Prius, he sized up the front lawn, the pale frost on the hedges, and began a voice-to-text email to his father-in-law. "Good morning, sir," he began, as he did weekly, starting the ignition. "Checking in with a little update on lawn care." It was one of the explicit terms of the arrangement: someone was to keep his in-laws apprised of the state of the home, just as regular tenants would, but more vigilantly, given their close relationship. Merritt had said she would do it, but the responsibility had gradually shifted to Anthony. He wouldn't even bother asking this time. Even if he did, she would say she didn't know anything about winter plant aeration, and still it would fall to him.

Concentrating on his verbal email, he drove slowly toward the main thoroughfare, casting a glance down Greer Lane as he passed. The school bus was stopped there, waiting; the stay-at-home mothers shepherded fleece-bundled kids inside. Lucy among them? Anthony couldn't tell; they were all pink and laughing, not so much as a brunette among them, everyone in a uniform of yoga pants. And now he had passed, *so mote it be*. What the fuck sort of word was *mote*, anyway? He had started to look it up after Merritt's first mention, but the headings on the search results—Wiccan shit, and Freemasons—had unsettled his Baptist-reared heart. His mother would have disapproved, and so he'd abandoned the research. The unease had remained.

"Anyway," he concluded, wrapping up a remark about fertilizer, "let me know if that sounds good to you. Thanks again, sir." And, send. He liked his father-in-law, who never turned anything into a pissing contest or exuded superiority, though he'd already been a few years into father-hood by Anthony's age, already owned the house on Ashburn Street. A professor of American economics, he alone among their family members had refrained from haranguing Anthony and Merritt about babies and home purchases. It was a relief. He knew how it was in this era, and in this town.

Anthony swung the steering wheel to guide the Prius onto the main thoroughfare, away from Ashburn Street, and his mood unclenched itself instantly. The neighborhood was beautiful, but darkly so. From the lack of lighting in the walk-in closet to the shadowy half memories Merritt kept uncovering, thanks to Lucy and her strange lies. Merritt cut off some kid's ponytail? Fuck that—not a chance. Anthony didn't believe it any more than he believed the reason her last job's HR department had given for her abrupt firing.

He thought of Merritt's face, contorted with panic as she hovered over a pregnancy test, wedlock still weeks away. Anthony had found the mo-ment a bit thrilling, but rules and benchmarks governed Merritt's life. She preferred to do things by the book. She was lots of things, includ-ing able to hold a grudge—but vengeful and roguish, she was not. A less-than-stellar performance review could alter her mood for months. At eleven, there was no way the straight-A student his in-laws had described would have risked falling out of the school administrators' good graces.

Lying Lucy. Anthony floored the accelerator, and Ashburn Street disappeared behind a wall of oak trees.

At the office, he shared an elevator with Loulou, the star of his team and one of the canniest people he'd ever met. "New suit!" she chirped, regarding him. He understood that she meant *Nice suit!*, and stood a bit taller.

"You ready for the thing?" he asked her, gesturing to indicate their big task for the day, a presentation that stood to make or break (but probably make) one of their most important client relationships. He was letting her take the lead, confident she'd represent them well.

"I think so," she said. "I double-checked my notes and practiced all weekend. I've been second-guessing my hair, though." She touched his arm briefly. "*You* know."

He did know. Early on, he'd worried about his locs, though he always pulled them back for work. Conservative clients and all that. But Loulou's Afro puff looked smart and professional, neatly secured with black pins that echoed the sheen of her blazer. Her dark eyes gleamed sharply behind the frames of her stylish black glasses. "You're good," he told her. She would understand that he meant, *You look good.*

At their floor, they parted ways. Once, Loulou had reminded him viscerally of his wife, all radiant confidence and vocabulary. But at the Halloween party the other night, he had noticed it was no longer true. Merritt getting drunk too quickly and deflecting all conversation with dull half-truths about her old job.

He sat at his desk and saw that tech had rebooted his computer over the weekend. His internet browser restored a series of old tabs, among them his unsettling Google search. *Mote.* He frowned and closed the window.

His phone chimed, a text from Merritt: *If you're getting sushi don't forget do the other place.*

His ears went hot. He had hinted the night before that maybe they should move away from the takeout-on-Mondays routine to save money. To which she had replied, *I did the math; even if I never find a job, look how much we'll save if we stay here for like three years.*

When only a few weeks earlier, they'd commiserated about wanting a place to call their own. Merritt had just come back from Lucy's and was disheartened by her failure to connect with her old friend over the desire for sovereignty. She, Merritt, felt inadequate, that she was taking advantage of her parents' generosity, if not stealing from them outright. Why hadn't Lucy validated or understood those feelings?

But Anthony knew why not. Merritt's parents were first-generation homeowners, while Lucy's had inherited their house on Greer Lane—just as Lucy now had. Lucy felt no less entitled to it than had her grandparents, who in turn had paid for it with money sown a couple generations earlier. Laughing heirs, or close to it. Old-rich cavalier. Anthony saw this sort of attitude daily in the faces of several of his reports, who wore four-figure suits but showed up late half the week.

His fingers tapped out a snarky reply to Merritt's text, then backspaced it. He was exhausted even before engaging.

After a moment, he texted Loulou instead, thinking of her manicured fingers on his arm that morning. *Lunch before the thing?* He would ask her what to do about this takeout issue, though her previous idea—*counter with a request; BFD?*—had crashed and burned. Her brand of intelligence was deductive and methodical. She would come up with something else, and something else after that if needed. Eventually, something would work.

III

The baby was crying—not the patient little warning bleats that made strangers comment on what a *sweet little thing* she was, but the guttural bloody-murder screams she saved only for after midnight, and for her mother.

Joey's elbow jutted out from beneath his mound of covers. "She'll wake them," he slurred. Their older kids had not acclimated to the late-night symphony.

Lucy slid her legs over the side of the bed. It was her turn to go. It was *always* her turn to go. Joey had work in, let's see, 4.5 hours.

Before the baby, before she'd left Stella Sport and her days had gelatinized, they had taken turns. Now her brain lagged sometimes, searching a stale schedule until she remembered. She had no place to be in

4.5 hours. Now and forever, it was her turn to soothe the baby back to sleep.

Pulling a sweater around her shoulders, she drifted into the little nursery adjoining the master bedroom and tried the first of her tricks: a hand in the crib, slow strokes to the infant's quivering shoulders. Sometimes it worked, but not tonight. Nor did increasing the volume on the white-noise machine. Nor the pacifier with the dumb-faced plush lamb hanging from its handle.

A baby was no different from any other challenge. You tried different things. You layered strategies until something clicked. Just like at Stella Sport. Some combination of cunning and luck, with a sprinkling of manual labor and old-fashioned wait-it-outness. Everything on earth was this way. If reporting a bully to the teacher went nowhere, you took matters into your own hands. You stole notes. You tried a binding spell. If the first spell didn't work, you practiced, got better at it. And if the white noise fell on deaf ears, you strapped the baby into the Tula wrap and paced the house awhile.

Lucy strapped the baby into the Tula wrap and paced the house awhile. Quickly there was silence, but she knew not to let her guard down just yet. She scanned her mental to-do list. It was Monday, a day of wall-to-wall domestic labor. Now was as good a time as any to chip away at the list.

She went to the linen closet and set aside fresh sheets for all the beds.

She went to her office—what had once been her office, now overgrown with Legos and old homework—and used the computer to order a delivery of diapers and baby wipes.

She went to the kitchen. She peeled and quartered four persimmons and dropped them into a Mason jar; she filled the jar to the brim with high-quality vodka. Merritt would love the infusion, when it was ready in two weeks or so. Lucy would invite her over for a taste, and she'd stay for a refill, and that would be one more day when the house didn't moan with loneliness. Meanwhile the garage fridge suffered no shortage of Rondel. You tried different things.

While she was in the kitchen, she fixed the kids' lunches. Turkey sandwiches with coarse-ground mustard and Swiss Lorraine, leafy greens from the backyard. They would pick at them and probably throw half away or trade them for Cheetos, but whatever. Her effort was what mattered.

She grabbed the navy cylinder of Morton salt from the cupboard and tucked it into a superfluous strap of the Tula wrap.

She went back to her office. She scribbled out a mildly spicy love note, borrowing the words from a book she'd read, and dropped it into Joey's briefcase. If adding a new baby to the brood didn't reignite the magic, well . . . you tried different things.

She went to the basement and pulled the laundry from the dryer, sorted as much of it as she could without disturbing the baby.

She approached the ancient mahogany bookcase, one of the few things her parents had left behind that she hadn't replaced with modern equivalents, and knelt at the level of the correct shelf. She sprinkled fresh salt around the cuff links Joey had inherited from his grandfather, her eldest child's first shed baby teeth, the ruby-red drawer pull. She murmured an incantation over each, and then a single conclusion: *So mote it be.*

By now, the steps came easily to her, the whispered words streaming out, fluid. It was more important than ever that it work. She hoped the drawer pull held even more potency than the earring, a tiny, elusive thing now housed in a ziplock to avoid its getting lost—though the earring had proved plenty powerful in its own right, at least back then. Although her own time spent practicing a perfect imitation of Merritt's handwriting surely hadn't hurt, either. The passed note had clinched the case, the school administrators tutting over their reading glasses. You had to come at things from every angle.

She grabbed the laundry and climbed both flights of stairs to the top floor. She spread the clothes on the guest bed and began folding.

Down the hall, her middle child let out a pitiful, howling whine. Lucy's shoulders tensed, but she composed herself. As in every room of the house, there were a few favorite books on the floor of the guest bedroom. She tucked one under her arm and made for the hallway, moving slowly to avoid waking the baby.

And if a story didn't work, there were the melatonin drops—shameful though they were—in the medicine cabinet between the kids' bedrooms.

You tried different things.

Dragonflies

After the service, Loulou's mother, Adrian—working her position as the eldest daughter of the deceased—ordered everyone back to the house to deal with the dragonfly situation. Do not pass Go, do not collect two hundred dollars, no tiptoeing over to the hotel to sleep off the repast. Grandma Lou's dragonfly collection spanned more than fifty years and every conceivable material (glass, ceramic, textile) and was the only thing she hadn't accounted for in any of the meticulous provisions of her last will and testament. Adrian would be damned if she was going to let everyone, all these assembled and *willing* extra hands, leave town without sorting it out first.

Nobody argued; since her ascension to the role of matriarch two days earlier, Adrian had already perfected Grandma Lou's sweetly authoritative tone, had already learned to flex. She sounded like a new person. She even *looked* different, eyes bright and determined under the black fringe of a fascinator hat. "See you all there in five minutes," she said, fixing a firm look on each person in turn as they all milled around on the fresh-air side of First Baptist's ornate wooden doors.

Only Cousin Nicole, with the onyx-eyed baby thrashing on her hip, was excused to go home, her husband trailing her dutifully through the church parking lot. Everyone else piled into cars; Loulou lifted the skirt of her black dress and swung her ascetic black heels, one after the other, to slide in beside her mother. "All right," she said encouragingly. "Dragonflies."

Adrian leaned back against the driver's seat, rolled her eyes heavenward. "Those cotton-picking dragonflies," she murmured in that strange new voice, then started the car with a resolute nod. This task was far from the last of many things that needed doing, though Grandma Lou—clear-eyed till the end, and not wanting things to turn out as they had for her friend Myrna, whose grabby passel of nieces and nephews had given the lawyers a real field day a few years back—had more than done her part on the front end. This had featured heavily in Adrian's eulogy this morning: the surge of admiration she'd felt for her mother, when, locating a particular book on one of Grandma Lou's shelves some weeks earlier, she'd found affixed to its title page a sticky note bearing Lou's curling script. *For Adrian.* A volume of Paul Laurence Dunbar poems, which Adrian alone among her siblings had appreciated as a child. It and every book on every shelf had a name stuck inside it, evidence of the deceased's conscientiousness. Loulou was getting a stack of *Southern Living* cookbooks; she'd brought along an extra suitcase for carting them home. She figured they'd make for a nice artifact in her otherwise Spartan kitchen, something for guests to page through while they sipped wine.

"I was thinking . . . ," started Loulou.

Adrian tensed palpably, like she'd been shocked. "Uh-huh," she said with a sigh. "You were thinking about what?"

It was the eulogy Loulou had been thinking about, how well it had gone; but she saw in the sudden stiffening of her mother's shoulders that Adrian was expecting her to bring up *the thing*, the one she'd promised to tamp down into the Save for Later file as long as Grandma Lou was still on earth. The realization offended her so deeply that the compliment died on her lips.

"Because," Adrian went on, "if it was about that *thing*—"

"It wasn't," said Loulou.

"—I guess I feel entitled to hope we can just get through the rest of all this without having to get into that."

"It wasn't about that," said Loulou. "Nice to get your vote of confidence on my tact level, though."

Adrian fell silent, her eyes on the road. They sailed past the exit to the freeway, where in her little sedan Cousin Nicole might be cajoling her baby to nap as her husband, the good-looking and attentive man who'd bounced the baby on his knee throughout the whole service, steered them toward their row house downtown. The baby had been angel-quiet until the very end of the service, his dark eyes widening at the sound of each sob and swell in the music. *Such good manners already*, Adrian had at some point stage-whispered to Nicole, who hardly needed compliments.

"So anyway," said Loulou after a time. Adrian's car crunched over

Grandma Lou's gravel driveway, pulling in just behind Uncle Charlie's, just ahead of Aunt Roz's. "Dragonflies."

Inside the little brick house, Uncle Charlie and Aunt Vanessa had already chosen stations, Uncle Charlie leading his boys—young men now, Loulou realized—up to the second floor to handle the moving of furniture. Over the long months of Grandma Lou's decline, beds and dressers had been shuffled around to accommodate medical equipment and her increasingly limited movements. Adrian and Aunt Roz had brought in a cot and had taken turns sleeping by their mother's bed—two weeks on, two weeks off. "Get it looking like normal," Adrian called up the stairs after her brother and nephews. Uncle Charlie tossed back a focused, affirmative grunt. The elder of his sons, who'd been promised the master bedroom TV to take back to his dorm room, had the hint of a spring in his step.

"Here's a few of them," said Aunt Kendra, waving to indicate the glass dragonflies lined up along the entryway table. "What do you think, Adrian?"

They were some of her prettiest ones, chosen for that spot because of how they caught the light that came in through the front windows on sunny days. "They'd be good for someone who's got a nice place to display them," said Adrian.

"Your other daughter," said Aunt Kendra. "What's her house like? How old are her kids now?"

"Too little," said Loulou, though she hadn't been asked. On her last visit to her younger sister, she'd had her glasses smashed and nearly lost a tooth playing roll-around with her niece and nephew. She imagined, and then tried not to imagine, the glass dragonflies chipped and shattered and eventually crushed into powder on some playroom floor.

"I'll find a place for them," said Adrian. "Let's wrap them up and put them away for now."

A day earlier, she'd sent Loulou out to the hardware store for cardboard boxes and kraft paper; she now indicated with a little gesture that Loulou should go find some. Heading out to the back porch, where she'd stored them, Loulou found Aunt Shell in the long hallway that connected the front and rear of the house. "Hi, honey," said Aunt Shell. She stopped what she was doing—dusting the picture frames along the walls, the painted dragonflies interspersed with portraits of the family—to wrap her arms around Loulou. "Didn't you look nice at that service. You doing all right?"

"Doing all right."

"Your man couldn't make it? Is he working?"

Loulou stepped sideways, out of the embrace. "No man right now," she said lightly.

A little crease appeared between Aunt Shell's eyebrows. "Mm," she said. "Are your brother and sister coming later?"

"Just me," said Loulou, taking another step toward the back porch. "'Scuse me, Aunt Shell."

When she got back to the front of the house, Adrian and Aunt Kendra had spread the glass dragonflies across the entryway table. Without talking it over, they formed a little assembly line: Aunt Kendra wiping off stray fingerprints with a cloth, Adrian wrapping the translucent bodies in paper and handing them off to Loulou, who laid them along the bottom of one of the boxes.

"Pretty," murmured Aunt Kendra every so often. And then, when they were down to the last few, she turned to Loulou. "You didn't bring what's-his-name, the doctor, the one who came to Nicole's wedding."

The specimen Adrian handed Loulou at that moment had a long black proboscis that wouldn't stay wrapped; Loulou did her best but finally let it protrude from between the folds in the paper, laying it on its back in a corner of the box. "We broke up not long after that," she said.

Aunt Kendra hesitated, then said, "Well, Charlie and I broke up at least twice before we got our act together. You never know."

"True," said Loulou, thinking that, in fact, sometimes you *do* know. According to the linked series of news bulletins she'd gotten since then, the ones from theoretically well-meaning friends and the ones that slipped through her Facebook filters, he'd *gotten his act together* and left for another city with someone else, someone much younger, young enough for Loulou to speculate that the leaving was probably for school or a first job. Not that there had been much credible doubt before that.

Adrian sighed loudly. "There are lots and lots of others out there," she said, as she often had lately. She turned to Aunt Kendra. "Have you ever heard of Eye-You-Eye?"

Loulou hated how she always did that, really drawing out the letters in the acronym to emphasize its pathological foreignness. They'd reached the last glass dragonfly, and Aunt Kendra seemed to slow her fingerprint wiping to a glacial pace. "Eye-You-Eye," she repeated, testing the term's familiarity in her mouth. "Give me a hint."

"I don't even want to tell you what it stands for," said Adrian.

"So then don't," said Loulou. "I thought you didn't want to *get into this* today."

"Oh, IUI," said Aunt Kendra, finally handing over the last glass dragonfly. "I do know. That's the one where they, you know"—and here she reached out a hand to pantomime the use of a tool, an invisible syringe or maybe a turkey baster, causing Adrian to avert her eyes in abject disgust—"up your you-know-what to make a baby. Right? What about it?"

"Here's my next question," said Adrian, giving the kraft paper a rough crumple. "Have you ever heard of someone doing that—*alone*—at this child's age?"

A flush crept up Aunt Kendra's neck. "I did think it was for, you know, *later*."

"Why are we talking about this?" asked Loulou. She dropped the last wrapped glass dragonfly into the box and slapped the cover flaps shut. "Glass dragonflies. Finished. What's next?"

Before Adrian could answer, the front door opened, and in walked Aunt Roz, a handle of vodka in the crook of her black-lace-clad arm. "*Here I come to save the day,*" she announced in a singsong.

The furrow in Adrian's brow deepened. "Ignore her," she said to no one in particular.

"What's next?" asked Loulou again.

Her mother handed her an empty box. "The étagère in the living room," she said. "There are a few of them on there. Do your best to decide where they belong. Oh, and Loulou?"

Loulou stopped in the doorway.

"You know that brooch she had?" Adrian drew its shape with her finger, a subtle stone-studded thing of two inches' width that Grandma Lou had often worn fastened at her clavicle. She waited for Loulou's nod, then said, "Keep your eyes peeled. I couldn't find it anywhere yesterday."

"Okay," Loulou said, proceeding through the doorway. In the living room, Uncle Wood and Cousin Aqil were cleaning behind Grandma's old sofa, tossing dropped tissues and scraps of paper into the open mouth of a garbage bag. Loulou sidestepped them with her box and considered the étagère, its contents arranged as if by the hand of an expert curator. A half pad of sticky notes and a pen were the only things out of place among the objets, left there by Grandma Lou herself, Loulou guessed, before she'd gotten around to labeling the dragonflies. Loulou started with a quick scan of the shelves: no brooch. She reached for a stone dragonfly figurine on the top shelf, one she recognized as having been carved by Uncle Charlie during his midlife foray into masonry. *Uncle Charlie*, she wrote on a sticky note, which she pressed onto the outside of the empty box.

"Hey, Loulou," said Cousin Aqil, his adolescent voice tight as he strained under the weight of the sofa. "Did you hear I'm getting the Volvo?" Together, he and Uncle Wood dropped the sofa flush against the wall and began smoothing out its marled gray fabric, which Adrian and Aunt Roz had chosen for the reupholstery job once Grandma Lou had finally agreed to part with the original madras plaid.

"I heard!" said Loulou. "Congratulations."

"There's only like ten thousand miles on it!"

"Remind me, though," said Uncle Wood. "What was the rule about it? What did Grandma say?"

Cousin Aqil rolled his eyes. "B average," he huffed.

"At least," added Uncle Wood.

"Sounds reasonable to me," said Loulou, reaching for the wire-rendered swarm of dragonflies on the top shelf of the étagère, a souvenir from a trip to Sedona. *Aunt Roz.*

"Do you still have to do the end-of-year assessment?" Cousin Aqil wanted to know. "Do they have that where you go?"

"Ha," she said. He had her age all wrong, was figuring it at something less than twice his own. "No, but I hear it's tough."

She recognized most of the pieces, but there was one she didn't: a set of hammered copper wings on a metal stand. Taking it in hand, she followed the sound of her mother's new voice—lifted officiously above the symphony of others—into the kitchen.

"Careful, careful, careful," Adrian was saying. She had Cousin Kira wrapping up the china plates—not the ones from the start of Grandma Lou's long marriage, already earmarked for Loulou's brother and his new bride up north, but the ones she'd bought halfway through it, silver-rimmed with a single understated dragonfly at the center of each dish.

"I haven't found that brooch yet," Loulou told the room.

"Loulou!" said Aunt Roz. "Come and talk to me."

Loulou joined her at the sideboard, where she stood pouring a batch of stingers. "Hey, Aunt Roz," she said, holding up the object in her hand. "You recognize this?"

Aunt Roz glanced over. "I gave her those wings when she finished her master's. I'll take it with me to give to the next graduate." She offered Loulou a full glass, the white crème de menthe swirling toward its surface.

Loulou set aside the wings and took the glass; there were, by her careful count, six days of freedom left this month before at least two weeks' abstinence.

"To Mother," said Aunt Roz, lifting her own glass to touch the rim of Loulou's. "To a peaceful end and a beautiful service."

"*Peaceful*," repeated Adrian from across the room. "Says the daughter who was three hundred miles away at the time."

Aunt Roz rolled her eyes. "Says the daughter who showed up exactly when asked. You're the one who scheduled the rotation, Louadrian."

"To Grandma Lou," cut in Loulou. She took a sip. The essence of mint tingled against her nose, sending through her a sharp memory: her grandmother kissing her forehead at the end of a long-ago visit, her finely lined hands the same color as Loulou's smooth ones. Sweet mint on her breath.

"So," said Aunt Roz. "You left Doctor Sexy at home?"

Loulou took a long sip. "In a manner of speaking," she said. "I left him at home for good, you might say."

Aunt Roz's mouth fell open. "No!"

"*Hhhh*," sighed Adrian. "I told you that *months* ago, Roz."

"You did *not*," said Aunt Roz. "What did he do? Or was it the other way around? What did *you* do?"

Cousin Kira pretended to whack herself in the head with a china plate. "*Seriously*, Mom?"

"I want to know," said Aunt Roz, pulling out a chair at the kitchen table. "Rights of the bereaved."

"He didn't do anything," said Loulou. "The issue was what he *didn't* do. It just wasn't going anywhere."

Aunt Roz's dark eyes widened like her grandson's had all throughout the service, as though this were a specific and salacious disclosure. "My goodness," she said. "Well, you know about your cousin."

She was, Loulou realized with alarm, getting ready to launch into the story of how Cousin Nicole had nailed down that husband of hers, the painstaking five-year domestication process that had, after some number of false starts, landed Aunt Roz her docile son-in-law and an onyx-eyed grandbaby. All of which, Loulou supposed, was meant to inspire the sort of hope she'd had at Cousin Nicole's age—the sort she wasn't so much worried about anymore. "I know," she said quickly. "Things have a way of working out."

"And you're still on the right side of thirty-five, aren't you?"

Loulou fumbled for an answer, reluctant to get into the details. Technically, yes, but the *wrong side* was just a beat away, better counted in weeks than in months or years. Across the room, her back to the group, Adrian let her head fall dramatically to one shoulder. "*Hhhhhh*," she sighed again, piercing the faltering silence "Roz, fix me a stinger."

Obediently, Aunt Roz got up and began pouring another glass. "What I mean is that maybe there's still something you can do," she told Loulou as she stirred. "Maybe not overnight, but in the long term. Nicole had to break down and learn to cook, for example."

Loulou bristled. "I can cook."

"You still have that apartment and that roommate?"

Loulou set down her glass and picked up the dragonflies, taking a step toward the door. "Apartment, yes; roommate, no," she said wearily. The roommate had gotten engaged and moved away but still emailed periodically to see how *the thing* was going. (*Not going*, Loulou had most recently written back. *At my mom's request, that and the rest of my life are on hold at the moment. My grandma down south isn't doing well. Can't do anything to upset her.*)

"You need a bigger place," said Aunt Roz, giving the sideboard a *eureka!* of a slap. "Men don't like being all crammed in like cotton-picking sardines."

"She doesn't care about that," said Adrian, coming over to get her glass before Aunt Roz could even drop the mint sprig into it. "Just wait till you hear what this child has decided to do instead of trying to make things work with a nice man."

Loulou marched out of the room and took the stairs two at a time, but not quickly enough to avoid hearing Aunt Roz from the landing between floors: "What on earth is Eye-You-Eye, Louadrian?"

Upstairs, Uncle Charlie and his sons had finished restoring the master bedroom to its pre-hospice state; the bedside cot Grandma Lou's daughters had shared in turns was gone, and the TV with all its accessories had been unplugged from the wall in preparation for their new life in Cousin Caleb's dorm room. The bed had been stripped of the outmoded linens Loulou had last seen on it, Grandma Lou's favorites since the seventies, and made up again in crisp unused sheets and a bright jewel-toned quilt. There was the scent of fresh paint and dabs of it visible at intervals along the buttercream walls. From floor to ceiling, the room looked brand-new.

Except for the dragonflies. Loulou approached her grandmother's dresser and saw that these were the more sentimental installments in the collection, homespun items not quite right for the elegant displays on the ground floor. Among them was a small crude dragonfly statuette Loulou had made herself in elementary school, still intact and bearing her little-girl fingerprints in the glossy yellow paint. Kept, all this time, along with a few other crafts she recognized as her own and those of her siblings and cousins. Tucked inside the pages of a photo album were dragonflies done in crayon and colored pencil and tempera paint, various grandchildren's names added in Grandma Lou's own handwriting where they hadn't been included initially. On the wall above it all hung a showy dragonfly-shaped panel of beaded lace in a frame speckled with crystals. Loulou moved along the edge of the dresser, taking in each of the objects.

Beneath her left foot, there was a *crunch*; unable to shift her weight fast enough to avoid it, she felt her thick black heel flatten against the hardwood floor. She saw it in her mind's eye first, the crushed brooch, and when she managed to look, it was exactly as she'd guessed: antennae snapped off, smashed wings asymmetrical, peridot tail stones loosed from their settings. A fine pale green dust coated the underside of her heel.

Later, adopting her former roommate's glass-half-full reaction to this part of the story, Loulou would learn to include in her retellings some quip about how glad she was to have been wearing cheap old shoes with heels fit for a nun. Anything nicer, with a sleeker shape, and she'd have twisted an ankle or—worse, and more likely—removed them the moment she'd walked through Grandma Lou's front door after the service and been barefoot by this point, tearing up her foot instead. She'd caught her mother's judgmental eye that morning and knew these shoes bordered on the inexcusably unfashionable, almost a disrespect to the memory of her elegant late grandmother. But new shoes hadn't been in this trip's budget, which had barely allowed for a round-trip plane ticket. Three failed intrauterine insemination rounds had cost her over four thousand dollars in the months before Grandma Lou's illness, and this upcoming round—which would not be the last—was another three-figure hit. Though by now she'd stripped the process down to its bare bones: a drugstore syringe and stuff hastily ordered off a website that seamlessly matched women with sperm donors at no surcharge—at the expense of reassuring FDA approval. It was better to have destroyed the brooch (whose little stones, it would turn out, could be salvaged and turned into what would become her nicest pair of earrings) than her foot, especially at a time when antibiotics were near the top of a long list of things to avoid consuming. *Glass half-full.*

But for now: "Fucking *shit*," she said, narrowly missing the brooch a second time as she stamped her foot on the hardwood floor. The dragon-flies rattled on the unsteady dresser.

Back on the ground floor, with the framed panel under her arm, she detoured through the living room and swept gnarled bits of metal from her hand into the garbage bag Uncle Wood and Cousin Aqil had left behind. The kitchen was alive with the voices of Grandma Lou's assembled offspring, and someone had put on one of her crackling old Earth, Wind & Fire records. *You can try,* said Grandma Lou's voice in the ear of Loulou's memory, *but you can't keep Negroes out of the kitchen.* Loulou peeked in and saw that the rest of the aunts and uncles and cousins had joined her mother and aunt around the kitchen table, that more stingers had been poured.

Aunt Roz spotted her in the doorway and slid over to make a space for her on the edge of her chair. "Find anything good?" she asked under the cacophony of voices. She peered at the object under Loulou's arm. "Is that the thing with the lace and the beads? Your cousin Nicole made that at summer camp."

"Ah," said Loulou, not taking the seat she'd been offered. "I thought maybe so. Is she coming by soon to help out?"

"Not today, I don't think. She says the baby won't sleep. They'll come by tomorrow or the next day to take a look around."

Loulou frowned. "We'll be all done here by then, won't we?"

"Hopefully, so they can move in right after your mother flies home."

"Move in?" Loulou looked over at Adrian, who was talking to Uncle Charlie about emptying the aging contents of the refrigerator. "Mom," she said, waving her hands to catch Adrian's eye, not caring that she was interrupting. "Mom!"

Adrian frowned and stopped talking, dispatching Uncle Charlie with a pat on the shoulder; he opened the refrigerator and began tossing old condiments into a nearby trash can. "What, Loulou?" said Adrian.

Loulou felt her blood pressure surge. She walked over to her mother, arms folded. "You didn't tell me Nicole was moving in here."

"Sure I did," said Adrian, lifting an eyebrow. "Maybe you were distracted and forgot."

"So it's hers now?"

"It's mine and Aunt Roz's and Uncle Charlie's. Nicole and them need the space. Your grandmother would be thrilled to have them use it. A yard for that baby to play in and everything."

Loulou stared back at Adrian, understanding suddenly that the unfamiliar quality in her mother's voice was more than just the assertiveness of a new matriarch. In the months she'd spent traveling back and forth to her hometown, nursing her mother to a peaceful end, Adrian had actually lapsed into a shade of her old drawl, the depth of which had faded in the decades since she'd moved away.

"We don't want to just leave it untended," Adrian continued. "You know how hard your grandparents worked to get this house paid off? What I want to know"—and now Loulou noticed the hint of a quaver in her mother's voice, the same voice that had carried this morning's eulogy steadily through to its impressive finish—"is what you think is going to happen to your father and me and *our* things when it's *our* turn, how you're going to manage all that while you're out messing around with Eye-You-Eye."

Loulou kept staring until it dissipated, the urge to strike out at the incredible faultiness in this chain of logic. She folded her arms and rolled her eyes heavenward. "Okay, Mom," she said softly.

Aunt Roz appeared at Adrian's side, sipping at a fresh stinger. "You find that brooch?" she asked Loulou. She turned to Adrian. "You tell her she gets to keep it when it turns up?"

"No," said Loulou, turning on her boxy heel. "I'll keep looking around."

Behind her, Adrian heaved another deep sigh. "She's mad at me," she told Aunt Roz in a stage whisper. "For telling her it's foolishness to do it all out of order like that."

"My goodness," said Aunt Roz as Loulou hurried from the kitchen, but not quickly enough to avoid hearing the end of it from the door to the back porch. "These children. What I'll never understand is why such a cotton-picking *hurry*."

Amicus Curiae

Since the strokes, their mother has preferred the front porch, content on her worn bergère whenever there is so much as a sliver of sun in the sky; and so they have decided to spend her birthday here, on the front porch, on rigid wooden chairs dragged out from the dining room. Her street is quiet, the neighbors at work or off gambling, but they have Noel Pointer humming from the old speakers. Two days of this, or however long it takes to feel they have been good daughters.

Opal doesn't require much these days, anyway. Tiny portions of soft foods the doctor has recommended: cottage cheese, applesauce into which one of them has thoughtfully sprinkled small amounts of nutmeg and ground cloves, for the fragrance more than anything. Someone to help her with the spoon and to clear the dishes afterward. Someone else to stand behind her and grease her scalp with Luster's Pink Oil, as nothing seems to agitate her more than the notion that her careful plaits might have grown dusty. She never talked much herself, even when it was easy, but seems to enjoy that they do, a corner of her mouth lifting contentedly whenever someone's cadence suggests a joke has been told. The slender fingers of her better hand fiddle with the fraying strands of the afghan in her lap. She is still prettier than any of them, and they all know it.

Cassandra has flown up from Atlanta, craftily combining the trip with business travel for write-off purposes. Suzette has driven in from Philadelphia in the new silver Bimmer, of which she seems quietly proud. Fay has emerged from the bedroom she's slept in since childhood and stumbled downstairs, only somewhat grumpily. And Lela walked over from the Port Authority, having taken a Greyhound up from DC with a friend now lost to the blackjack tables at the Tropicana. Fay and Lela are handling the food and drink. Suzette brought the Pointer record and now stands behind Opal, working the hair grease with her deft fingers.

Cassandra is bossing everybody around, sending this one to the refrigerator for more applesauce, that one to Opal's vanity in the master bedroom for a better hairbrush. It's an amplification of a persona they've all tolerated for years, anxiety coloring the edges because she'll be defending her dissertation in a few weeks. And, of course, because of their mother's deteriorating faculties.

"Miss Doctoral Candidate acting like her shit don't stink," said Lela to Fay just now at the kitchen sink, where they stood refreshing the Waterford pitcher. "What else is new."

Fay stood on tiptoe to pull a bottle of rum, her secret, from a cabinet Opal can't reach anymore. "What else is new," she said back. She offered Lela the first nip, then remembered. "Sorry, Lee," she said, smirking, and poured an ample helping into her own water glass.

The last time they were all together like this, their mother was a pillar of pearls and elocution. *DOESN'T stink*, she would have corrected Lela. *And don't swear.*

It's the cusp of evening but feels earlier, a trick of cloudless October. They've been talking about nothing, the children, their jobs. Cassandra told a dull five-minute story about the influential amicus brief her husband submitted in a high-profile assault case down in Georgia. The others stifled yawns; none of them saw the news coverage. Now there has been a lull of a few seconds, long enough for the Forbidden Topic to surface. With Opal seeming to follow only the lowest-hanging threads of conversation, there's nothing to stop it from coming back up.

Once again, Cassandra is the culprit. "Look at the time," she says loudly, interrupting Suzette in a story she's just starting about performing Dvořák in front of a crowd that included Senator Wofford. Cassandra shows the others her arm, the slim silver Bulgari watch proclaiming the top of a new hour.

Fay purses her lips and out trickles a stream of nine familiar notes. *The five o'clock whistle.*

"Quitting time," says Opal. "They'll be getting off now, won't they?"

"Mother," says Fay, who is sometimes cruel. "Who is *they*?"

Cassandra whirls on Lela. The others whirl on Lela. "Call your man, Lee," says Cassandra.

"Stop it," says Lee. She shares a look with Suzette, whose eyes flash in sympathy. Suzette knows as well as Lee knows that Lee's husband,

Linwood, hasn't once in his life held a nine-to-five. And that even if he had, even if somehow Lee had managed to hog-tie him into working regular hours for a Bell Atlantic call center, there is nothing in this life or the one after that would move Lee to call him just now. Five o'clock or not, Lee is all fiery determination, the scorched earth steaming in her eyes. Her children, two sturdy boys, are safe with a neighbor who will help them complete their homework and then put them to bed in their sleeping bags.

Linwood doesn't know which neighbor, doesn't have the house key, doesn't know that Lee—who hid the key in a flowerpot—is here in Atlantic City with her mother and her sisters. Only God or the devil knows what Linwood is doing back home in DC. What widespread pair of thighs will offer him her pillow tonight.

"Mother," says Lela, changing the subject. "How's your food? Do you need any more cottage cheese?"

"Of course, there was a lovely cottage," says Opal. "A lovely little cottage just outside Biloxi. We had to wash the floors with—with—"

"Lee," says Cassandra. "You have children. What you're doing is foolish and short-sighted."

Opal turns to Suzette. "What did we use to wash the floors?" she asks. She turns to Fay. "What did we use to wash the floors?"

"You're going to raise two boys by yourself?" presses Cassandra. "Two boys and . . . ?"

Suzette clasps Opal's hand. "You used lemon oil," she says.

"That was it!" says Opal, and smiles.

Lela covers her belly with both hands. She is bigger than you would think for just five months, her symptoms more intense. She still naps in the back room of the consignment shop she manages, retches up anything that isn't hamburger meat or a plain saltine. By this point in her previous pregnancies, she felt luminous. She worries this baby is infected with Linwood's monstrous callousness, concerned only with itself, doesn't care whether she lives or dies.

"You can't," says Cassandra. "I'm frankly amazed you would try." She jerks her head in the direction of the front door, indicating the house telephone on the other side. "Go call your man!"

She hisses the words, not wanting to upset Opal, who has returned to the laborious process of spooning her dinner into her mouth with

Suzette's careful assistance. Opal has no idea what her third daughter has done, that two of her grandchildren will spend the night at a neighbor's. Aside from Cassandra, they have been careful to preserve her innocence, because she would never understand. Opal worships God first and men second, and not only because she believes they are made in His image.

Where are the limits of Opal's forgiveness? each daughter wonders separately. Her own husband, their father, died young and charming, his slate clean or his secrets uncovered. Whereas everyone has known forever that Lela's Linwood is a dog. Everyone except perhaps Opal, who at the wedding practically shoved Lela toward the altar.

And now Linwood has taken everything. Even the red of Lela's hair is less fiery, the coils snarled and dirty. She owes her hairdresser fifty dollars and so hasn't had a relaxer in months. She tried doing her own, applying Dark & Lovely over the kitchen sink, but this is the nineties; there is no YouTube; she ripped a hole in her latex glove and mislaid the chemical globs and had to holler for her sons to come and rinse her with water from a Kool-Aid pitcher. All while Linwood slept through the day after playing what he said was yet another late gig.

When she told this story to her sisters this afternoon, in hushed tones as they greeted one another in the foyer of their childhood home, this was where the chorus of incredulous tutting began. *Late gig my ass*, said Fay. *A gig pays money, doesn't it? He's the king of late gigs and his wife can't square up with her hairdresser?*

Lela was too tired to get defensive. *Anyway*, she told her sisters, letting her battered duffel drop onto the Persian rug. Money had been tight for a while—that much was true. Linwood had broken his leg in a bar fight and spent most of the summer convalescing. Now that he was no longer laid up, Lee had urged him to make up for lost time, taking work where he could get it. Maybe some of the gigs went late, maybe not. But most of this time, she said, *late gig* was just another name for this light-skinned broad he was seeing out in Landover.

She looked so beat-up when she said it, no one told her not to say *light-skinned*.

But there was more. Miss Landover had expensive taste; and after her whims swallowed up Linwood's meager gig ducats, he had to scramble. A Sam Goody receipt Lela found in the couch cushions told the rest of the story: that he'd spent nine hundred dollars in cash on a LaserDisc player and a copy of *The Shawshank Redemption*. LaserDisc? Their own living room was still outfitted with an eight-year-old VHS machine, and Lela had never seen that film.

Right after finding that receipt, she told her sisters, she'd run to the bathroom and upchucked what seemed like everything she'd eaten all week. It wasn't so much the evidence of infidelity—such was, sadly, part and parcel of the Linwood experience—as it was the fact that, this time, he'd apparently seen fit to dip into their communal funds for his romantic pursuits. Normally he had the decency to keep his other women in the shadows, which meant sticking to gifts he could afford with his own money. This time he'd been lazy enough to leave giant bread crumbs for his pregnant wife to find.

Worse, she told them, she didn't think it meant she was losing him. That would be easier. If anything it meant she was stuck with the version of him who shamelessly stole from her. Just a few hours after his Sam Goody purchase, he'd been at Lela's dinner table, complimenting her beef stew between large, lusty bites. Afterward, rubbing up against her from behind as she stood at the sink washing their dishes. If only she'd known then! She would have put ex-lax in the broth.

Her sisters laughed at this, then cut themselves off abruptly. Opal was approaching, just up from a nap in the adjoining living room. *Girls?* she called. *Cassandra? Suzette?*

Now Fay takes a long drink from her water glass and laughs aloud to herself. "Shawshank," she cackles. "Shawshank!"

The others glare at her and huff nervously, but Opal's expression remains unchanged. "Darling," says Opal to Fay, and gestures toward the bud vase on the table, the tangerine-colored pansy inside. "Pour me some of that water, will you?"

No *please*, and they all notice the creep of her long-discarded Southern accent. Fay sighs. "That's your flowerpot, Mother," she says. She picks up the Waterford pitcher and fills their mother's glass; but Opal, reaching for the glass, knocks it to the floor. It's partly Opal's fault but mostly Fay's, her grip having loosened too soon, and her sisters notice. The full glass lands on its side and the water spills, a dark stain blooming along the length of the wooden floorboards. Opal's eyes cloud over; she hates herself this way. Her daughters notice.

"It's all right, Mother," says Suzette, and produces a rag, which she uses to push the excess water over the lip of the porch. She rises with the empty glass.

"We'll get you a clean one," says Cassandra, and pulls Suzette by the arm into the house.

In the kitchen, they quickly find Fay's rum and pour it down the drain. After rooting around a bit, they also find a handle of vodka under the sink with the cleaning supplies, a potent-smelling flask on the table by Fay's unfinished crossword puzzle. There's nothing to say, so they say nothing.

Then, as Suzette is locating a new water glass, Cassandra breaks the silence. "Those children," she says. "Lela can't leave Linwood over some silly shit like this."

Suzette winces at her language and stares down at the glass. "But she's so unhappy," she says.

"Be that as it may. Haven't you ever wanted to poison your man and then a few minutes later the sun comes out?"

Suzette's mouth twitches, but you'd never catch her saying a negative word about her Micah.

"And Mother doesn't have a clue what's going on, so I feel that somebody needs to weigh in. *I* need to, if no one else will."

Suzette nods and squeezes Cassandra's arm. "I understand, Sandy," she says. "I understand. You're just worried for her."

Cassandra abides the contact for the moment, then disengages abruptly to move toward the porch. "And for *us*," she says. "Who do you think will be looking after those children, number three included, if that whole thing goes pear-shaped over this silly shit? I have all the kids I want already, thank you."

Back on the porch, Lela has strong-armed the conversation in some other direction. She is babbling about her sons' grades, little astrophysicists in training to hear her tell it, and Fay is rolling her eyes. Taking long swallows from her water glass.

"Mother," says Cassandra. Her voice slices officiously right through whatever Lela was saying. "Do you want to tell us a story? Maybe about a birthday that was especially nice for you?"

Opal blinks at her.

"Because today is your birthday," Cassandra thinks to add. "Was there a birthday that was particularly special?"

The others know exactly the one she is thinking of: Opal's thirty-fifth, which she spent working at the club. As Opal paced the floor, seeing to the door monies and dispatching orders to the bar staff, their father had the swing quintet seamlessly transition from "Mack the Knife" into "Happy Birthday," surprising his wife, and then presented her with a little velvet box in front of everyone. An opal pendant on a filament of buttery gold. Once she had it around her neck, their father made a show of dropping to his knees and faux smooching the floor before her feet as she stood there blushing and laughing.

All her daughters remember it like it was yesterday, the original memory amplified by her retellings over the years. Opal then was around the age they are now; they relate in a new way. They lean in, even Fay, who has always turned a cynical nose up at the stories about their father's performative adoration.

But Opal stares back blankly. "Well, I—"

"The birthday with the band, and the necklace?" prods Lela.

Opal looks around, stammers a bit. "I don't want to bother you," she says finally. She pulls her gaze from theirs and stares up the road. "I just sure am glad you girls are here."

Disappointment settles over them like cement. "Hasn't this been fun," says Fay, and starts heavy-handedly clearing Opal's dishes.

Cassandra whirls on Lela. "Like I was saying," she says.

Lela pantomimes hanging herself from a noose. "Please," she says. "Don't feel like you have to finish what you were saying."

"No marriage is perfect," says Cassandra. "Surely you don't think he gave her opal necklaces every day of her life until he died. Up and down is how it goes for *everyone*."

"So that was your point," says Lela. "I knew you had one."

"My point was—"

"Come on, Sandy," says Suzette. "Let's give it a rest until after—you know. Mother will be in bed before long."

"My point was, you picked him and made babies with him. That was my point. You know how sorry she"—she jerks her head in the direction of their mother, who is looking off into the distance—"would be to know you're giving up like this?"

Lela lets out a noise that is almost a growl. "If you don't shut your—"

"Here he come right now," grumbles Opal, squinting. Her voice is guttural, her accent all Mississippi.

They all look at her, Cassandra and Fay and Lela and Suzette. "What now, Mother?" says Fay.

With some difficulty, Opal lifts her good hand. "Here he come," she says again, more urgently. "Here he *come*. Here come this motherfucker *right now.*"

Suzette's eyes widen at the language. The sisters' eyes follow the line of Opal's hand to see, some fifty yards up the quiet road, Linwood himself walking toward them.

Opal is getting to her feet. She says, "You see this dog on my street? You want me to tell him to get on, Lee?"

Lela is all shock and confusion. Her sisters are silent. As Linwood draws closer, they see in his hands a bouquet of chrysanthemums, autumnal fuchsias and yellows. He's working hard to maintain his usual confident stride, hiding all but the hint of a limp despite his newly healed leg. His full lips pursed, he's whistling "Perdido." A knapsack hanging from one shoulder like the layabout wanderer he is.

"Did you tell him where—?" starts Fay.

"I didn't tell him shit," says Lela. She turns and slams herself into the house.

Opal is practically baring her teeth, all five feet and three inches of her squared off against their approaching company. "Say!" she calls out.

Linwood slows his approach, drops the melody he's whistling.

Opal fans the air with her hand like she's clearing someone's overapplied perfume. "You, you can just—*get on!*"

Linwood's face signals confusion, but he's still coming. Now he's at the top of the walkway, now ambling up to the house. He's in a too-tight T-shirt from the Gap, newish Chuck Taylors on his feet. His brown skin shimmers with a sheen of Greyhound perspiration, one triceps pulsing under the weight of his promiscuous knapsack. He's trimmed his goatee. His flowers are beautiful.

Between Lela's sisters, there courses a sudden bell-sharp awareness that if Lela sees this man up close, his dark eyes and deep Cupid's bow, she will take him back. There is a sexiness to even the slight hitch in his gait. All will be forgotten: his Landover field trips, *The Shawshank Redemption.* If he is let into the house, he will sweet-talk her, and she will fall even further into her salon arrears. His whiskey-shot smile will shatter whatever brittle armor she has about her, and the honey on his tongue will do the rest.

Fay is the first to act. She scrambles to her feet and pushes their mother gently to the side. She tosses the remaining contents of her glass over the balcony, dousing their guest.

Linwood scowls and stops at the bottom of the stairs. "Let me talk to Lela," he says in his velvety low voice.

Fay feels the warmth of a body at her side: Suzette's shoulder, pressing against hers. Together, they form a wall at the entrance to the porch. "You should just go home," says Suzette. "Or wherever it is you came from. Leave a number, if you'd like. Lela will contact you when she's ready."

"You women better move," snarls Linwood. "That's the mother of my children in there. I just want to talk to her."

Fay's got the bowl of cottage cheese now. She heaves it and the curds land in a pulpy pile at Linwood's feet. As he's working that out, though, she tosses the applesauce, and this lands wetly on one shoulder of his Gap T-shirt. "Get," she says. "The. Fuck. *On*."

"Fay," says Cassandra. "Fay, *stop* it."

But here is Opal's voice, clear as a bell: "Get him off my property," she says. "Get him away from my girl!"

The others watch as for an instant Cassandra weighs it, this unambiguous new charge against a lifetime of the opposite. In six months, Opal will be gone, her teachings left for the new matriarch to interpret as best she can; and, grief aside, it will be a simpler state of affairs. Mistakes can then be made without detection. If Cassandra gets it wrong, who will ever realize? She's known Opal longer than any of them.

But for now, there remains a clear pecking order.

Cassandra rises and parts her sisters' shoulders with her hands. "Linwood," she says evenly. "You need to leave."

For a harrowing second, the three of them—Cassandra, Fay, and Suzette—register the look in his eyes, and wonder what they'll do if he just charges through their little barricade. They stand taller than their mother, but not much; slim, snappable wrists and ankles run in the family. And Linwood has always hated Cassandra the most for the obvious reasons. Pretentious. Uppity. Sends his children Christmas gifts he could never afford himself. No matter that she's spent most of this afternoon trying to singlehandedly salvage his marriage.

But he fears her too. The others see it in the way he falters on the stairs. They seize the moment and take a synchronized step forward.

To their surprise, Linwood takes a step backward. Just like a sort of fucked-up front-porch tango. They see him wondering what they've just wondered: What if he just . . . ?

"Leave," says Cassandra again.

And then they watch him give up. All of them know that a man is simple, linear. Linwood is doing nothing more than connecting one dot to the next. At some level, Cassandra is just as fancy as she purports to be. Her husband helped get a man sent to prison: five years for what amounted to a lovers' quarrel out of control. It was on the news.

Linwood lifts his hands in surrender, and the mums *sh-sh* against one another.

Opal, back in her chair, says, "Those sure are pretty flowers." She yawns.

They turn and look. They've lost her again. Linwood extends the arm with the bouquet.

Suzette takes it. "Thanks, Wood," she says, and crams the flowers into the bud vase.

Linwood does a sarcastic little bow, faux genteel. "Ladies," he says in a tone that changes the word into something else. He pivots on his Chucks and starts back up the street with his freed-up hand in his pocket.

They look at one another, eyebrows high, and try not to laugh. It isn't funny—Lela's life in upheaval, her children soon to be without their father, and all of it due to avoidable, garden-variety pussy-hound misbehavior—except that something about it is. And so they *do* laugh. Fay is the first to break, but the others follow quickly. Lee, they know, will be fine. She just has to get Linwood out of her system, pull herself together, figure out something new to do with her hair. Ill-timed pregnancy aside, she is as pretty and charming as ever, failed homespun relaxer and all. And they are, all of them, still so young, with so much life ahead of them, most of it bursting with unknowns.

The Opal Cleft

Here was Cyrus at the door on a Saturday, unannounced and with a leather duffel hanging from each arm, asking to crash for *a night or two—three at absolute most.* In the half year since Theo had last seen his cousin, Cy had perfected the all-over look of bohemian tragedy: down ten pounds he couldn't afford, a premeditated shabbiness to his winter coat, and his hair tied back with a shoelace. He had shows coming up in DC neighborhoods Theo recognized vaguely by name; at the last minute, his Airbnb had fallen through, and then his phone had died on the bus ride down from Brooklyn—"so thank God you were home," he finished, breathless. "Is it okay?"

"Sure," said Theo. He stepped aside, flooded with gratitude as Cy entered the apartment. Saturday now meant cleaning, a relentless litany of tasks that required rubber gloves and had to be done well for the subsequent Sunday to be worth a damn. A distraction was welcome. He peeled the gloves from his hands and took one of Cy's duffels, deposited it near the sofa.

Cy looked around, his eyes widening at the folded afghan on the sofa, the framed photos lining the bookshelves. "Look at you, Mister Lives-with-a-Woman! Is she home? Should you ask first?"

It was a smart question, but Theo bristled anyway. "She's at brunch," he said. "I'll text and make sure." Though of course the answer would be a thirsty-ass *yes*, Aja long having hoped to meet this particular cousin of Theo's. Thanks to YouTube, she was a superfan. One of those twenty-five-to-thirty-four-year-old women whom Cy found charming at his shows except when he didn't, who drank too much on empty stomachs and tipped stupidly well but got their low-hanging earrings snagged in his good wigs when he agreed to photos. Theo wondered whether to say so, to manage expectations.

But Cy had already plugged in his dead phone and installed himself in the just-scrubbed bathroom, where he now spilled the contents of a vinyl makeup bag across the sink. "If it helps," he called, "I can get you guys tickets to one of the shows. Tonight's sold out, but probably for tomorrow? Or Monday or Tuesday?"

Theo added this proposal to the text he was drafting, leaving out the Sunday and Monday offers. The whole point of cleaning the house on Saturdays was to reserve the next two days for the catatonic consumption of football and takeout wings, one of few rituals that had survived Theo's move from Brooklyn into Aja's U Street apartment.

And on second thought—he hesitated at the part about Tuesday too. For Tuesday evening he'd loosely slated drinks with Brandon and Tiffany, old college friends who'd both recently made manager at their respective consulting firms and seemed poised to reach down a hand. Engaged, too, to each other—which meant Aja's presence would be expected if not mandatory.

But drinks with Brandon and Tiffany, if done correctly, could be contained to a neat ninety minutes; long enough to connect and get loose, not long enough to get sloppy. Anyway, how often was his cousin in town? Basically never. Theo cleaned up the text, skimmed it, pressed SEND.

"Tonight you wouldn't like, anyway," added Cy, yelling a little over the whine of his electric clippers. "Seems like a pretty white crowd, bunch of girls doing Top 40, you know? But on Tuesday I'm soloing at Maisie's. Jazz. Not sure what your lady's into, but I'm thinking that's more your speed?"

Theo's phone buzzed, a reply from Aja: *Omg YAY! Everything clean, right?*

His mind cast back to the previous Saturday, a brief but irritating fuss over some grease buildup on the stovetop. He retrieved his gloves from the counter.

"Wipe up when you're done, man," he thought to call when a few minutes later the clippers went silent.

"Of course." Cy leaned out of the bathroom, the point of his chin coated in honey-colored powder. "Oh, and *thank youuuu*," he trilled in a voice Theo recognized from their roommate days, when he'd half watched dozens of these metamorphoses on Cy's show nights. In the early stages of transformation, Cy basked in the playfulness of it, trying on ever-campier personae as incrementally his face disappeared behind the makeup. But another eight layers of paint or so and he would no longer be Cy but Heaven, azure shimmer everywhere, highlighter dappling her cheekbones; and her speaking voice would follow suit, a languid contralto like a cloud floating majestically past. Or so it had been explained to Theo. And that was to say nothing of what happened when whichever wig went on, the inexplicable shoes. Cy already stood even taller than Theo, a willowy six-foot-four, the extra height inherited from the towering Danes on the other side of his family tree. Heaven on heels was a spectacle. Aja would lose her mind on Tuesday.

Aja, "Anytime," said Theo, and leaned in close to inspect the surface of the stovetop. Clean, as far as he could tell.

"Oh, Jesus Christ," called Aja, skimming a towel across the bathroom sink. She held it up to show Theo, the hot pink microfibers matted with stubble and powders. "He *saw* the bathroom like this?"

Theo paused the TV. "Babe," he said, keeping his tone light. "He *left* it like that. I just haven't gotten around to redoing it yet."

A brief silence as Aja confirmed that the hairs on the towel were Cy's, fine and sandy, and not Theo's coarser, darker ones. "Ugh, oh well," she said, and came out to nestle on the sofa beside him.

Her head was heavy and her voice raspy from an afternoon's worth of brunch cocktails, which could have one of two diametric implications: either she'd be all talked out, her girlfriends having absorbed her every microdroplet of gossip—

"Oh my God," she murmured into his armpit. "You wanna hear what Brielle said?"

—or else exactly the opposite. Someone would have pissed her off, necessitating a meta-download. Brielle was the only other Black associate at Aja's firm, and thus a necessary ally. Big, unwieldy breasts and no ass. Who, at the house party Aja had thrown to celebrate Theo's move-in, had more than once let a hand graze Theo's dick when they found themselves together at the drinks table. On this point Aja had escalated from incredulous to argumentative for months until Theo finally dropped it, baffling though it was, her protectiveness of this person who he quickly learned was always this way, desperate and predatory as fuck around partnered men, which half the time Aja herself was first to point out—but anyway. These days he kept his distance.

Aja had propped herself up on his chest with both elbows and now stared at Theo, her dark eyes wide and lovely and sparkling with brunch makeup. "She said"—fruit and syrupy liqueur on her breath; *bellinis*, he thought—"that if Kyle doesn't put a ring on it by her birthday, she's getting her IUD out anyway. She already has the appointment. Kyle has no idea, and we're all, *That's fucked*, but then again, what's she supposed to do? Give an ultimatum, a.k.a. admit defeat and strap in for like four to seven miserable years of resignation?"

There was a Kyle? Theo had never heard of Brielle's having any sort of relationship within striking distance of an ultimatum. "Wow, babe," he said. "That's wild."

"Right? *God* I'd hate to be her."

Theo's mind groped. He knew better than to cosign on the sentiment, pondered a better reply. But now Aja was sort of straddling one of his legs, her locs brushing his shoulders, a black bra peeking out of her collar and her skirt bunched up beneath her ass, which still regularly struck him as extraordinary. She moved the afghan gingerly to the coffee table, and that was the sign. His mind stilled.

He'd lived with women all his life—a mother and twin sisters, three chaotic but familiar presences; a fastidious exchange student in his senior year of college; the Manhattan trust-funders who'd graciously offered up a glorified hallway into which his bed just barely fit during the lean year before he'd learned to handle his ephemeral start-up salary; the Park Slope screenwriter who'd yielded him the master suite during the more bountiful Goldman Sachs years that followed; Heaven, in the moments after she emerged from their shared Williamsburg bathroom and before she flounced out the door to one of her shows—and the well-known generalities held. The main things were to (1) mind his business, and (2) invest in a TubShroom.

But then there was Living with *a* Woman, a different animal entirely, complicated further by the fact of her name all by itself on the lease. It began and ended with the strange humiliation of handing her a check for a nominal amount on the final day of each month. (And why a check, when everything else—down to splitting the bill at meals on Dutch days—was digital? "It's our business," Aja always said with a wink, tucking the limp slip of paper into her wallet. "Venmo doesn't need to know how much this pussy is worth.")

And in between were the other surprises. The sudden disappearance of most of his books, which turned up eventually in a plastic storage crate at the back of the coat closet, the bookshelves apparently reserved for framed photos and a curated handful of Aja's books of equal shape and size. His offer to bring home takeout when she seemed stressed at work, only to be told that it actually relaxed her to cook elaborate meals. The deep offense she took when he fell a step behind in the saga of her friends' relationship statuses. Her little bolts of bawdiness (Venmo!), after all the work he'd done to sanitize his vocabulary.

And then it would be the end of the month again, and there he'd sit at the teak table she owned, scrawling out another check in his shitty handwriting. The amount, which they'd settled on when he'd received his first bleak contractor's paycheck, embarrassed him. Worse, she'd given him May free, before the job materialized, and never let him square up for it.

He'd once watched his father, then a gig bassist, empty his pockets of cash tips, a dirty little pile building on the counter. His mother's mouth set in a grim line as she watched, counting silently, and then scooped the ones and fives into the rent envelope along with the hundreds she'd already taken out of the ATM.

Aja didn't want to hear about that any more than he wanted to talk about it. "I'm just glad you're here," she'd say, et cetera. He tried different ways of making up for it, but all their favorite takeout places were cheap, and she'd never eat that many wings anyway.

"Whoops." Aja giggled, wriggling back into her tights. "We should have hung a sock on the door or something, just in case."

"Ha," said Theo. "Cy probably doesn't even go on for another two hours. Those shows go late."

"Better save up my energy for Tuesday, then." Aja started for the bedroom, then paused at the door and pointed toward the bathroom. "Could you, um?"

His eyes followed her gesture and he understood. Wipe down the sink, again.

"And then finish whatever you were watching?" she added from behind a sheepish little smile, then disappeared into the bedroom and shut the door.

Well. He would do it, but he would finish his *Black Mirror* episode first. Didn't matter that it was a rewatch. He waited till Aja seemed to quit stirring behind the bedroom door, then resumed the episode.

As an afterthought, he went to the (spotless!) kitchen and found a Dogfish Head in the fridge. It was, after all, a Saturday night.

In the morning, he left Aja reading in bed and Cy snoring lightly in the living room and exited the apartment, taking the stairs instead of the elevator. In the lobby, he ran in place until he thought he could deal with the November cold sans outerwear, then pushed through the revolving door and began jogging the length of U Street. He took the long way around to Meridian Hill Park and then jogged the perimeter, glaring at his own Fifteenth Street office building from across the street. God, what a depressing place, particularly on a Sunday morning, a few North Face–clad drones beeping in to close out the week that had just ended, or jump-start the one coming up. Thirsty asses.

Not that he didn't relate—in his Goldman Sachs days, he'd spent more Sundays that way than not, hunched at his desk. Relegated to following Cowboys games by refreshing the stats on the team's website rather than risk streaming anything on company computers. In a way, it was better now. At least no one here expected him to spend weekends in his sad little hole of a government office. Certainly they weren't paying him to do so; and even if he'd wanted to, they made it insultingly difficult for a lowly contractor to gain access outside of business hours. Even his access badge was a different color, the photo horizontal instead of vertical.

He stopped at Starbucks for bagels and coffees, remembering at the last moment to get extras for Cy, and then chugged home, the cold catching up to him. Before the elevator door opened, from all the way down the hall he heard familiar voices. He had to set the Starbucks on the floor to unlock the apartment.

In the kitchen, Aja and Cy, their heads thrown back in exaggerated laughter. She at the stove, pushing something savory around in the big skillet; he on a barstool in a bathrobe, one long leg draped over the other. "Theo!" they said in unison as he entered, and Aja dropped the spatula, came forth with a performative kiss. Along the countertop: the open-mouthed waffle iron, batter drooling from its edges; a plate of waffles punctuated with chocolate chips; another plate of fat chicken sausages split longways; a half-empty bottle of brut rosé, a nearly full bottle of orange juice. A mimosa at Aja's elbow and another on the counter in front of Cy.

For reasons unclear, irritation surged in Theo's throat. "Wow," he said. "Everybody's up already!"

Cy rose and pulled a third champagne flute from an overhead cabinet. "I'm getting to know my hostess!" he said. "Also, last night's crowd sucked and I was in early."

Early still had to mean after 2:00 a.m., when Theo had finally gone to bed after a while spent tooling around on ZipRecruiter; but all right. Cy was grown.

"Here," said Cy. The mimosa he handed Theo was no more than 10 percent OJ, and it dissolved some of Theo's unexplained annoyance. The cousins clinked glasses, like in their roommate days.

"Tell him what happened last night," Aja prompted Cy. "The money thing." She tipped the skillet and poured sautéed mushrooms onto a clean plate, pan sauce over top. Drippings of butter and herbs landed on the counter and there they remained as she arranged servings of each food on yet another plate.

"Oh, that," said Cy, waving a hand. "Typical group-project bullshit. There was this flimsy little group number in the middle and two of the girls didn't know it."

"And you *have* to know it," Aja interjected. "It's a whole political, contentious thing."

"Which they knew," continued Cy. "Posted everywhere backstage. They dock you if you're late, they dock you if you don't know your lip-synch, they dock you the most if you fuck up the group number. Which these two knew."

"*But then!*" said Aja, and set the plate before Cy. She'd added whipped cream to the waffles and a little sprig of fresh parsley on the side. Theo eyed it.

"But then, this place, they also pool tips," said Cy. "And one of the girls, the ones who didn't know the number, is tight with the manager, and got him to divide what was left *after* docking those two."

"*Such* bullshit," said Aja. "Basically, they ended up dividing the penalty."

Theo's head spun. Aja had settled on the other barstool, opposite Cy, so Theo went to the cabinet to seek out his own plate.

"Let me know if you need more whipped cream," said Aja, leaning halfway over the counter to watch Cy cut into a waffle. "If I can't be as thin as you, then I need you to be as fat as me."

Laughter from both. Theo shut one cabinet and opened another. "Are we out of plates?"

"And then it's so annoying that you have to go back tonight," said Aja.

"But on the bright side," said Cy, spearing a minuscule bite of waffle with his fork, "where else would I wear that other basic-ass, low-rent Disney princess dress I brought to town? What a waste *that* would be."

"At least there's Maisie's," said Aja.

"Whole different thing, thank God." Cy nibbled and swallowed dramatically. "I've done Maisie's twice before—night and day. Actual art appreciators in the audience. Worthwhile tips. And that was before I even"—here he pantomimed creating and completing some craft with his hands—"had Heaven together. You know?"

"That's *so* great," said Aja. "*So* great. I can't wait."

"So glad you're coming," said Cy, and reached across the tabletop to clasp her hand in his.

"Gotta shower," Theo said, and headed that way, tucking the Starbucks bag—all three bagels still warm inside—under his arm.

He understood, of course, what Aja imagined. What anyone would imagine, clouded with *Paris Is Burning* references and encountering Cy's waifish thinness, the shoelace in his hair. Cishet persecution and starving artistry. Lazy coworkers stealing the communal tips when poor Cy had already had to pay out of pocket for the bus ride down.

How very fucking annoying. *Did you have to look out for him a lot as a kid?* she'd asked once, when Cy was still just a vision from YouTube.

And, well, sure he had. Boys in the nineties, what could you expect. At summer camp, willowy Cy, taller than everyone else their age, would sign up for dance and fiber arts and spend free periods on the fringes of deep fields, talking to birds. He'd embodied plenty of the stereotypes, and Theo remembered that sometimes a shoving match had been necessary to shut some bully up.

(And, yes, he'd omitted the occasional salient detail, the times he himself had been the instigator or had waited perhaps longer than he should have to intervene in the face of an outside threat. No one was perfect at that age, were they? Not even Cy himself, with his short fuse and surprisingly fierce right hook.)

But between their mothers—Cy's the sensible elder sister and Theo's the younger and flightier—Cy's had been better suited to raise the son she had. Aunt Cassandra and her husband, the towering Dane, had chosen Quaker schools with progressive values and rich arts programs, paid for outside dance lessons, all that shit. Whereas Theo had once, due to his mother's fumbling a resignation deadline, spent a whole semester in the wrong public school; not the rigorous one he'd tested into, but the one rumored to be for—well, you couldn't even say the word anymore. That chunk of wasted time, his first introduction to the tragedy of a false start.

So, whatever the fuck. It was sad, of course, losing a few bucks to a couple of flakes. If the loss cut too deeply into Cy's bus fare, maybe Miss Waffles-and-Moneybags would spot him the difference.

"Thought you weren't coming today!" said the guy at the wings place.

"You thought wrong," said Theo. "We play the Vikes in ten minutes."

"Cutting it close!" said the guy. "Let me guess: your lady."

"Ha," said Theo. He wondered whether his domestication gave off an actual scent. Maybe the brain-cell-killing artificial lavender of Fabuloso, at least a cup of which he'd had to use on the war-ravaged kitchen countertops.

"Here," said the guy, and dumped in an extra dozen before sealing the Styrofoam container. Half buffalo and half rosemary. For the first time all day, Theo's mood brightened.

Some three hours later, though, he was grouchy again. A loss—especially one that narrow, four freaking points, and *especially* on home soil—really was a shitty way to launch another grinding DC workweek. It was true what a buddy of his had once said: You didn't need to lay down money to feel you had skin in the game. The highs were there either way. Though so were the lows, of course.

Cy had stayed out someplace overnight, and Aja slept in and teleworked on Mondays, so Theo drank his reheated day-old coffee in the kitchen in peace before bundling up for his commute. Unlike at Goldman, where everyone had found hyperpromptness exhilarating, coked up on their own high standards, here there was no reason whatsoever to clock in before the expected 8:30 a.m.

If there was a reason to be grateful for this job beyond the excruciatingly obvious, it was that one could finish all one's assignments within the first half of the day and reserve the rest for nobler pursuits. After lunch, Theo rewatched several key segments of the previous night's game, pinpointing exactly where the Cowboys had gone wrong. Turnovers right out of the gate, and then a terrible onside kick attempt in the third quarter.

His hand twitched toward his phone. But instead of navigating to a fantasy roundup or some other forbidden website, he texted Brandon, of Brandon and Tiffany, consulting-firm power couple: *Where for drinks tomorrow?*

While he awaited Brandon's reply—to hear Brandon tell it, life as a manager was both a sprint and a marathon: constantly busy, sheer productivity its own metric—he scrolled the internet, adding to his research file on both firms. Either would represent so drastic an improvement that it was hard to rank them. Though there *was* the fact that the junior associates at Brandon's firm tended to be a year or so older than those at Tiffany's. So said the application-gaming message boards. But how much did that really matter now? He, king of the false starts, would be older than every underling at either place, regardless.

He followed up with a second text: *Aja's and my treat.*

Someone poked their head into his office—they didn't knock around here—and asked him to make copies of a stack of documents. Menial but time-sensitive, the worst combination. He got up and did it. By the time he came back, Brandon had replied: *No, it's our turn to treat this time*, it read, and offered the name of a bar.

To pass the day's final hour, Theo googled his father's name, as he did from time to time, following it up with words that seemed pertinent. *Bass. Jazz. Music.* Each returned results that skirted his intentions. A ran-

dom bassist—not his father, but a man around the age he'd be now—
giving an informal interview in which he mentioned contemporaries he
admired, among them Theo's father. A middle school jazz band butcher-
ing a piece of music Theo had determined was one of his father's notable
compositions. Et cetera.

Frustrated, he googled Cy's name next, and of course the results were
in the hundreds of thousands. Most of it, of course, was garbage, bad cell-
phone videos of trashy lip-synch gigs like the previous nights', though
Heaven herself was luminous and, judging by the cheers that rendered
her act inaudible, pleasing to her audience. This, for the record, was the
reason Theo had never managed to get to one of Heaven's shows, despite
Cy's periodic invitations. What was there to like about spending the evening being trampled by a crush of rabid fans? Each crowd was bawdier
and more boisterous than the last.

Without meaning to, Theo finished the day that way, following one
link to the next. Pop song after pop song. Wig after wig. Smoothly waved
chestnut, racially ambiguous blond, teased-out Diana Ross Afro. Once or
twice Theo startled at how Heaven resembled a young Aunt Cassandra,
though differently proportioned. And aside from the glittery bluish glow,
of course.

Aja and Cy were at the teak table. "Theo!" they said in unison, again, as
he entered.

Aja reached for his hand. "Look!"

They'd pulled out an old photo album, an unsolicited gift from Theo's
mom, which they must have found tucked away in the coat closet. Theo
sat obligingly and let Aja show him a photo of himself and his cousin
at around five years old. Two little reeds with arms slung around each
other, one a sunbaked brown and one less so. *Atlantic City*, read someone's handwriting in the corner.

"Soooo cute," cooed Aja.

"I sure was," said Cy. "Kidding!"

"Well, you were," said Aja.

"But there's a family secret," said Cy, "which is that basically one person in each generation gets the looks, and then everyone else is just an
also-ran. Anyone else who wants them has to paint them on."

He took the book and flipped back several pages to an older photo:

their shared grandparents at their peak. Aja leaned in and drew in her breath. "*Gorgeous.*"

"Ha," said Theo. "So, yeah. It was our grandfather, and then here's his dead ringer, plus some Denmark."

"Yeah, but no," said Cy, furrowing his brow. "Mom and I look like Granddad. But the *beauté originale* was Grandma Opal." He turned to another page, later, their by-then-widowed grandmother on the Boardwalk holding some infant sibling or cousin of theirs.

Aja leaned in again, and gasped again. "Oh my God, *weird*," she said. "Theo, you look—"

"*Just like her?*" supplied Cy, triumphant. He framed a portion of the photo with his hands. "The little chin dimple?"

Aja reached up and ran a hand across Theo's chin.

"I always called it *the Opal cleft*," said Cy. "Theo and his mom have it, and no one else. I have this pointy shit! That's why I've spent a fortune on little teeny-weeny contouring brushes. I draw one on myself for worthwhile gigs."

Theo leaned in. It was surreal, hearing himself described this way to Aja, who'd surely looked through these photos with him before, though probably not this closely. And to have his own vague misinterpretations so summarily dispelled. Sure, he knew about *the family secret*, but it had never occurred to him it wasn't a glamorization of the good looks of his late grandfather, who'd died young and handsome. And the so-called *Opal cleft*—he'd never given that any thought at all, more concerned with his relief at what his mother *hadn't* passed down.

"Speaking of which," said Cy, rising, "anyone need to get into the bathroom anytime soon?"

The guy at the wings place had his back to the door and sat alternating his gaze between the ancient television mounted on the wall and the display on his phone. Theo recognized the orange and green of the DraftKings website. "Hey," he said. "Picking up an online order."

"Oh—hey, man." The guy turned and started assembling Theo's order. "Who's the naked ones for?"

"Huh?" said Theo, distracted. On the old TV, a panel of commentators sat dissecting the 49ers' first string, running scenarios for the evening's home game.

"The plain wings," said the guy. "I never seen you get plain ones before."

"Oh, yeah," said Theo. "My lady eats them without sauce." He shrugged. "She doesn't like getting her hands dirty."

"They be making us do things," said the guy, returning the shrug.

Indeed. Aja almost never watched football with him; on Monday nights, she absented herself to meet up with friends or lingered at work. Her offer to join had come as a surprise—a little dose of happy-couple theater for their houseguest's benefit?

The guy sealed the Styrofoam container with Aja's naked wings and heaped in another dozen with Theo's, spooning barbecue sauce over the extras. "Oh well. More for you."

The guy's phone dinged: A DraftKings notification? Theo wanted to ask whether he had money on the 49ers, or maybe a fantasy team poised to advance pending the night's outcome; but look at the time, only ten minutes till kickoff. Instead, he handed over his twenties and took the bags in silence, dawdling only briefly before the TV.

"Ugh, this *bathroom*," said Aja the moment Theo walked in.

Theo set the wings on the table and peered in. Again, Cy had left behind a storm of cosmetological offal, a sinkful of stubble, a dusting of blue over everything. "I'll get it after the game," said Theo. He set the takeout bags on the countertop and reached into the fridge for a Dogfish Head.

Aja watched him crack the bottle open. "Could you, um?"

"Could I what?" He sank onto the couch, remote in hand, irritation surging. "Babe, I'll get it after. Or, better yet—Cy's grown. Let him handle it when he gets in."

On-screen, the 49ers were jogging onto the field, a few minutes behind schedule. Thank God. But then Aja wandered into his sight line, arms folded. "He's company," she said tightly.

"He's family. I cleaned up after him once already. Can you sit, please? Can I—*we*—watch the game?"

Aja perched on the arm of the sofa. "Can I ask you something?"

Theo sighed and muted the television.

"Back when you lived together," said Aja.

A vision of the Williamsburg apartment snapped into Theo's mind:

Spartan, serviceable furniture dotting the living room; Cy's dead house-plant and Theo's long-empty fish tank on the windowsill; bare kitchen cabinets; a counter perpetually covered in takeout containers. A faint dusting of shimmer that thickened as you approached the shared bathroom.

"Toward the end, I mean," continued Aja. "Didn't Cy have to spot you once? Rent, utilities?"

Theo's jaw tightened. "You know he did," he said. It was one of the things they'd talked about once so they never had to again. His lowest of low points. With his final Goldman paycheck already spent, the Cowboys got knocked out before the conference championship. His phone, exploding with notifications from various betting sites, a string of bad decisions coming home to roost. Debts piling higher than the dishes in the kitchen sink.

And Cy, affable as always, no detectable judgment in his kohl-ringed gray eyes as he tapped the numbers into his cell-phone calculator, then sent over a sum to cover the bulk of Theo's share of the bills.

Not once, in fact, but twice. Which of course Aja knew.

"I actually find it bewildering," she was saying. "That you don't feel more—"

What was the word on her tongue? *Appreciative, indebted,* maybe *pathetic*? Theo sat up straight and drummed his fingertips on the remote to keep from hurling it at a wall.

"That you aren't more supportive," she finished finally. "If it were my cousin? I'd be at all his shows, even the bad ones."

"We're going tomorrow, right after drinks with Brandon and Tiffany."

Aja's eyes narrowed. "Right after what now?"

Another source of *bewilderment*: that two people could share twelve hundred square feet of space and still bungle a simple transfer of information. Aja's face registered zero recognition as Theo explained the plan, Brandon and Tiffany's new managerial statuses, the bar Brandon had proposed.

"You did *not* tell me," she said when he finished.

"*Absolutely*, I told you," repeated Theo, slapping the back of one hand into the palm of the other for emphasis.

"I would have said no. I *hate* networking this early in the week."

"It's not networking. It's drinks with friends! You would have said no to like ninety minutes of sitting at a bar two blocks away?"

"If you had actually *asked*, I probably would have *considered* it. But you're springing it on me at the last minute, and it's on the same night as Cy's show, and it's *definitely* networking."

Feeling ridiculous as he did it, Theo grabbed for his phone and searched his text history, trying different word combinations. *Drinks with Brandon. Drinks with Tiffany. Drinks on Tuesday.* Nothing, nothing, nothing. What the fuck. "We talked about it," he said, his voice thin. "Like yesterday."

Aja laughed dryly. "Yesterday? While you were slamming around the house being rude to your cousin and then going into a football coma?"

"I wasn't rude!"

Aja got to her feet and did a hulking imitation. *"No one's paying attention to me, wahh. I'm gonna go eat bagels in the bathroom.* Meanwhile Cy's trying to tell us about losing half a night's pay—"

"Half a night's pay," repeated Theo, the words cutting at the insides of his mouth. He jabbed at the remote and sound burst from the TV. "You know what, forget it. Forget it. I'll just go by myself."

Aja stared, stunned, and finally stalked off toward the bedroom. "Great," she called over her shoulder. "Have fun not networking."

She was out first the next morning, per Tuesday's norm, and Cy didn't stir on the sofa when Theo reheated another deferred Starbucks cup.

The bar Brandon had chosen was wood-paneled, with rich-looking espresso chairs. The sort of place the Goldman bros would have chosen, laughing if you looked agog upon entry. Theo supposed that was Brandon and Tiffany now: effortlessly resourced, no longer impressed by places with two-for-one rail specials.

They did, to their credit, limit themselves to asking once each—where was Aja, anyway? Brandon asked it as they were seated, before he'd even removed his moneyed leather coat; and then, while Brandon was in the restroom, Tiffany leaned close, peering over her Warby Parkers, and asked again, as if the answer might change.

That thing couples did as they situated themselves further into coupledom. Losing their ability to socialize in odd numbers, unsure how to physically orient themselves at a four-top, even how to order drinks. After overtalking Theo twice, Brandon finally grinned apologetically at the server and said they'd have a round of mezcal mojitos.

Their new jobs? Wonderful, wonderful! Everything falling into place, their leadership skills really progressing, even the rigorous schedule an easy adjustment since they were both on it. And it made the wedding planning so much more efficient, ironically, if he knew what they—well, of course he'd let them know when he was ready for the inside tip on wedding planning, right?

But, yes, the jobs, everything fantastic. And his? Just great also, nice to have more of a work-life balance for the moment after Goldman, though he was beginning to think maybe it was time for—

Here were the drinks. *God* it was nice to go crazy and have a sugary mixed drink on a weeknight, responsible old grown-person wine got so boring, though of course it made mornings easier; could he believe there were still people his age who did this every night and kept their jobs?

During a lull, peering into the phone in his lap, Theo found he had a text from Aja: *Hope you're having fun drinking casually with your friends. I'm heading to Maisie's early. Stopping at the ATM. Don't forget cash for tips.*

He resisted the urge to ask just how well she planned to tip. His own perception of Cy's charlatanism aside, it was her money to spend. None of his business.

Though maybe after Cy had left, safely on a bus back to Williamsburg, Theo might pose the question in some non-asshole way, leading Aja to draw her own conclusions. How exactly *did* she think Cy was making ends meet, lo these six roommateless months, in gentrified Brooklyn, on a few nights per week of pooled tips? The same simple money-earned, money-spent hamster wheel Aja herself had been on throughout adulthood, or was there a more realistic explanation? An indulgent mother and a towering, deep-pocketed father, perhaps? Cy could do whatever he wanted and fall up. Not everyone was so lucky. Some people had to try other things.

Theo returned his attention to the table and managed to reach the bottom of his cloyingly sweet drink, admired Tiffany's ring once more, offered again (unsuccessfully) to pay the check.

And when, just before they reached the door, Tiffany doubled back to hit the restroom, he found the balls to touch Brandon's arm and say: *You know, if either of you has an opening anytime soon, I'd love you to keep me in mind.*

In another chapter, this sort of thing had been so easy for Theo. Evidently that chapter had closed, giving way to this awkward and domesticated DC chapter. Back in the empty apartment, he gave the kitchen another thorough cleaning, until he reached the bottom of the tub of Lysol wipes. Just to settle his nerves.

Maisie's sat tucked just off the main strip, behind a row of more conventional and brightly lit gay bars meant to invite foot traffic. You had to know it was there, which until this weekend Theo had not. He paid the cover, had his hand stamped, squeezed into an open sliver of space at the bar, searched the crowd until he found Aja and, by her side, her dick-grazing friend, Brielle. Both laughing and wearing low-hanging earrings. Their purses full, presumably, of law-firm cash.

Well. He turned and ordered a drink, something simple and cheap, pleased to watch the bartender's heavy-handed pour. The crowd here was mostly male, and nothing like the screaming legions he'd seen on YouTube. Jazz fans, he supposed. Professional dress, neat haircuts.

He claimed a seat at the bar and checked his phone. An email from Brandon, brief and to-the-point:

Really enjoyed catching up with you, man. Shared what you said with Tiff and we'll both keep it in mind. We think you'll find a good fit soon. Wanted to say that we think it's good you're taking a break from some of that for now. Wouldn't want to see you burn out again so soon, or get caught up in anything else. Just enjoy the extra time with Aja.

Theo took a sip of his drink and swallowed. Returned his phone to his pocket, just as the lights dimmed.

A spotlight swung over a stage at the back of the room, a standing microphone stretched to maximum height. Music started up, prerecorded but voluptuous in the high-end speakers, and touched off a scattering of whistles throughout the room. A bass line, the skitter of a hi-hat, a crescendo of piano melody.

Then Heaven appeared onstage, first one endless leg and then the other, the blue dermal shimmer toned down to emphasize a glittering blue gown; and there indeed was the painted-on cleft in her chin, though nothing looked painted at this distance and in this light. In her shoes, remarkable pale gray platforms with sequins down each stiletto heel, she must have stood at least six-foot-seven; somehow, though, she was lithe and glittering, feline, not the least bit gawky. The room around her stilled and Theo felt his mind quiet along with it, all thoughts of the night's failures receding.

As many dozens of metamorphoses as he'd seen, as many times as he'd watched Heaven emerge from the bathroom, a sky-colored spectacle with a blizzard of cosmetics in her wake, somehow he hadn't expected what now stood before him. Where in there was his cousin—overtall, underweight Cy, who'd tripped over his own feet as a child? Pampered Cy, whose parents paid his rent? Nowhere to be seen. He stole a glance at Aja and saw her full-bodied gasp, her pretty hands covering her mouth exactly as they had the first time she'd seen a Basquiat up close.

He turned his gaze back to Heaven. He watched her shine a demure smile around the room, seeming to make playful eye contact with every member of the audience all at once; and then she began to sing, a contralto like a cloud floating majestically past, and you had to admit maybe there really was something to this whole thing.

Three Guests

One of my mother's sisters showed up unannounced one night after dark, toward the end of our third-to-last week together. A Friday night. Bedtime had come and gone, but Daddy was working in his office and my mother had fallen asleep on the sofa, so Aubrey and I were sneaking a last half hour of Nickelodeon. Time and routines had gone strange by then, but there were little gifts to be found.

My mother startled awake at the sound of the knock on the door. What in the world, she murmured, and looked at her watch. That couldn't be Barry, could it? On the wrong day?

We hadn't had much company in a while, but it just so happened she'd invited over her general manager for Saturday dinner; there was already a slab of salmon marinating in the refrigerator, a litany of preparations planned for his arrival. But that was a day away.

She got slowly to her feet, pulling her sweater around her shoulders. Aubrey and I followed her to the door, having lost interest in our cartoon. Our mother looked through the peephole and sighed, then turned the knob.

We were delighted to see our aunt standing there, but surprised she'd come alone, without our cousins. Stranger still, she was all dressed up, the sort of party dress women sometimes wore in perfume ads, but she had her shoes in her hand. Strappy, fancy grown-up shoes with metal nubs for heels. Bare feet standing there on our concrete doorstep in the night air.

We searched our mother's face for cues, but she looked just as surprised as we were. She stepped aside so her sister could come in. Lela, she said. I didn't know you were in town.

I came up for the weekend, said our aunt in a voice that shook. I was supposed to be—I didn't mean to—

She looked over our mother, reached out and touched the thick sweater around her slender shoulders.

God, Suze, I'm sorry, she said, and her voice cracked on the last word. I came over here in a cab. I really should have just gone back to my hotel. This man I was with—

Don't be silly, said my mother, straightening. Anytime is fine. Anytime. I've got a bed all ready for you. You'll just have to let me fix it up a little bit.

She led our aunt over to the couch and sat her there; Aubrey plopped down beside her and turned her attention right back to the TV.

My mother touched my arm and nodded toward the stairs. Help me, Bell, she said.

I followed her up to the linen closet, where she talked me through pulling out a set of sheets dotted with watercolor violets. Together we went into the guest room and spread them across the bed.

Rule number one, said my mother, is you make a little mark on the fitted sheet so you know which end goes at the foot of the bed.

She pointed to show me where she'd done just that.

Back downstairs, she let me and Aubrey watch the last few minutes of our show, our aunt petting our heads as if we were kittens. Wrapped in her sweater on the other end of the sofa, she dozed until the credits came on, then roused herself. Girls, she said, blinking her tired amber eyes at me. Go on upstairs to bed.

I brushed my own teeth and Aubrey's and got us both into bed. Aubrey was asleep almost immediately, but I lay there for an hour in the quiet, trying my hardest to make out what was going on downstairs. I heard my aunt's distressed, expressive voice rising and falling around the contours of a story, my mother's softer one murmuring reactions. Every so often, a sharp intake of breath.

I could make out a word or two for every ten, enough to fire up my imagination but not enough to truly follow the thread. Eventually, though, I heard a laugh pass between them. It was low and quick, but it was enough. I'd stayed up almost two hours past my bedtime, and suddenly I didn't have another second of fight left in me.

In the morning, the first thing I did was check the guest room. My aunt was gone, the bed stripped and the sheets folded hastily on a chair.

I found my mother downstairs, getting ready for Barry. Here, Bell, she said when she saw me, and dropped a bag of fingerling potatoes into my arms before I could ask a single question. Go find the colander and rinse these off. We've got a lot to do today.

She spent all day in the kitchen, cooking the salmon and side dishes and shining the nice glasses by hand, running a microfiber cloth across the baseboards, mopping the foyer. Daddy and Aubrey came into and out of rooms, bringing chaos, undoing things, until finally she sent them out of the house for ice. How exhausted she must have been! I think about it every time I've had to stay even half an hour late at the office and I find my hand twitching toward the speed-dial for expensive carryout. She looked more and more tired from all the bending and slicing and scrubbing, grayness creeping across her face, but she didn't sit or even slow down until the food was all done and the kitchen looked like it had never seen a lick of cooking. She spread the food across the buffet table and checked her watch; only when she saw she had time to spare did she lower herself onto a kitchen chair to catch her breath.

I'd hovered nearby the whole day, trying to help, but she'd been moving too fast for me to do much other than watch. Now I drew near. Smells good, Mom, I said.

She looked over the buffet offerings and gave a resolute little nod. Then she checked her watch again. She was still in her pajamas; bracing herself with an arm on the table, she got to her feet. Time to get dressed, she said, and sent me upstairs to find the Vaseline.

When I saw her again half an hour later, she was dressed in a skirt and a cashmere sweater, and her skin and lips were bright with color. All the tiredness had vanished from her face, and she got Aubrey and me into our Hanna Andersson dresses, brushed lint from Daddy's fresh-cut hair.

When the doorbell rang, she put on a smile like sunshine. In walked Barry, carrying a dark green bottle; when he handed it to her, he gripped the neck for a second or two before letting go. He wrapped a hand around her forearm and murmured something into her ear, his white mustache touching her face; she laughed a strange laugh, lovely like a tinkle of music but one I'd never heard her do before. I looked around, but Daddy was busy straightening out the dining chairs, and Aubrey, already bored of the whole thing, was hiding under the sweeping white cloth my mother had laid over the table.

At dinner, I remembered just in time not to serve myself first, instead waiting as my mother cut a slice of herbed salmon and heaped it onto Barry's plate.

I waited a beat and then took my own slice. On Daddy's lap, Aubrey squirmed and whimpered; she didn't like salmon then and she never did develop a taste for it, but it would become one of my weekly staples.

I watched my mother work without seeming to, passing plates, hopping up to pour refills, opening a larger brown bottle when the green one was empty. Every so often she issued one of those tinkling laughs, parting her bright lips to show a hint of teeth. Barry liked her laugh; every time, he returned one of his own. Whereas sometimes Daddy did and sometimes he didn't.

Hours later, as my mother moved through the empty kitchen stacking dishes, I stood upstairs in my pajamas and practiced that laugh in the mirror. She hadn't had time to tell me directly, but I thought it was probably important. I didn't get it quite right that night, or even that year, but eventually I nailed it.

Over wine and pizza, I ask my sister whether she remembers the time we had Barry over for dinner.

Barry, she says. Who the hell is Barry? She swipes at her eyes and her hand comes away blackened with eye makeup. Mascara and liner have tracked halfway down her cheeks. At thirty-two, she's still wearing Wet n Wild, still boo-hooing over breakups. She's wearing a bathrobe I've lent her and there's makeup on the collar too.

He was the general manager of the orchestra, I say. We had orchestra people over for dinner a few times, and then one time just him. So Mom could tell him she was, you know, leaving.

I dig my phone out of the sofa cushions and try to pull up a photo, but the Philadelphia Orchestra website doesn't go into that much detail. And anyway, Barry was old even then. I think of his white mustache brushing her cheek.

Anyway, I say. I'm bringing it up because I always think of that night when I'm going through something rough.

Because?

This was the first week of that June.

Aubrey stares back at me blankly and I remember I have to connect the dots for her, every single one. She was only four then; not every detail of that time is etched in her memory or her old journals.

And Mom was gone three weeks later, I say. So she should have just been resting. But she put on this big dinner for him. She didn't want to let everybody down. The weekend after her last rehearsal, she had him over to let him know she was going on a hiatus to focus on her health.

Aubrey wipes her nose with her sleeve. *My* sleeve. I'm not exactly following your point, she says.

Just, *the show must go on* is my point, I say. She barely ever cooked by then, but she pulled everything together and had Barry over. And actually—

I'm about to tell her what happened the night before the dinner with Barry, how Auntie Lee dropped in and sapped the last bit of the energy our mother was saving to host her boss, but just in time I think better of it. I don't need Aubrey to think it's my passive-aggressive way of complaining that she's once again shown up unannounced with man drama when I've got things to do tomorrow. Even though in fact I *do* have a child to drive to soccer practice in the morning, a brief for work looming over what remains of my weekend.

—actually, nothing, I finish, and Aubrey, refilling her wineglass, doesn't care anyway.

Nice pep talk, she says.

It wasn't really a pep talk, I say. Anyway, come on up whenever you're ready.

She sinks into the sofa and covers her streaky face with the lapel of my bathrobe. Mmph mmhmmph mmph, she says.

On my way to bed, I peek into the guest bedroom, but I already know the bed is ready. Good, soft sheets the color of wheat, upper-middle thread count with the subtlest sheen.

I also know my sister is just going to sleep on the couch in my bathrobe, unwashed face and all, because that's the sort of thing she does and nothing anyone says or does is ever going to change that.

Company

This house was too small for six people, woefully so, but it's too big for one; the empty rooms fill up with spirits. My father's parents, who built the place from loam in the forties, turn up in the kitchen every so often to tut about the oven mitts I leave on the countertops. Every time, the same tired confrontation: *That's what the hooks are for*, they say. They were lanky people, arms much longer than mine, and I keep telling them the damn hooks are too far from the stovetop to be any help when I've got something sizzling. Once, I hurled a blistering wedge of apple at the opposite wall with my burned-up hand, just to prove the point, and got the sort of tongue-lashing you can get only from a Club Harlem barfly beyond the reach of retaliation. *Fay, you lazy so-and-so*, they said. *Can't even walk three feet for an oven mitt.* Cackling like witches while I cussed and fumbled for ice.

If I run into Mother anyplace, it's in the first-floor powder room, where she spent even her last days hollering instructions: *This room is for company. No nasty business in here, just hand-washing.* A rule I've kept to through twenty-some years of almost no company. Wash your hands, then tidy the powder room back to pristine conditions and skedaddle, because company could turn up anytime. Mother gets firm about this and not much else, probably because she gave up on me forty-five years ago. *Fay, you sure is ornery, but maybe you'll listen to me about this one thing.*

On the other hand, Daddy doesn't limit himself to a single room. He's in all of them, or sometimes out front considering the skyline, ready for a talk day or night, his smile gleaming like new parquet. It's years now that I've been chatting with Daddy nearly every day, not idle chit-chat but those real conversations that go deep and last all night, and I'm always refreshed by his vigor. He's young enough to be my son now, his close-cropped hair eternally the color of a well-traveled penny. *Fay, Fay,*

Fay, he sometimes says, and he raises his glass toward me with a wink and a grin sweeter than the spiced rum inside it. Cassandra may have inherited his vulpine brain, and lucky Lela holds this generation's monopoly on that hair of his, but I'm the only one of us whose glass he ever clinked like that on earth, and I don't ever let anyone forget it.

For example, this one Monday morning in the boil of July, here came this girl up the walkway in black leather boots with their heels worn down to shit. I heard her coming from a block away and found her from the master bedroom's bay window, watched her *clackety-clack* her way toward the row house in broad daylight with the uncertainty of a person on two-foot stilts. A heavy-looking duffel bag hung from her shoulder, half-unzipped.

Lord, I said to Daddy. If that isn't a beautiful mess.

She got a little closer and I saw that she was prettier than what the Borgata usually spits out at 10:00 a.m., but every bit as bleary-eyed, tugging and hiking to keep her bag and her miniskirt in place. She collided with my mailbox and whipped her head around as far as it would go in either direction, obvious shame all over her keen little face.

I said to Daddy, If I didn't know better, I'd think we knew this child from somewhere.

Downstairs, I had the front door open a half second too soon, thanking God I'd had the presence of mind to have my cuticles pushed just that week. She stood there poised to knock, blinking fast. "Oh, hi," she said, lowering her delicate fist with its chipped turquoise nails. "Are you Felice Collins?"

Up close, her face crackled with Suzette's prettiness, the same features arranged just a little bit differently on a canvas that same shade of sugared pecans. I could see she had slept on her hair funny, her high-piled bun ringed with fuzz, and she had pulled a trick Lela used to call *the whore's beat*: dabs of new makeup right over the old. She smelled fine, though, notes of vanilla and powder rising from her July-dewy skin. Even on heels, she stood barely taller than I did in my slippers. "I am," I said.

She smiled a perfect how-do-you-do smile and stuck out her little hand, all manners and teeth. "I'm your sister Suzette's daughter," she said.

You think I don't know that? I managed not to say as she told me her fancy little name, gave me a finishing-school handshake.

"Sorry I look a hot mess," she continued. "I was up here with friends for the weekend and I just now missed my bus back to DC."

DC, how about that, I said to Daddy, who was looking her over with frank curiosity from his perch on the porch railing. "There are buses every hour or so, I think," I told her. "Do you need a ride to the Port Authority?"

She shifted her duffel from one slender shoulder to the other, dipping a little under its weight. She had her father's inky eyes, not Suzette's saditty amber ones; and now they darted from side to side, trying to see around me into the house. "I could probably walk to the Port Authority, though," she said. "I was actually thinking more along the lines of, um . . . "

Daddy was pleased with her, present condition notwithstanding. Even when she faltered like that, too shy to ask outright to come inside, we could hear her tongue was silver and had been all polished up in high-end District schools. The kind of diction we four girls used to practice for hours upstairs in our bedrooms, trying like hell to wring out all traces of western Mississippi—a place we'd never been but that flowed all through the house in our parents' speech. Cassandra did the best at exorcising her accent, and Lela just stopped trying when she realized no one was more than half listening to her anyway. Suzette, by the time she left Atlantic City, spoke to me so little that until now I couldn't have guessed how it had turned out for her. Now Daddy was nodding at his granddaughter like she was telling him the answer to a question he'd been asking for a long time.

"The thing is more that I've never actually seen this house," the child continued. "Or any pictures of it, even. And they keep telling me my mom's stuff is probably still here—and also that *you're* still here, so . . . "

Fay, said Daddy. *You're going to invite her in, aren't you?*

"But I get it if this isn't a good time. I just googled to find the address. I didn't have a phone number to call or anything."

And they *didn't give one to you?* I managed not to say, thinking wasn't that just precious of Cassandra and Lela, setting the child up to think I was out here curating the goddamned Collins family museum.

"Also," she added, switching her duffel back to the original shoulder, "if you don't already have lunch plans, maybe we could go someplace on the strip?" To which she added, when I didn't immediately reply, "Or I could walk to the grocery store and cook for us, or something?"

Just as I was thanking God that Mother was tucked safely away in the powder room, unable to offer up an opinion on the audition I was putting this child through, Daddy jumped in with one of his own. *Fay*, he said, crossing his muscled arms. *You invite the child into my house.* She lifted a cell phone from a pocket in her bag and thumbed futilely at its dark screen. "If I could even just charge my phone for a few minutes," she tried, finally, her voice thin with desperation.

I found my company smile where I'd packed it up and put it away years ago and stepped aside, opening the door wide. "Don't be silly," I said, nodding her in. "I don't mind a surprise visit. We used to have them around here all the time. I'd love for you to stay for lunch. I have steak medallions marinating, but I suppose you'll tell me Suzette didn't raise you on red meat."

"I eat red meat!" she all but shrieked, and her happy expression nearly sliced me in half with its familiarity. Had buttoned-up Suzette ever beamed like that, a full-bodied smile that pinked her cheeks and curled her slender fingers? Not in my memory; but it reminded me at least a little of Daddy in life, how when he grinned he appeared as if onstage and floodlit from behind. This child had a bit of that in her.

In the foyer, she carefully released the heft of her duffel bag, and I heard the ring of glass against glass as she lowered it to the wooden floor. She stood there for a moment, taking everything in, the goddamned Collins family museum I had never meant to curate. Daddy had followed us inside and stood watching her with his chin on the shelf of his fingers, just as tickled as could be.

I left them there and went to see that the powder room was company-ready, an unnecessary trip that put me face-to-face with Mother. Your granddaughter is here, I told her crossly as I straightened out the seawater-colored soaps, smacked the dust from the hand towels. One of Suzette's. Looking like you wouldn't believe what a mess. Like she just left last call ten minutes ago.

You see what I mean about the powder room? was all Mother had to say.

Back in the living room, Suzette's daughter had found the row of paintings that hung gallery-style on the far wall. All the ones I'd never

sold, not so much for lack of interest as because I'd simply gotten used
to their being there, entries from a series that had swallowed up my free
time for a couple decades. "I had forgotten Auntie Lee said you liked to
draw and paint," she said, running her unwashed fingertips over one painting's raised acrylic ridges.

"That's right," I said. Thinking, wasn't that just typical Lela, Miss
Casual Understatement, reducing all my higher learning and my life's
great passion to the insignificance of a childhood hobby. As though she'd
ever learned to do anything a person could do standing up, in front of an
easel or otherwise.

Suzette's daughter stood right up close to the first painting and
stroked each of its four faceless brown-and-gold figures in turn, linger-
ing especially on the smallest. "This is you four," she said with real wonder. "The four sisters. Right?" She considered the others in the row, their
slight variations in composition. "Oh, they all are," she murmured, a
hand at her slender throat. "Right?" She turned to look at me, more interested than Suzette had ever been.

"If you please," I said. "But I try not to talk about it as literally as
that." Families all over the city and beyond, people who knew nothing about any four sisters, had purchased my paintings throughout the
years and hung them in their homes for their own reasons. One buyer
had spent her weeklong blackjack winnings on a piece I'd done using a
nylon brush frayed beyond repair and told me she planned to hang it
in honor of her four dead angora rabbits, to which I'd had no response
other than, *You hear this, Daddy?* I relayed some of this now to Suzette's
daughter. She laughed a laugh like Daddy's, loud and a little destabilizing, but she covered it up with one hand, like Suzette. "They may have
started out being about us four," I concluded. "But they're easier to sell
if I don't say so."

"Oh, you sell them," she said, nodding at the canvases with admiration.

"Right," I said, also thinking how very irritating of Cassandra, Miss
Bottom Line herself, to fail to mention there was monetary value in how
I spent my days.

"Does this one have a title?" she wanted to know, her fingers still
griming up the brown-and-gold painting on the left.

"I don't name things," I told her, and reached out to straighten the frame so her hand would fall away. "But you can see there are these four figures, you know, one for each of us. Your aunt Cassandra, and me, your aunt Lela, your mother."

"I guess when you're one of four girls, that's something that matters a lot to you," she murmured.

"Sure. Especially four girls that came one right after the other like we did. It's something people mention a lot, part of who you are."

That's because you were all just so lovely together, called the ghost of a neighbor, the nosy spinster who was born and then died in the row house just west of ours and who in between used to keep Mother company as she hung our little-girl pajamas from a clothesline in front of the slatted porch. If she ever resented Mother's fecundity, or that the signs of it flew like flags out there in the form of many garments in stair-step sizes, she managed through admirable restraint never to say so. Instead complimenting us, playing with us, bouncing Lela on her knee while Mother nursed Suzette in a rocking chair in the corner. That spinster gave me my first set of finger paints and taught Suzette violin after school. When my parents' club opened up the block, she happily took over the nightly four-way bedtime duties, reading us to sleep before pouring herself a glass of Daddy's rum and settling into her own untroubled sleep on the bèrgere sofa.

None of this seemed worth telling Suzette's daughter, who'd moved on to look at the next painting, a study in blues and greens inspired by a composite of Boardwalk memories. Once Cassandra was ten, we four were allowed to go up the walk on our own as long as we stayed together, holding hands, which we did till we were around the corner and out of the spinster's sight. A textured, fiery sun hung in the corner of that painting, directly above the littlest figure in the back, and naturally Suzette's daughter reached up with those fingers in need of a manicure and touched all over it. *You don't know how to look with your eyes, child?* I managed not to say, turning my back on her to resist the temptation.

Isn't it nice, challenged Daddy with his arms folded, *those things being appreciated finally? Instead of just hanging there?*

Real nice, I shot back. What I want to know is what kind of finishing school taught her to touch all over artwork like that.

Fay, said Daddy. *Fay, Fay.*

You just like her for what she looks like, I told him. There's more Grey Goose in her than there is Suzette.

Easy, Fay, said Daddy. *She'll stay awhile, and then you and I will have a nice chat about it out on the porch. You be nice to her until then, Fay, you hear me?*

"How about this one?" came her voice from behind me.

I found my company smile again, turned around to find her drifting toward the one with the four figures rendered all in white, surrounded by black shapes vaguely suggestive of musical instruments. "That one is about your grandparents' club," I forced myself to say.

"Ohhhh, right," she said. She grinned, touching it, bobbing her head a little like she could hear the *tsk-tsk* of a hi-hat. "Little Suzette's. Right?"

"Well, but usually we just called it *the club*. And it's called something else now, anyway."

"Because they sold it?"

"Right, your grandmother sold her part of it. Your grandfather's partner bought her out in the early seventies and redid everything. Trying to lure in some white people. But that took a while and it changed hands a few more times before then. Anyway, though, your grandmother got what she needed from it."

Suzette's daughter smiled bemusedly, as if at the quaintness of what I'd said. "Did she buy this house with the money from that?"

I snorted a little, thinking how between the two of them, Cassandra and Lela could have done a much better job of laying all this out for the child, offered up more details besides just the club's goddamned name. "Not at all," I said. "She sent us to college with it. All four of us. She didn't want us throwing cards in a casino. She didn't want us stuck forever serving drinks or sitting backstage at a show somewhere doing go-gos' hair and makeup. That's what they did at first, while we were small—worked shows. Tending bar and fixing up the talent. They saved and saved and bought the club with what they earned, doing that."

"Grandmother did hair and makeup? Wow. That's just so not what I imagined, from what they told me. I always pictured her like a—like a schoolmarm or something. Real proper, real organized. That's how I imagined her."

Of course you did, I managed not to say, unsurprised that *they* had wiped Mother clean of any whiff of hair grease, of cheap perfume, in their retellings. When, in fact, until she didn't have to anymore, Mother had continued to operate as the club's de facto stylist-in-chief, dipping her whole hand into vats of pomade before night shows so she could walk around smoothing down the go-gos' edges. Wearing an apron that bulked up her trim little figure, a great sacrifice for someone like her, just so she had a place to store clean makeup brushes and jars of foundation powder in hard-to-find shades from high yellow to sable brown.

Any night they let us four come to watch a show, she'd keep a little toothbrush in her pocket, constantly wetting her fingers on her tongue so she could slick our fine little baby hairs across our foreheads with its soft bristles. She ended every night soaked to her skin, her face flushed, wearing a bit of each go-go's perfume.

Proper and organized. Well, all right, she was that, too, thoughtful enough to dress four of us in white before trips to the club so we'd be easy to round up right at 10:00 p.m., before anyone got drunk enough to mistake Cassandra for a baby-faced go-go in street clothes. Proud enough to keep our block-away row house fastidiously clean at all times, because in those days company really was constantly possible. Women who'd fought with their dates and couldn't find their way home till morning. Men who got so drunk they couldn't have found their own car keys even if Daddy, acting as manager and bartender, hadn't snagged them for safe-keeping. At a Black-owned club that got that joyfully noisy, you did what you could to keep the AC police at bay. Even if it meant stretching the limits of your own hospitality sometimes.

Someone overserved this Negro, Mother would tell us if we four woke up in the wee hours, crept out to the stairs to watch Daddy guiding some brown man onto the sofa. *You girls get your behinds back upstairs before you wake him.* That led to the implementation of Mother's favorite rule, the one she enforced with a switch: *When there's an overnight guest in this house, you never open the bedroom doors. You lock up and wait till I come get you in the morning*, she said. In our rooms at night, we'd dutifully turn the locks while downstairs Mother started the bustle of setting out blankets and guest towels. And at dawn we'd wake up one by one and wait patiently in our little pairs, Cassandra and me twittering over magazines in one room, Lela and Suzette playing dolls on the floor in the other, till Mother's officious knock sounded on our doors in turn, signaling that an overserved Negro had safely departed.

Of course, there were those occasions when someone didn't listen. That time Lela flooded the toilet in the shared bathroom between our little-girl bedrooms and marched resolutely out into the hallway for spare towels against Mother's orders, earning a switching she said was worth it to peek over the balcony and lay eyes on the handsome man sleeping on the sofa. *I mean it, you four,* said Mother afterward, slapping Lela's switch into the palm of her small brown hand. *Y'all keep your behinds in these rooms until I come get you, and ask Lela if I'm kidding about that.*

(*You all just wouldn't believe how handsome,* said Lela later, rubbing her raw behind.)

"Mother was organized," I told Suzette's daughter, after a moment's thought. "But she still did hair."

"What about Granddad?" she asked now, looking again at that bright red sun hanging over the painted Boardwalk.

"What about him?" I asked, suddenly exhausted.

She faltered. "Just—anything, I guess. What was he like? I know he was good-looking. That he loved music. Auntie Cassandra and Auntie Lee, though, most of what they say is that he was strict. About school, about boys."

I laughed aloud. "Do they really! Well, he was, with them." Cassandra, who to her great mortification hit puberty just a beat too early, so that for the next two years the rest of us referred to her exclusively as Miss Tits. Lela, who was born with a terrifying sparkle in her eye and hair like a matador's flag, who at six would march up to a grown man at the club in her little white pinafore and ask whether she could see what was behind the front flap of his trousers. Of course Daddy had to deal with those two a certain way, developing hawklike vision and a tone of voice that could snap them to attention from fifty feet away.

He had none of those troubles with me, his helper behind the bar, stirrer of cocktails and squeezer of lime slices. The only one of us who never tired of watching him pour shimmering liquids into snifters and highball glasses. He only had to tell me once not to steal nips of things from the bottles at the club. *This here is for guests, Fay,* he said that one time. *People who come here to pay us for it. It's our job to give it to them and to keep our wits while we do it. You understand me, Fay?*

I was ten then, and I did understand, and was shamefaced enough about it that he smiled and laid his palm on the crown of my head to show that all was forgiven. On his next night off, he poured a little bit of his rum into my juice cup, shook in a few sweet brown spices, and took me out onto the front porch to watch night fall over the skyline. *To good drink and good talk*, he said, clinking the rim of his glass against mine, and there we sat, chatting in the moonlight.

Had Suzette known him as strict? If so, you had to think it was because she herself was that way, inside-out strict, all abstinence and precisely placed hairpins. Even when she was still practically a baby, she wept under Mother's stylist thumb, miserably submitting to the indignity of having her baby hairs smoothed down with a graying communal toothbrush. Some years later, she begged Mother to press her out with the hot comb instead, so she'd look fancy when she took to the club stage to perform on the violin in an immaculate white linen dress. Daddy never even had to beg her to play; she *wanted* to accompany the band to some esoteric bebop interpretation of a Debussy piece that the crowd first twitched at and then hollered for. Just a little goddamned prodigy, her tiny fingernails painted primrose pink because she knew there'd be people watching her draw that bow across the strings of her child-sized instrument. Daddy and the spinster cheered loudest of anyone, but the whole club went bananas for her. After it was over, she looked down with surprise at the litter of dollar bills around her feet, gathered them up into one hand, and skipped right offstage to deliver them to Daddy. *My little Suzette*, he whooped with a grin just about too big for his face, as the crowd whistled like worked-up wolves.

"I wouldn't have called him strict," I told Suzette's daughter. "He was a good man, a good father, and a good business owner. There isn't a lot else to say."

She nodded, her fingertips already on the next painting. The one on the midnight background with the inverted heart shape at the center, three brown figures all around it and the fourth one, the smallest, tucked shrunken in the corner. She stared at that little figure and I saw the next question bubble on her tongue, knew what it was before she'd formed the first word. "And," she said. "Sorry, I'm sure this is hard, but what about my mom?"

"It isn't hard," I said.

She looked over at me. "Oh," she said. "Well, okay."

"Pretty. Obedient. Sweet. Easier on our parents than the rest of us were."

Suzette, Suzette, Suzette. Not as smart as Cassandra, but still got straight As nearly every term. Had nothing close to Lela's natural sex appeal, but could steal your boyfriend without trying. Preferred Debussy and Ravel, but somehow got a jazz nightclub named after her. The kind of person who threaded every needle on the first try. Who tattled on me for saying I'd heard spirits through the Ouija board, working our parents up into thinking I was playing with the devil's tools. They cut the board in half and threw the planchette into the trash can, spooked by the words of the youngest person in the house. I popped the head off her favorite baby doll in retaliation, and somehow only *I* got spanked.

"She scared easily," I added, now. "Didn't like my Ouija board. That's basically what this painting is about."

"To the extent that any of them is *literally* about anything," supplied Suzette's daughter with a wink.

"Exactly," I said. "Which, as I mentioned before, I try not to say is the case."

She needed a midmorning nap, she said, and asked if a bed was available in her mother's old bedroom. The sclera of each eye nearly as red as the sun over the painted Boardwalk.

"This house isn't as big as you think," I told her. "Three bedrooms, two for us four girls. Suzette and Lela shared."

Her eyes brightened at this. "She shared with Auntie Lee," she said. "Must have been fun."

"They didn't think so," I told her. "Grab your things."

We climbed the stairs, her bag jangling with heavy bottles, and stood at the mouth of the upstairs hallway. The bedroom I shared with Cassandra to the left, Lela and Suzette's to the right. Daddy frowned at me from straight ahead, in front of the bathroom we'd all shared. Ignoring him, I turned left and pushed open the door to Cassandra's and my old room.

"Here you go," I said.

She stepped inside, let her bag fall a little recklessly to the ground. "This is it?" she asked with wonder, approaching the reclaimed wood furniture, roughly flinging open an armoire that had already been old when Mother bought it for us.

"This is it," I said, making sure not to look in Daddy's direction.

She reached into the armoire and pulled out the sleeve of Cassandra's faded denim jacket from high school, lifted it to her nose, and breathed in. Without letting go of that sleeve, she did the same thing with the hem of a shift dress the spinster next door knitted for my thirteenth birthday. She held them for a moment against her face, then turned around. "These things were my mom's?"

I managed not to lie: "You think Lela would wear anything that classy?"

She smiled at that, pulled the dress off its hanger, and sat with it on one of the twin beds, slid her feet—bare, no socks or pedicure—out of her leather boots.

"Sleep as long as you want," I told her. "I'll just be painting across the hall and then I'll start lunch."

She swung her body to horizontal, still clutching onto my shift dress. "Thanks, Aunt—" She hesitated. "Aunt Felice. Is that okay?"

I said, "Fay is fine."

"Thanks, Auntie Fay," she said around a yawn, eyes already falling shut.

The oven mitt hooks are *too damn far away*, I groused at my grandparents, who just rolled their eyes at me. Minced garlic and aromatics sizzled in the hot, hot oil.

Smells real good, Fay, said Daddy. *But what did those mushrooms ever do to you? You trying to wake up my granddaughter?*

She could stand to get up by now, I said crossly, but I didn't let the knife fall quite so heavily after that.

You should be kind to her. You can see what kind of weekend she's had.

Into the pan went the sliced mushrooms, the bay leaves, a little more rosemary. I wiped my hands on Mother's old apron and took a long sip of my spiced drink.

You could give her a little more than what you've been giving her. You could let her have one of your paintings.

Ha! I told him. I could send her home with that whole armoire too. I could let her just move right into this house, while I'm at it.

Fay, he said, shaking his head. *More than just that her mother scared easily, is all I'm saying.*

I poured in the beef stock and cooking wine early, sending the whole dish up in a fragrant hiss, just to drown him out. I took my spiced drink to the porch while it simmered, and naturally Daddy followed. Persistent as always about seeing our chats through to the end.

There are a hundred things you could tell her about Suzette, he went on. *And she's here, asking.*

Of course he was right, but she'd have to go to Cassandra and Lela for a report on the fullness of Suzette's transcendent humanity. Myself, I didn't have much more to say than that she scared easily, hollering down the house about the witchcraft I was trying to do on my two-dollar Ouija board. That she wanted everything cleaned and shined, company-ready like the powder room, and that you could just see in her little face that she was pretending the club was Carnegie Hall when she took to the stage with that uppity violin.

Or maybe my niece *wanted* to hear that her mother had an ugly side too. That she eventually got too big for her little white britches and started faking sick on club nights, claiming she couldn't play the violin because her stomach hurt. Obvious as any little child pulling that gag. They left Miss Carnegie Hall home with the next-door spinster a few times, and would you believe the only thing anyone ever said to me on those nights was *Where's the little one who plays the violin?* While I ran around on my tiptoes squeezing limes into two drinks at once.

Finally admitting she wasn't actually sick, just scared of the men there. Which she had no reason to be, until that last one. We'd been going there for years with no funny business, Daddy's hawklike eye watching over any interaction that took place between a grown man and a girl in white. And by that point three of us were technically women by biological standards, only Suzette still a baby, and *she* had the nerve to be scared of the men there.

We have to go through this again, Fay? She knew. The littlest children see what we don't.

I downed my drink and walked back to the kitchen for a refill, to stir the thickening pan sauce. Daddy, Daddy, Daddy, I said. You're never going to convince me that simple child knew a thing. She just thought she was too good for all of it. She was always like that. Too good for us, too good for everything.

Where's the little one who plays the violin? some overserved Negro slurred in my ear one night, just after Daddy slipped his keys from his pocket with expert fingers. *Home sick!* I yelled back at him, at my peak of irritation from saying that all night.

Later, we four listened from our beds as they laid him on the sofa, noisier and chattier than surprise guests usually were. *Jesus*, said Cassandra in the dark. *It's like he's giving a speech down there. Would he just pass out already?*

Right after that, we heard our mother's key turning in our lock and then, echolike, the same sound from across the hall—an extra precaution for our extra-boisterous guest. Cassandra was asleep again instantly, dreaming her big-brained dreams, but I was awake to hear the creak of footsteps on our hallway. I broke Mother's rule number one, unlocked the door from the inside, and peeked out at him, our overnight guest, who had his back to me and was fiddling with Lela and Suzette's doorknob. First carefully and then wildly, like maybe he could just pull the whole thing off, screws and all.

Suzette broke it, too, Mother's rule. Little Miss Model Citizen just opened the door without a thought and looked up at him, her eyes bleary under her silken headscarf, simple and not understanding shit. He put his hand on the shoulder of her nightgown and bent down to her eye level and she kept standing there, dumb as a plastic doll. *Daddy*, I called out, because someone had to, while she just stood there like all the noise that followed—the crack of a fist on flesh, of bone on the brick wall— just rolled right off her. Like she didn't even hear it.

And would you believe that? Cassandra was the one we called Miss Tits for years; I smiled beautifully at everyone I fixed a drink for; Lela at six marched right up to grown men and asked them to unzip their trousers. All that, and *Suzette* was the one that man came for, later insisting that he just wanted to hear her play the violin. Not that I spent much time trying to work out what was going through his short-eyed mind that night. *Some things will just never make sense*, Mother said later, *and a man like that is one of them. We just walk forward in faith and we thank God he didn't get his hands on our little Suzette.*

We do, Fay, Daddy said now, reminding me, like anyone ever said I did otherwise. *We thank God for that.*

My chat with Daddy ended when the steak medallions turned a savory brown. I ladled pan sauce over each plate and was just about to call upstairs for my niece when I found her already at the dining room table, in a new outfit and with her hair refreshed, smelling of the pomade she must have found on Cassandra's old nightstand. She'd brought down her duffel bag and laid it by the front door. Cleaned up like that, and with some sleep behind her, she looked more like Suzette than ever. She had found my downstairs Bible and had it open to the inside cover.

"Lunch is ready," I said, setting a plate in front of her.

"Smells great," she said absently, tracing her finger across the hand-drawn lines of the Collins family tree.

"The earlier handwriting is your grandfather's," I said. "Up through your mother's generation. After that, it's mine."

"He died young," she murmured, touching the dates beside his name. "They told me it was an accident. Kind of a weird story."

Wasn't that just like Cassandra and Lela, I thought. Power-washing all the ugliness off it, like a press release. But of course you had to do that, scrub away all traces of any connection between Daddy's death and the club, like what we'd done back then because nobody wanted any mess from the AC police.

"A car accident?" she asked. "They never specified."

"A house accident. He got his skull cracked open in a fistfight with someone from the neighborhood."

"A white guy?"

"In this neighborhood? Not back then. Why do you ask?"

"No reason." She raised an eyebrow. "Was he drinking rum at the time?"

Daddy chuckled in the corner; I frowned. "No," I said, stabbing at a steak medallion with my knife. "He wasn't a drinker. Rum was his drink, but not to where he'd get into fistfights because of it. The other guy was drunk. Your grandfather was stone-cold sober, which didn't help. Drunks don't fight fair."

She held my eye for a beat and then looked back at the book. "I want to add something," she said.

"Such as?"

She went to the door and unzipped her duffel bag, pulled out a pen. I stiffened as she scribbled for a second on the family tree. "Look," she said, turning it to face me.

I took a bite of steak, chewed, and swallowed it slowly. "I see," I said. "I had your name wrong."

"It happens a lot."

"I thought that was a boy's name, actually," I said, nodding at her edit.

She shrugged. "I assume they were hoping for a boy the second time around. They got all the daughter they ever needed with that first one." There was a familiar coldness in her voice, something that made me ache. Daddy reached over like he wanted to stroke her hair.

I studied her revisions again, the vertical line she'd drawn down from her older sister's name. Married some time ago, a wedding I dimly remembered avoiding, and apparently the union had been fruitful. "They didn't tell me the news about your sister," I said. "Isn't that just like Cassandra and Lela."

"Why not, I wonder. She's due this winter," said my niece. Finally she set fork and knife to her first medallion and began cutting it into perfect, evenly sized pieces.

"No good reason," I said. "At some point, they got it into their heads that I couldn't be happy for anyone who had something I didn't, like a big mansion or a husband and babies."

"When in fact?"

"When in fact of course I can. My best to your sister."

I never understood it, why they tiptoed around trying to hide their triumphs and joys like I wasn't having a fine time watching with Daddy from the sidelines. Or sometimes from up close. After Mother was gone, they all came back to the row house for holidays, to pluck old belongings from their bedrooms and use them to feather their nests in new cities. Leaving behind only the entirely obsolete.

Cassandra turned up unexpectedly one Christmas on the arm of a white behemoth, and Daddy studied him carefully from the corner. *I knew one of you would go that way*, he said. *I just figured it would be Suzette.* But his natural distrust dissolved as the man revealed himself to be solicitous and nearly as smart as his fiancée. Lela married a man she said reminded her of her days at the club, a moody musician who let her see behind the front flap of his trousers whenever she wanted. Suzette, of course, married not the football player she pulled out from under me while I was away at college and helpless, but someone even better than that, a man it almost hurt to look at, who naturally kissed the ground she walked on and gave her perfect children.

Years of staggered visits, each of them throwing me a sorry look if ever she forgot herself and rubbed her round belly or kissed her child's face. Like anyone asked them not to do that. Lela turned up once with babies loaded under her arms and in infant carriers, looking like the punch line to a joke. *You're in the wrong place,* I told her. *You should be looking for a shoe to move into. And by the way, couldn't you have tried to make one with red hair?* She gave me a self-deprecating laugh and made her little joke. *I really don't know how this happened,* she said. *You could say it was one too many chats with Daddy lately. Too much fun with that husband of mine and we just weren't careful.*

Like any of it bothered me. Sometimes, early on, I'd meet a man for drinks at the place the club had become, but invariably he'd want to follow me home, and it was just too crowded here. Sometimes I painted the child I might have had, or my best guess, but I could never get the brush to do what I wanted it to. That's why I returned instead to the comforts of my famed four figures. It was what I knew.

We owned the house in four parts, Mother having seen to that, but one day Cassandra rounded everybody up and said, *Fay, it's all yours.* Her big lawyer husband had drawn it up in writing; only signatures were needed. As if to say that since I couldn't get a man to stick, maybe I'd like playing wife to a row house. A kindness, for sure, but the worst type of kindness: a pitying one. Still, I never forgot the generosity underneath it, never took for granted that I got to paint my life away in a paid-off home. That I didn't have to sell any pieces I didn't want to.

And so then I *didn't* feel cruel joy when Cassandra's children finished growing up, both of them unimaginable messes even after an expensive childhood in a mansion, all riding lessons and tutors. When the younger one renamed himself the Heavenly Sky and took to dancing around in dresses and wigs, which Cassandra never mentioned but which I learned anyway from running into the child on the strip while he was in town for a show. I bought a ticket, afterward making sure to call up Cassandra and tell her how much I had enjoyed myself.

Nor did I smirk, privately or otherwise, when Lela had to throw out her hot-blooded musician, who for all the liquored-up fun they were having had apparently never stopped chasing strange. I cooked her weeks' worth of meals and took them to her, along with an extra set of hands willing to scrub her bathtub, rock her fussy babies. Teasing her only a little about how she'd been born with a taste for hound dogs.

And, of course, I was devastated about poor Suzette. Sick so suddenly and then gone before I ever got around to replying to any of her
letters. Before I got to compliment her on the photos of her pretty, pretty
daughters.

My niece offered to help me clean up after lunch, but I turned her down,
worn out from the togetherness. To think six of us would all sit packed
in one room, I told Daddy in the kitchen. And now one visitor and I'm
crowded. I was kind to her, though. You saw me. I was kind. *And I'm
glad for it, Fay*, he said. *I still say you might think about it, finding something to send home with her.*

I lingered over the dishes, scrubbing the lipstick from the tines of my
niece's fork by hand. She'd consumed every mushroom and every last
drop of pan sauce, but had left her cut-up medallions untouched, spread-
ing the pieces around her plate. An old trick of her mother's from the
days when she decided she didn't have the stomach for root vegetables
or fried food or anything otherwise *impure*. I tilted the plate and pushed
the wasted meat into the trash can. She was gone from the dining room
when I returned there, leaving her duffel bag unzipped and open wide,
her tiny, bright garments and two half-drunk liquor bottles exposed. I
found her on the front porch with her feet in my chair, sipping something golden from her lunchtime water glass. A bottle of bottom-shelf
rum, pre-spiced, sat on the floor in front of her.

"What are you doing?" I asked.

"Just thinking about everything," she said, and lifted her glass. "Having
a little chat with Granddad."

Even in the July heat, my blood flashed icy. "Are you, now."

"It's just that this morning has been surreal. Meeting you, sleeping in
my mom's old room . . ."

I walked up close enough to smell the rum in her glass, cheap and
syrupy. "Who told you to call it that?"

Daddy had followed me outside and was in the corner shaking his
head. *Fay*, he said warningly.

"To call what what?"

"Out here drinking alone at noon. That's *a chat with Granddad*?"

Her dark eyes narrowed. "It's one thirty, actually. And the rum is what I meant. That's what they call a rum drink. Auntie Cassandra and Auntie Lee. My mom used to say it, too, my dad told me."

Well, wasn't that just precious. Wasn't it just perfect. Already Cassandra and Lela had tested my patience with their liberal use of that phrase. Cassandra booking herself one ticket for an island cruise because work was stressing her and she needed *a few days to chat with Daddy*. Lela blaming him for her prolific maternity, when surely in life he would have told her not to go near that husband of hers with a ten-foot pole.

Saintly Suzette, meanwhile, using the term to make fun of all of us, to elevate herself above it, never touching a drop of anything, and anyway least able of all of us to remember what a *real* chat with Daddy had been like.

The spinster next door chuckled to herself. Her nose as far in Collins family business as it always was.

"I wanted to ask you something about those paintings," said the child, Suzette's daughter, bringing her glass back to her lips. "The ones in the living room."

Fay, said Daddy warningly. He looked on her fondly, still charmed somehow by the sight of her, those bare toes hanging off the front of my chair.

"Yes?" I said quickly, before her liquid courage could take hold. Before she could ask to take what was mine. "What about them? Those ones in the house, they've all been sold. I just hold them here till the buyers can come for them."

A pause. "Oh," she said. "Well, that answers that, then." She lifted her glass to her lips and tossed back the rest of her drink. Her hand went for the bottle.

"You don't need another one," I told her, taking her glass. "There's a bus at two and I need to get back to painting. You still prefer to walk yourself to the Port Authority?"

Back up the walkway she went, still wobbling under the weight of her ridiculous duffel, minus a few ounces of rum. *Fay*, said Daddy as we watched her go. *Really, now. I don't know what I'm going to do with you.*

I left him on the porch and went upstairs with her left-behind bottle under my arm, looked in Cassandra's and my old bedroom. The child had stripped the linens and tidied up after her nap. She'd also helped herself to Cassandra's denim jacket and my old shift dress, so I helped myself to a swallow of her cheap liquor. Artificial spices crackled on the back of my tongue.

I left the room, shutting the door behind me, and crossed the hallway, let myself into the younger girls' bedroom. There sat Suzette on her old twin bed, shadowed by all my easels, her usual look of disapproval tinged with a particular sadness. *I don't believe you sometimes, Felice*, she said as I picked up a brush and situated myself in front of my latest. *That you would treat my baby that way.*

I don't know what you mean, I told her. You heard me offer the child a ride.

She just shook her head at me, her hands in her lap, judgmental and uppity as ever. As though *she* never ran out of patience for unexpected company. As though Mother didn't slick down her baby hairs with the exact same old toothbrush she used on mine.

The Everest Society

Eight days before the social worker's home visit, Liv squeezed into the lobby of her apartment building to find that the elevator meeting had already started. She scanned the crowd until she located her husband, Dante, who'd apparently arrived early enough to score a seat near the front of the room, now crowded with residents. Liv tried to catch Dante's eye, but he was preoccupied, his brow furrowed as the conversation thrummed toward a fever pitch.

Nishan, their neighbor from the eighth floor, wanted to know what the hell was taking so long. It was starting to get ridiculous, he said, slapping a knee for emphasis. Trudging up and down seven flights of stairs like goddamned mountain climbers. He and his neighbors on Eight— they had taken to calling themselves the Everest Society—had started a group text among themselves, a perpetual flurry of notifications about who'd be hitting the mailbox soon, who didn't mind carrying home an extra carton of milk, and so forth, thereby sparing the, forgive his expression, *older aunties* of the eighth floor—Silvia and Tomasina, who huddled together and winced at this but urged him on—from having to make the trek for basic necessities. "Not that I mind helping my neighbors, but we have it the worst of anybody," he concluded, waving a hand to indicate the members of the beleaguered Everest Society, the dozen or so nodding heads scattered throughout the lobby crowd. "Fix this, or tell us how much longer!"

Liv caught Gracie, the arthritic brunette from Seven, rolling her eyes at *the worst of anybody*.

"And, Nishan, I want you to know we hear you." Noelle, addressing the group in her capacity as board president, raised her voice over the sudden eruption of applause, the bleated *amens* from the fourth-floor Robinsons. "*All* of us, and that includes management and myself, everybody in this room was expecting a working elevator by now, and we're—"

"How much longer?" Josette from Five, a bag of Doritos perched on the meat of her folded arms.

Noelle's mouth snapped shut, and she knelt behind the stack of folded chairs that served as her podium, an arm supporting the weight of her belly. She reappeared holding aloft a sheaf of papers, from which she read aloud as if to a roomful of kindergarteners: "'We apologize for the delay and for any inconvenience residents may experience as we complete the renovation. We have enclosed an updated work order, including a new projected completion date.'"

Liv leaned forward and strained to hear. The back row: land of the day-late and the dollar-short. Normally you could show up to these things right on time and still get a front-and-center seat, inches from Noelle and her chair-stack podium and her binder smugly labeled BOARD. Hardly any owners and absolutely no renters cared about the usual substance of board meetings: budget stuff, and whether to cover the bald spots in the wretched hallway carpets. Liv came, always, because patching the carpets meant incremental increases in property value, and normally she luxuriated in the front row with her notepad in one hand and her voting paddle in the other. The voting paddles, lime-green index cards on Popsicle sticks, had in fact been Liv's idea. You could tell each time Noelle reluctantly called for a vote that she was pissed not to have thought of it first.

They had voted months earlier on replacing the elevator, first on the initial question of *whether*: a unanimous *yes* from board members frustrated by its chronic outages and concerned about rental appeal. Then they voted again on *when*: the winters (Liv among them) greatly outnumbering the summers. The elevator did its most egregious stalling in the witch's-tit chill of January, once trapping Liv and Dante between Three and Four for several minutes before Dante succeeded in wrenching the doors open—an experience that went from harrowing to momentarily sexy to outright mortifying in the time it took him to pull her to the safety of Four's threadbare hallway floor, where a clutch of Robinsons stood in pajamas, cheering.

Anyway—it turned out *everyone* came to board meetings that concerned the elevator, defunct until its pricey replacement was installed. Make that *everyone and their sister* when the projected completion date had come and gone a week earlier. Workers still roamed the halls in the mornings, babies still woke to incessant drilling, and—the big problem— the only way up from the lobby was the steep cinder-block gauntlet of the emergency stairwell.

"'New completion date,'" read Noelle from another page. She paused, cleared her throat, shifted her weight from one chubby leg to the other. Enjoying the others' suspense, of course, was the main reason to take on a thankless job like this one. "'Monday, March fourth, or week thereof.'"

A brick of hot clay formed in Liv's throat. The social worker was due just a few days after that. She coughed loudly, trying and failing to get Dante's attention.

"What the *fuck*," shrilled Nishan.

Josette gave her bag an indignant crumple, crushing the chips inside.

"Guys, guys," said Noelle, yelling a little over the din. "It's still right around the corner. Less than a week to go."

Silvia and Tomasina gripped each other's hands, their bird shoulders twitching.

Dante raised a hand, which Noelle acknowledged with a nod. "All due respect," he started carefully. Liv drew in her breath. "They got off to a late start, they moved slow those first few days, they already missed one deadline. Should we be weary about putting our money on March fourth as the guaranteed completion date?"

Weary lodged itself like a fish hook in Liv's brain.

"Well, March fourth *or week thereof*," said Noelle. "I wish I had a good answer for you. In the meantime, if I could just remind you all . . ." She riffled again through her papers, produced a familiar-looking sheet of sparse bloodred text. A notice from the fire department, the patronizing reply the board had received to its queries about whether anything could be done for the residents of a building facing this sort of self-induced crisis. Liv had helped draft the letters. Were there county services available to assist those most fucked over by this sort of thing? The infirm, the pregnant, the *eighth-floor aunties*? Did off-duty firefighters schlep groceries when they weren't rescuing kittens? Again as if to small children, Noelle read directly from the fire department's reply: "'We encourage you to be patient and neighborly during this difficult time.'"

"Patient and neighborly." It was the refrain she'd posted in every public space throughout the building, omitting the part that went, *This department does not offer services of the type requested.* The part that meant *Good luck, you're on your own.*

They climbed the stairs in practiced formation, Noelle and a few others peeling off at Two. "Good night, Noelle," intoned a few people, almost no one nastily.

At Three, the Valdez kids hugged the Robinson kids goodbye, and the noise level dropped several blessed decibels. Dante caressed Liv's knuckles with the pad of his thumb.

Four: "Good luck!" cried the Robinsons, meaning this mostly for the Everest Society but also for everyone still trudging. Kevin Robinson caught Nishan by the elbow. "Tell me if you need help with them old aunties," Liv heard him murmur.

Inside Liv's unit on the sixth floor, Dante did the locks from top to bottom and made a show of sorting the mail, leaving Liv to collect herself in the bedroom, to double-check the dates, though she couldn't have been surer. Sprawled across the sleigh bed, not quite ready to thumb through the calendar on her phone, she stared instead at the puckered paint on the ceiling and counted breaths as she'd been taught. This was marriage: endlessly kicking the can of conflict into the future. The *canflict.* In spite of herself, she laughed.

Dante found her, tossed a handful of bills onto her nightstand. "What's so funny?" he asked, kneeling beside the bed. He knew better than to nestle beside her just then.

She turned to face him. "*Wary,*" she said. "Or *leery.* They both mean 'suspicious.' We need to be *suspicious* of whether they'll finish the elevator on time. *Weary* means 'tired.'"

He stared back. "What?"

She returned her gaze to the ceiling. They would need to pay yet another contractor to point it up, flatten the little cracked peak in the corner above the bed. "The home visit is March seventh," she said finally. "What are we going to do about it?"

"Oh," he said. "Well, still do it, right?"

"If the elevator's still out?"

Tentatively, gingerly, he climbed onto the bed beside her. "It's only five floors. We would have explained. We can offer her water."

Water. Well, of course they would. "Sure," said Liv. "I guess."

Dante tried to take advantage of the long silence that followed, his slim fingers finding the buttons of her work blouse.

"Ugh," said Liv, pushing his hand away. "Can you believe Noelle?"

In the morning, she woke to the relentless thrum of a riveter muffled only slightly by the wall and the door and the other wall. She smoothed the duvet over her side of the bed and replaced the ikat-print throw pillows. She showered and zipped herself into her fourth-Wednesday black sheath dress and worked a grape-sized blob of pomade through her edges. She found her staple charcoal work pumps and buttoned them into a tote bag, slipped her feet into battered ballet flats. She nodded goodbye to Dante, who slept on.

In the stairwell she met Gracie from Seven, clutching her bad hip as she descended. "Screw this shit," said Gracie.

It was an extreme version of the sort of greeting that had become standard over the past six weeks, though normally you heard it on the way *up* the stairs. "Not much longer," said Liv lightly, and veered around the other woman.

On the Metro, she squeezed into a seat beside a mother feeding her toddler cheese puffs from a bag. The child's eyes were wide with dark lashes; a dimple appeared in his chin when he smiled at Liv. Their elbows collided as Liv struggled one foot out of its ballet flat and into a pump. "Sorry," said Liv, wincing at the resulting cry of surprise, and she waited—a pump on one foot, a flat on the other—until the mother and child disembarked a few stops later, then completed the switch. She scanned the other faces on the subway car: no one from work. But still.

She arrived early, having overcompensated for the elevator outage. Walking the final segment of her commute, she passed L'Occitane and Papyrus and Swarovski, the usual hostess-gift garbage meant to imitate opulence, and stopped mid-footfall when a thought struck her. Probably the social worker—Margaret was her name, according to the emails she and Liv had exchanged in the weeks leading up to the home visit—would use the guest bathroom, where they normally kept Dove bars rubbed down to piles of ivory slime. Margaret would find a reason to check out the bathroom even if she didn't have to pee, Liv figured. At the very least, she would peek under the sink for improperly sealed household cleaners, which by then they would have tossed and replaced with gentle organic alternatives, odorless, screwed tight.

But just in case she did have to pee—from the *water* Dante planned to offer her. In case it was absolutely critical that she wash and moisturize her hands mid-visit before they got back to the work of dissecting Dante's work history and Liv's credit report like they were frog cadavers splayed wide open, Margaret iron-hearted under her enamel of unwavering politeness.

Liv doubled back. In L'Occitane she bought a bottle of verbena hand soap and a wee tube of shea-enriched moisturizing cream, receiving pennies in change for her fifty-dollar bill.

At lunchtime, she huddled in the office of Claire, her lateral coworker and sometimes friend, browsing produce displays online.

"Here it is," said Claire. "This one is pretty close to what I have."

Four tiers, copper-mesh basket you could hang from a hook in the ceiling. Williams Sonoma was selling it for slightly more than Liv's last two phone bills.

"But, I mean, get anything," said Claire around a forkful of microgreens. "Ikea will have something identical for, like, five dollars."

"Definitely," said Liv, swallowing her disappointment. Claire's lower-Bethesda townhouse was wall-to-wall ecru with pitch-perfect copper accents, every last element in harmony. Liv had been there twice for after-work cocktail gatherings, shushed into self-conscious silence by the hammered kitchenware, the professionally framed wall art. Taking particular note of the gleaming baskets advertising their bounty of Fuji apples and ripe avocados.

Back at her desk, unable to help herself, she navigated to a website she bookmarked: a resource guide for prospective parents planning for the home visit. What the home visit was: your private life on the tines of the social worker's fork. Relationships and daily habits, finances, diet.

What it supposedly *wasn't*: a housekeeping inspection. *A certain level of order is necessary*, read the website, as it always had, *but some family clutter is expected. A comfortable, child-friendly environment is sought.* Could there be a clearer way to intimate you were fucked if your spice rack wasn't alphabetized? And while fortunately Liv *had* alphabetized the spice rack, some weeks ago now, the list of what still needed doing seemed to keep growing.

She switched to Google, found the nearest brick-and-mortar Williams Sonoma, and mapped a homeward route that minimized carrying time.

"We have it in silver," said the saleswoman around a faux-apologetic wince. You could hear in her voice that her house was paid off. Working retail to dodge not poverty but a retired husband. Liv had learned about this sort in her own days working retail for the former reason.

"But not copper," said Liv.

"Sorry, no," said the saleswoman. Her wince deepened, a practiced effort to look sorrier than anyone had ever been in human history. "Maybe online . . . ?"

But the shipping time. "I'll just take the silver," said Liv.

The box was comically enormous and unwieldy. Trudging home from the Metro in her ballet flats, she tried everything: carrying it in front, behind her back, on her shoulder. Finally she began a process of shoving it forward and then lurching after it at two-foot intervals, hoping durability was baked into the price.

At the front door, she tried Dante's cell phone. To her surprise, the call went straight to voice mail. "Motherfuck," she murmured, remembering. Dante was working late, filling in for an injured coworker. She paced awhile in the lobby, thinking maybe someone? But no one. A workman lazing at the elevator opening had pocketed his phone and disappeared into the wire-lined shaft at the sight of her. The Everest Society and others from the upper floors had tightened up their routine, these days leaving the building only as necessary.

She pushed the box into the stairwell and began the ascent toward the first landing, rolling it homeward one step at a time. At Two, she flipped Noelle the bird. Even if it was unreasonable. Even if Noelle wasn't home.

At Four, she collided with another solid mass, stopping her in her tracks. She circled the box to look. In the corner of the landing sat a massive Magnavox box, turned so its insides were exposed to all passersby, its bottom lined with a careworn flannel Baltimore Ravens blanket on which someone had arranged a rectangular platoon of unopened water bottles. FREE read a handwritten construction-paper banner taped to a flap of the box. The handwriting was a child's; the medium: scented marker. A number of the bottles had been plucked from the spread.

"Jesus Christ," she panted, and resumed hefting the Williams Sonoma box. It was two fucking floors; she made it, of course.

Dinner was a cheap stir-fry, lentils and broccoli and not much else heaped over brown rice, a fried egg and a drizzle of hot sauce on top. Dante, the Wednesday cook, ate his creation hungrily.

"Did you see the thing at Four?" asked Liv, spearing a broccoli floret with her fork. She wondered what the best way was to display microgreens. Did you have to refrigerate them?

"Huh?" said Dante.

Why even ask? Change could happen right under Dante's nose—for example, the kitchen ceiling sprouting silver-toned produce baskets, which then miraculously filled with vivid jewel-colored fruits and vegetables—and 1,000 percent of the time, he failed to notice. Overlooked, her after-work hours of joist-hunting and hole-drilling and almost breaking her neck trying not to slip from the kitchen stool as she guided a dime-sized metal loop onto an equally tiny hook. Liv squeezed her eyes shut and pressed her temple.

"What thing at Four?" Dante tried again.

"Someone put out water bottles at the landing," she said softly.

"Oh, right," he said. "I saw that. Nice! Right?"

"I was thinking it's kind of unsightly. And stupid, considering it's the seventh week and this bullshit is almost over."

"*Hopefully* almost over," said Dante. His eyes twinkled. "Unsightly? We care about the aesthetics in the stairwell now?"

"Jesus Christ," said Liv, rising. She gripped her bowl with both hands and marched over to the kitchen sink. Just in time, she stopped herself from dumping her untouched stir-fry down the garbage disposal; instead, she pulled a tube of plastic wrap down from an overhead cabinet and yanked out a square whose corners immediately folded in on themselves and clung, a useless, shriveled triangle.

"I'm lost," said Dante carefully.

"Margaret!" said Liv, more loudly than she'd meant to. Her face went hot and her vision blurred momentarily, but still she could see his thorough confusion, the question on his lips: *Who?* She cleared her throat and counted breaths. He waited.

On Thursday, she left early in her Ann Taylor tweed. Heeled leather boots in her tote and leftover stir-fry for lunch. The morning was noisy: a chorus of power drills grinding at the elevator shaft, the reedy wail of a sleepless infant.

She slowed as she descended past the fourth-floor landing. Only a handful of water bottles remained; where there had been others, someone had dropped an envelope scrawled with a note: *Many thanks plus a gift from the Everest Society.* The paper was thin; you could see the cash (a five) right through it.

She charged past the third floor and crashed into the door at Two as it swung open. "Sorry, sorry," she said, backing up.

"Watch it," came the voice of the startled figure behind the door. Noelle, her brow furrowed deeply. She waited a dramatic beat before emerging, shielding the curve of her belly with both hands.

"Sorry," said Liv again. "Just trying to get out on time."

"*Patient and neighborly,*" huffed Noelle, and pointed at the door to Two, the posted notice which read the same.

To give her aching calves a break, Liv took a risk and wore her ballet flats on the walk past L'Occitane and Papyrus and Swarovski and through front-desk security at the office, meaning to slip into her boots on the elevator. But when the elevator doors parted, there stood her boss's boss, whose eyes did a darting once-over. "Good morning, Vanessa," he said, and smiled. *Vanessa* was the other Black girl's name.

An email from Dante awaited her at her desk. In it, he apologized anew for not noticing the new produce basket and insisted that even if he'd forgotten Margaret's name, *of course* the social worker's visit was on his mind, just as it was on Liv's. *Of course* he had not forgotten the upcoming Weekend of Final Preparations, had scheduled a haircut, had found work coverage for March 7—everything they'd discussed, he would do exactly.

If perhaps there was one thing he *didn't* understand, his message continued, it was why, after all they had done to prepare, well, who cared that the elevator might still be out? People climbed stairs all the time. The world was full of stairs. Margaret the social worker probably lived some-place with stairs. To imagine they would flunk the home visit—a sub-jective and therefore technically unflunkable thing—because of some stairs, to start second-guessing whether to proceed with the home visit altogether, was frankly crazy-bitch behavior.

This was marriage: reading your spouse's carefully chosen words, hearing in your mind's ear the ones he had refrained from using in-stead. For example, Dante would never have typed the words *crazy bitch*. Nor did he remind her, as he must have wanted to, of the seven-story Petworth walkup in which he had spent his childhood, humping back-packs and siblings and furniture up and down stairs, growing stronger for it with no conscious yearning for an elevator.

And so, pounding out her reply in what few minutes she could scrabble together before the first of the morning's deliverables came due, neither did she remind him of the crumb of family history he'd dis-closed in the middle of their courtship—the 1990s: a cousin of his, se-verely asthmatic, found dead in the Petworth stairwell between the fifth and sixth floors.

Casual Friday. Liv started the descent in the relative comfort of burgundy corduroys. At Five, narrowly missing a window of opportunity, she found herself caught behind Josette, who moved slowly and sipped what looked like milk but smelled faintly of coffee. The cardboard box at Four bore new fruits: glorified candy masquerading as breakfast bars, loose hot-pink tubes of Go-Gurt. A note read: *Happy Friday! You're halfway there.* Josette stopped to browse.

"Sorry, could I please—" started Liv. She was interrupted by the fling-ing open of the door to Four, a sudden stampede of young Robinsons, braids and backpacks streaming behind them. The cacophony echoing off the cinder blocks.

"Aren't they just so sweet," murmured Josette, reaching for a Go-Gurt.

Over bitter arugula salads, and perhaps against her better judgment, she sketched the scenario for Claire.

"I don't mean to negate what you're feeling," said Claire around a forkful of chicory. "But is it really such a big deal? A few flights of stairs and some junk food?"

"I don't know," said Liv. "Either it is or it isn't, but by the time I know, it'll be too late to do anything about it." She took a tiny bite and considered her words. Chewed and swallowed. "It's like I've done so much work to get ready—we both have—and then this. A social worker shows up and we look like—like—"

"But it's *someone else's* junk food," said Claire. "I mean, you have to assume she'll come with a checklist and that she can't dock you for anything that happens outside your personal front door." She took a swallow of Sanpellegrino, tucked a flaxen lock behind an ear. A teeny copper stud winked from the lobe. "You know what I mean? It's a whole formal, standardized thing. A lot of things like this are just, you know. *Objective*."

According to Redfin, though, Claire had managed to score a mortgage nearly twice Liv's, on her identical salary.

"If you're really worried," she continued, "just postpone. Waiting longer will suck, but maybe the peace of mind is worth it. And then Margaret comes and she just"—with one hand she pantomimed a swift elevator ascent—"right up to your place." She shrugged and stabbed at her salad with her fork. "I mean, if you're so worried. I bet they'd give you a mulligan."

Well, sure they would. In fact, they *had*. Though Liv had bitten back this part of the story: The home visit had originally been scheduled for December, for an evening before the board even signed its contract with the elevator company. She and Dante had spent the first iteration of the Weekend of Final Preparations tidying and ironing, had put out their holiday decorations early, readied the sound system to play gently upbeat classic jazz.

Liv had wiped down her grandmother's Waterford pitcher and bought an orange to slice. Dante had hung a mirror over the sofa and moved the rest of the furniture into every possible configuration until they found the one that felt most spacious. Almost a sort of second honeymoon, the two of them working seamlessly in tandem, making each other laugh with a hammy rendition of "Blue Skies." At breaks, they'd nestled together on the floor, Dante showing her the plans for a toy chest he wanted to build. The finish line so close.

And then, cleaning out the kitchen, sweeping behind the refrigerator—a tiny little floof of fur, a tail.

Glue traps, snap traps, steel wool. Phone calls to the property manager, who offered only the usual blah-blah-blah about how the cold of winter drove mice indoors and even to the upper floors of buildings like Liv's. *Call back if you're still seeing them next week.* This, two days before Margaret's originally scheduled home visit.

Dante, not understanding the severity, had joked about bringing home a feral cat for the night. Onto the sparkling, just-waxed floors.

In corresponding with Margaret, she'd smoothed it over, capitalizing on an undercurrent of flu-season paranoia. Margaret was only too happy to reschedule, except that with the holidays coming up—so sorry she was!—both she and the alternate assigned to Liv's case had vacation plans that would make it difficult to firm up another visit until the new year. How was early March?

The board had just begun collecting proposals for the elevator replacement. Early March was fine, of course.

But you couldn't ask for *two* mulligans. Could you? *No*, said the message boards, agreeing on this, if nothing else. Habitual unpreparedness in prospective parents was at least as bad as a messy kitchen. *If you're that worried, just hire a onetime maid*, someone suggested.

A notice in the lobby announced a board meeting to take place the following Monday, March 4. The notice promised an update on the elevator. Liv frowned as she opened the door to the stairwell, uneasy and unsure why, until she realized. *March 4*: the projected completion date. *Or week thereof.*

Liv began the climb. Top 40 radio and children's voices echoed off the cinder-block walls; there was an olfactory flood of garlic and oregano. Noelle stood on the stairs past Two, rubbing her belly, deep in conversation with the mother of the Valdez kids. Liv caught part of it: blah-blah-blah *gender reveal*. "I don't know, though," Noelle was saying. "What if I'm disappointed, you know?" The Valdez mom nodding sympathetically.

Liv charged past. Imagine worrying about such a thing.

The stairs around Three and Four were dotted with little Valdezes and Robinsons, and at the fourth-floor landing sat an open pizza box. Behind it was the cardboard Magnavox box, piled high with grocery-store snacks and old magazines, their covers screaming neon. The HAPPY FRIDAY! sign remained.

Wren Robinson tugged at the hem of Liv's corduroys. "We're having a pizza party!" A gap in her grin where her front teeth should have been, doll lashes, a dimple in each smooth brown cheek.

An ache formed in Liv's belly, her mind filling with unbidden thoughts of dressing a child like this one for school—neatly ironed dresses, dabs of pomade to smooth the fuzz around her braids—and of offering her a snack from the bounty of the produce basket. Of the muscles going taut in Dante's arms as he lifted her from the convertible sofa, drowsy at bedtime.

Wren nudged forth the pizza box, which contained a single, jaggedly half-torn slice dripping with grease. "You want this piece?"

It smelled delicious, and Liv did want it. "Do I," she said, and sat. Her pants had just enough give to them, the thick burgundy fabric hiding any trace of the tomato sauce from Wren's small fingers.

The workers worked only weekdays—the board had saved several thousands of dollars by opting out of overtime—and so the second Weekend of Final Preparations got off to a late start, Liv rising naturally from a dream about mountains. She made the bed the hospital-corners way and distributed the ikat-print throw pillows along the headboard. She brushed her teeth and dressed in leggings and a knit tunic.

She found Dante in the kitchen, cajoling the capricious coffeepot. "Ready?" she asked, slipping her feet into her worn All Stars.

He gave the machine a frustrated pound. "Ready."

She let her hand brush his arm as she passed. "Almost there," she murmured, hoping he felt the little current of sympathy in her fingertips. Just this one last thing, and then.

He nodded, a crease between his brows. "All right," he said.

She opened the door to the unit and stepped into the hallway. The first time around, they'd started here; she had simply pivoted and knocked on the same door she'd just stepped through. This time, though, she had to account for a broader swath of possibilities. She let herself into the stairwell and descended in a rush, covering her eyes and using the banister as a guide, muscle memory steering her around the known obstacle at the fourth-floor landing. She let herself peek between her fingers when she'd counted four and a half flights and sailed through the door to the lobby.

She inhaled deeply and removed her hands. She imagined herself a no-fuss fifty-something with ice-blue eyes and blond hair going silver, who had seen a lot and wanted to put babies into the arms of parents who'd shape them into high-functioning adults. Who could sniff out a lie meant to cover up addiction, insolvency, or other forms of dysfunction. Who scrubbed her own bathroom sink at least twice a week.

As Margaret, she considered the lobby. Spacious and brightly lit, well-kept, an ugly but inoffensive faux schefflera in one corner. The mailboxes: orderly, bearing names that proclaimed a comfortable degree of diversity. She found the one belonging to the prospective parents, their surnames presented in pluralistic egalitarianism. She nodded with approval.

The prospective parents had mentioned an elevator outage. (Or hadn't.) She found the stairs. (Or didn't—this version of Margaret pressed the button to summon the car and after a moment's wait was off to see the residence.)

She stepped inside the stairwell and tutted immediately at the poor industrial lighting, the dust. She made a mental note to grill the parents on basic logistics: Did they intend to carry an occupied stroller to and from the—what was it—*sixth* floor anytime the elevator went out? She began the climb.

At Two, she regarded a posted notice urging the reader to be *patient and neighborly*. A nice, community-minded message. The door swung open and a young woman, clearly pregnant, unrelatedly pudgy, stepped out and brushed past her. No ring. Still—the promise of other children nearby. A good thing overall.

The third floor delivered further on that promise: Behind the door, small voices chattered and rose in laughter. The unmistakable sizzle and smell of Saturday-morning bacon. She made a mental note.

But then, at Four—carefully she sidestepped the battered armchair-sized cardboard box and leaned in to inspect it. Inside were leavings that might have been trash: magazines, candy wrappers. A faintly garlicky odor wafted forth. Had someone dumped it here as refuse? She had seen collections like this one evolve into uncontrolled garbage heaps, had signed the paperwork to have children removed from homes where rodents overtook first common spaces like this one and then private residences. The prospective mother certainly didn't *seem* like the type—on the phone she'd been thoughtful and mannerly, perhaps even a bit stiff—but you never knew.

She continued upward, her joints beginning to complain. Nearing Five, she passed a woman older than she, pouring the contents of a bag of Doritos directly into her mouth. Margaret thought of the foster mother she'd had to refer for a consultation with a nutritionist, someone to explain the limited value of greasy, processed foods within a balanced diet. She made a mental note.

By Six, her calves burned and she felt cranky. Ungenerous. She exited the stairwell and found the prospective parents' door. She knocked.

The prospective father pulled the door wide open, revealing freshly swept floors, bright walls, a set of silver-mesh baskets spilling a glorious rainbow of fruits and vegetables. "Hello there," he said carefully. He wore a crisp button-up shirt. From the stereo speakers trickled a stream of piano melody, "Pennies from Heaven."

Everything exactly as they'd discussed.

"Please come on in and have a seat," said Dante, stepping aside.

Liv took a step forward and felt it, the little crackle of static or sympathy; whichever it was, it called to mind her words of a few minutes earlier—*Almost there*, she'd said. But even if all went to plan—even if they charmed Margaret with gleaming pears and soap that smelled like old money—well, that would only be the beginning. Next there would be sleepless nights and piles of dirty laundry, a level of chaos like the one Liv had worked tirelessly for years to stave off. There'd be decisions: Cloth or disposable? Public or private? And so forth. Unsolicited advice from Petworth aunties and Metro strangers alike.

There would be money troubles, yearning for a place with a yard. Budgeting to feed three without resorting to cheap trash. Loosening the reins to allow for certain greasy pleasures, if only occasionally. *Teachable moments*, the unending discussion of how not to fold at adversity: big things like being fired without cause, small ones like being called the wrong name. The challenge of imbuing a brand-new person with the sort of generosity you saw, for example, in the little Valdezes and Robinsons— but also, maybe there'd be room for a bit more fastidiousness? They'd have to give it some thought, refine the message. If all went to plan, there'd be years to get it right, or not.

All the stuff she couldn't afford to let crowd her mind at the sight of every pregnant belly and doe-eyed baby, but that lingered there, just off-stage. In spite of herself, she laughed. Because, of course, what could be more laughable than the notion that they were *almost there*? Regardless, there was this: if they flunked the home visit, it certainly wouldn't be because they'd failed to queue up just the right jazz selection.

At the sound of her laugh, its uncharacteristic wildness, Dante tensed, unsure what to make of it, whether he was dealing with Margaret or Liv or someone else entirely. "I'm not—I don't—you okay?"

All at once Liv was spent, too tired to proceed through the rest of it, to accept his offer of water or an Aranciata Rossa, to playact the interrogation, to steal away and evaluate the guest bathroom in all its L'Occitane–outfitted lushness. She was tired enough to collapse onto the strategically fluffed convertible sofa and sleep for hours. Tired enough to sleep until she'd missed the home visit. Until she could start collecting Social Security checks. She slumped against Dante, grateful when his sturdy arms folded around her without the slightest betrayal of surprise.

"We done?" he asked after a silence.

"Done enough," she said. "It's still early. Should we go back to bed?"

Good evening, Ms. MacHale, read Margaret's Sunday-night email. *I'm looking forward to our visit at 4:30 p.m. on Thursday, March 7. Please let this message serve as your reminder to gather the documents listed in the attachment to this email, and as always please feel free to reach out if you have any questions or concerns.*

Liv took a sip of her Aranciata screwdriver and inhaled deeply. Down the hall, diced Spanish onions and russet potatoes crackled in fragrant oil. Dante whistled as he cooked. *Thanks for the reminder, Margaret!* she typed. *We're also looking forward to it. While I don't think we have any further questions at this point, I do want to give you advance notice that our elevator may not be working on the day of your visit.*

It was, by far, less difficult than she'd imagined. The drink loosening her fingers, she described in a few breezy sentences her position on the homeowners' board, the decision to replace the sometimey elevator, the workers' minor delay.

On the bright side, if you do have to take the stairs, you'll get to meet some of our delightful neighbors, she wrote. *Wear comfortable shoes!*

She took another sip, contemplating her final salutation. Tart carbonation tickled her nose.

With great anticipation, Mariolive MacHale

Thank God for vodka: For once she didn't mind signing her full name, its clutter of superfluous syllables. Didn't wish it were simpler, Jane or Kate or Claire. Didn't worry what Margaret might infer about her devil-may-care parents. Still, for clarity, she made one final addition before sending:

("Liv")

At Monday's meeting, Nishan from the eighth floor wanted to apologize for his behavior at the previous week's meeting. The dramatics, the profanity—chalk it up to impatience with what was at the end of the day a minor inconvenience. He had been to visit apartment-dwelling relatives in the grinding mayhem of New Delhi; hell, he knew litigious Washingtonians who spent years trapped in lawsuit volleys with their next-door neighbors. Surely it could be much, much worse. No one liked climbing seven flights of stairs, he said, but at the end of the day, when would he otherwise have bothered so much as trading phone numbers with the people who dwelled just a few yards away? "Shout-out to the Everest Society," he concluded, inviting a dozen or so whistles and exclamations from around the room. Silvia and Tomasina, flanking him, slipped their petite hands into his broad ones when he took his seat.

Kevin Robinson from Four wanted to thank whoever had helped his daughter Wren carry her scooter up the stairs over the weekend. Dante acknowledged them both with a wave of one muscled arm and tightened the other around Liv's shoulders.

Behind her chair-stack podium, Noelle nodded and straightened her papers. "That's nice, guys," she said. "Patient and neighborly, so great." Patronizing as ever, but seeming to really mean it, for once. "Okay, so other new business, before I get to the elevator update?"

Liv raised her voting paddle, figuring it was okay under nonvoting circumstances, if necessary, to be seen here in the back row, land of the day-late and so forth. Noelle acknowledged her with a head tilt; Liv stood, smoothing the A-line skirt of her dress. "I owe someone money for pizza," she said, projecting in the direction of the Valdez and Robinson kids, who took up a whole corner of the room. "I crashed the party on the stairs on Friday!"

The little Valdezes looked ready to send her a hefty invoice, but their mother cut in. "The pizzas were a gift," she said. "Pay the Everest Society."

"Don't!" said Nishan. "Don't you dare!"

"Well," said Liv, and gave Dante's hand a squeeze. "Will you take booze? We've got some perfectly good vodka we need to get out of our place by Thursday. If it happens the eighth floor is taking visitors."

A thumbs-up from Nishan, a smattering of applause from around the room.

"Nothing further," said Liv.

"All right, so," said Noelle, and gave her papers a shuffle. "Let's talk new projected completion date."

Acknowledgments

Several of these stories have appeared in other publications: "The Good, Good Men" (2019) first appeared in *Puerto del Sol*'s Black Voices Series and was later reprinted in Catapult's *Best Debut Short Stories 2020: The PEN America Dau Prize*; "The Everest Society" (2020) first appeared in *One Story*; "Mote" (2020) first appeared in *Joyland*; "Dragonflies" (2019) and "Rioja" (2020) first appeared in *SLICE*; "Company" (2020) first appeared in *Strange Horizons*; "Rule Number One" (2020) first appeared in *Hobart*; and "The Gatekeepers" (2019) first appeared in *Juked* (print edition).

For this book to come into existence when it did was no easy thing. I will always be thankful to the following people and institutions for their incredible support as *Company* developed from overheard anecdote to swirl of ideas to, finally, its current form:

My agent, Reiko Davis, who supplied just the right balance of enthusiasm and patience as the start of the pandemic upended all my writing plans, and whose faith in the book kept me going through several unexpected curveballs.

My editor, Yuka Igarashi, who brought such brilliant ideas to the revision process, and the rest of the team at Graywolf Press for giving me the debut experience that should be every author's dream.

The late Robert Bausch and the Writer's Center in Bethesda, Maryland, whose workshops planted the seeds that became eight of these stories; and my early readers in those workshops, many of whom became friends and incredible champions of this project. And especially my first teacher and good friend Jen Buxton Haupt, who is the closest thing this book has to a godparent.

Everyone who provided the bricks that became the foundation of my rustic literary education: the wonderful people at *One Story* and especially

Will Allison, who edited "The Everest Society" for publication there; StoryStudio Chicago's StoryBoard program and Danielle Evans for her sharp coaching and her work that has always been a north star for me to fumble toward; CRIT and the incredible Tony Tulathimutte, who taught me 1,000 things including how to schedule writing around the arrival of new babies.

All the friends who were kind enough to take my book-writing dreams seriously, and who have been wonderful cheerleaders.

My family, whose voices and fingerprints can be found all throughout these pages. My mom and dad; my brother; my incredible grandparents and other elders; my cousins. And of course my aunties—those related by blood and otherwise—who inspired the ten or more aunties throughout these stories. Aunties are very special.

My three sons, who are ultimately the reason for everything I do and who I hope will someday enjoy these stories, or at least enjoy knowing they sat on my lap while I wrote them.

And my husband, who truly did everything he could think of to make this happen, and whom I appreciate so deeply for that. Always and forever my Dante.

SHANNON SANDERS is a Black writer and attorney. Her fiction has appeared in *One Story, Electric Literature, Joyland, TriQuarterly,* and elsewhere, and was a 2020 winner of the PEN/Robert J. Dau Short Story Prize for Emerging Writers. She lives near Washington, DC, with her husband and three children.

The text of *Company* is set in Adobe Garamond Pro.
Book design by Ann Sudmeier.
Composition by Bookmobile Design & Digital
Publisher Services, Minneapolis, Minnesota.
Manufactured by Friesens on acid-free,
100 percent postconsumer wastepaper.